Praise for *A North So True*

"The best book I have read in so long...I was awake until
4am! I couldn't put it down!"
– Amazon reader

"*A North So True* combines the best of so many worlds...
from ice skating and snowmobiling to gut-warming shots
and hot baths, my senses soaked up every description."
– Random Book Muses

"Everything you'd want in a novel. Romance, mystery,
suspense, a hero who you fall in love with and a leading
lady who you almost wish you could be. A great read that I
couldn't put down."
– Amazon reader

Praise for *All Over the Place*

"Filled with rich, deep emotion, engaging characters and
dialogue, and plenty of intrigue that kept me turning the
pages...Ms. Clarke is certainly an author to keep an
eye out for!"
– Storm Goddess Book Reviews

"This book reminded me of a great chick-flick kind of
movie, only in book form. And everyone knows the book
is always better!"
– SMI Book Club

"One of the best, most romantic, awe-inspiring and
awwwww-inspiring happily ever afters I've read in a long
time. Brava, Serena Clarke! I plan to read more by you."
– Random Book Muses

Praise for *The Same But Different*

"You can't help but want to keep reading. It's not just romance literature, but also a story about sisterhood, loss and finding yourself. Extremely glad I found this book and *All Over The Place!*"
– Amazon reader

"Plenty of steamy tension…a recommended fun, feel-good story with some unexpected twists and surprises."
– WiLoveBooks

"A beautiful story about one woman's adventure of a lifetime."
– Written Love

Praise for *One Distant Summer*

"What an amazing emotional love story. *One Distant Summer* was my first Serena Clarke book, but it won't be my last. I thoroughly enjoyed reading her writing style, the story flowed flawlessly."
– Mommaleena's Blog

"A touching story filled with broken teenage hearts, loss, disappointment, hope, love and more…a story I loved as I read more and more…one that I would also highly recommend!!"
– Cozy Corner Reading Nook

"What an emotional read! I really enjoyed this book—the setting was beautiful and I felt that both Jacinda and Liam were deeply developed characters…the chemistry between them was undeniable."
– Sasha Says

A North So True

SERENA CLARKE

FREE
BIRD
BOOKS

Copyright © 2016 Serena Clarke
www.serenaclarke.com

A North So True
Free Bird Books
ISBN 978-0-473-32870-2

Cover design by Books Covered

For everyone far away, but near at heart.

Chapter One

" **S** omeone has to go."

As her boss scanned the room, tapping a manicured fingernail on the meeting room table, Zoe Bailey kept her eyes on her notepad. Obviously, it was vital to make detailed notes about this client's requirements. She only hoped that Alcina Sutton, the fearless and fearful head of Vertex PR, wouldn't walk to the end of the table and see that the notes were mostly scribbled variations on *not me not me not me*.

Taking a quick glance around the table, she tried not to laugh. Everyone else was deeply involved in checking their phones, taking a very slow drink of water, or finding something fascinating in the sweeping view of London out the window. The prospect of an undercover trip to a wildlife lodge in the north of Sweden—in the middle of winter, no less—was beyond ghastly to the designer-clad people in the room.

"Is it really ethical though, Alcina?" one of them asked, looking for an out. "Are we on solid ground with this?"

That was rich, Zoe thought. In the years she'd worked here, she'd constantly seen Vertex strolling across moral quicksand in the name of creativity and innovation.

Alcina—or Sutton the Shark, as she was known behind her back—sighed deeply.

"Niall," she said, as though addressing a toddler. "Clearly I wouldn't ask you to do anything outside the law. We are simply going in and observing on our client's behalf, seeing what any wildlife volunteer would see. Do I need to explain it for you again?"

Niall shook his head. "No."

She had already explained enough. The client was actually a group of wealthy landholders in the north of Scotland, vehemently opposed to the proposed reintroduction of wolves to their countryside. On the other side was a group dedicated to seeing the wolves run free in the Highlands again, who had been using case studies from Sweden to support their cause. Now, Alcina had decided that someone must go to the village of Lillavik, posing as a volunteer wildlife enthusiast, and find the chink in their armour—some detail that would bring down their case.

Unfortunately, it was February, and the more Zoe's colleagues heard, the more their worst fears were confirmed. This wasn't après-ski, hot toddies and luxury chalets. It was trudging through the snow in sub-zero temperatures, documenting wolf poop finds, and probably getting frostbite. Their faces said it all: *just no.*

The last thing Zoe wanted was to draw The Shark's attention, but she'd thought of a point that seemed relevant.

"What if someone googles the person who goes, and finds out they work for Vertex? Their cover would be blown."

The Shark sent her a thin smile. "That's not something *you* have to worry about, Zoe." She forced out the 'Z' with a harsh buzz. "You're not on the website."

A titter went round the room, and Zoe felt herself flush red, but stood her ground. "Yes, I am."

Alcina pursed her Louboutin-red lips. "We did some... reassessment recently."

Reassessment? With everyone's eyes on her, Zoe decided to say no more, and check for herself later. But her smouldering animosity for The Shark—shared by every single person at the table—flickered and flared into a steady flame.

Now her boss turned back to the room at large. "Here's the deal: if I don't have a volunteer by Monday lunchtime, I'll choose someone myself. Be warned."

She gave Zoe one last look and left the room, her heels tapping on the industrial-chic polished concrete floor. The door clicked shut behind her.

Around the table, there was a collective release of breath.

"Sutton the Shark strikes again," Niall grumbled.

"I only just got over that terrible flu," announced Cosima, sniffing ostentatiously. "I can't possibly go."

"I can't either," said Lydia, looking smug. "I have my holiday in Mykonos already booked."

Cosima nodded. "You can't cancel that. Anyway, I think she already has someone in mind."

Seven pairs of eyes flicked towards Zoe, then away.

She gathered her things and stood up. No Friday night drinks for her tonight. And if she was the one to go? This had never been the job of her heart...but she'd show them all, including Alcina Sutton, that she was a match for any one of them.

Chapter Two

Zoe lay across the lid of her suitcase and wrestled with the zip. Nope, it just wasn't happening. She cursed and stood back up, considering the selection of bulky jumpers, jackets and socks. Something would have to be left behind. Hello, frostbite.

Her flatmate (and workmate) Denise—one of six of them squeezed into the warren-like Bayswater flat—stuck her head around the door frame.

"I still can't believe you're going."

"Yeah...I can."

She came in and perched on the end of the single bed, the only size that would fit into the tiniest of all the small rooms in the flat. Fortunately—or unfortunately—it didn't see much action, so its narrow confines weren't really a problem.

"That woman truly is a cow," Denise said. "Didn't your mum have any idea what she was getting you into? Wish I could have warned you."

Denise was the receptionist at Vertex—storehouse of company knowledge, source of all juicy gossip, and unashamed proclaimer of truths. She was straight-talking and brassy, not PR-slick, and Zoe loved her for it.

She shrugged as she started pulling things back out of

her suitcase. "She was doing me a favour."

"You don't have to work where *she* tells you to." Then she paused. "On the other hand, if it wasn't for that, we would never have met."

Zoe smiled at her friend's U-turn from indignant to reflective. "Very true. And let's face it, jobs weren't exactly leaping at me in the street." She squished a pair of socks down the side of the suitcase. "Anyway, plenty of people would kill to work for Vertex."

She was trying to convince herself as much as Denise. She knew that her opinionated mother—a school friend of Vertex's owner—was probably why The Shark didn't like her. But when the last PR company she worked for folded, and her mother pulled a few strings to get her an introduction at Vertex, Zoe wasn't going to refuse. Maybe she should have been more principled...taken the high road...but she wasn't, and she didn't.

Each of her parents was as high-powered as the other— her mother Madeline a PR consultant, her father Anthony a lawyer—and they travelled the world consulting as a team for international firms who'd got themselves in sticky situations of one kind or another. As a kid, Zoe had tagged along, mostly feeling like just another piece of luggage, although less stylish than her mother's matched Louis Vuitton. An inconvenient sort of luggage, that needed to be fed and schooled and taken into account. She'd gone to a string of international schools, never staying long enough to settle in and make proper friends. On the surface, it was glamorous. In reality, for a shy red-headed kid with an unpredictable stutter, it was miserable.

Somehow, at fourteen, she'd convinced her parents that she didn't want to go to the next posting in Bahrain while they rescued an American oil company from some highly dodgy crisis. Miraculously, they'd agreed that she could stay in London with family friends—if she promised to commit herself to her career studies, as chosen by them. She promised, hardly believing her luck. At the time, university or college seemed a long way off.

As it turned out, her parents decided she should study

communications, which was a relief, considering the other option was law. If it seemed odd to others that her parents dictated her choice of degree, well, she didn't really care. She had no clue what to do with her life anyway. All the years of being plucked up from one place and set down in another had left her feeling permanently scattered. At least the stutter had stopped at the same time as the moving around.

Now she held up two coats. "Blue or grey?"

"Grey. I like the fur. The contrast with your hair is so pretty."

Denise was always telling Zoe how lucky she was to have naturally red hair, pointing to her own expensively-maintained blonde highlights. People—including herself—paid ridiculous amounts of money, she said, to achieve what Zoe had naturally. But having grown up being teased about it at every school she went to, Zoe remained ambivalent about her gingerness.

She hung the rejected coat on the back of her door, and threw the other one over her suitcase. "I knew she'd pick me. Everyone knew. And she'd taken me off the website already—it was a done deal. But I'm going to show her I can do it."

Denise shook her head. "What a complete witch she is. Good for you."

Zoe threw a lip balm into her bag. Chapped lips seemed likely, even if she avoided frostbite.

"Actually it's fine, because there's something else I need to do while I'm there."

Denise squinched up her nose, puzzled. "What?"

"Claire."

Her eyes widened. "Claire who disappeared? What about her?"

"Well...you remember the story, right?"

When Zoe had finally negotiated her way into a normal life, she'd said goodbye to her real parents, and moved in with Paul and Sarah Evans, the parents of her dreams. They lived in a regular house, on a regular North London street, went shopping at Tesco, watched *Coro*, gardened on the weekends, and had fish and chips on Friday nights. Paul was the son of Anthony's godfather, a tenuous connection at best, but Zoe guessed that her parents were probably as eager to be free of the teenage her as she was to put down her suitcase at last.

Paul and Sarah's tech-mad daughter Claire was the only girl Zoe had known her whole life, even if they'd only seen each other once every few years. At the grand age of fifteen, Claire seemed effortlessly cool to the still-only-fourteen Zoe, and she was desperately excited to have a friend...maybe even a sister. And for four years, it seemed like she did. Until Claire disappeared, leaving behind a letter crushingly final in its rejection of her parents, Zoe, and the life they'd shared.

Over the following weeks she'd watched Sarah and Paul grieve, and then harden against their daughter. Sarah in particular was cut to the bone, so painfully heartbroken that when the shock started to subside, she refused to discuss it or consider trying to find Claire. She shut the door on her daughter's room, and that was that.

But now, a decade later, Sarah was in the hospital, struck down by a devastating stroke. And when Zoe went to see Paul the weekend after The Shark's ultimatum, he'd surprised her by tearing up when she told him about the threatened trip to Lillavik.

He stood up. "Come with me."

He led her upstairs, through the silent house, and opened the door to Claire's room. It was exactly as she'd left it. For the first time since Claire left home, Zoe stood in the room where they'd shared so many laughs, tears and secrets. Well, not *all* their secrets, as she'd come to discover. Claire had lived a whole other life online— headphones on in front of her computer, talking to gamers all over the world, figuring out some tricky coding problem, sketching out characters and inventing game worlds. Some of her character sketches were still pinned to the wall above her desk—quirky, tough avatars, full of sass and grit...a lot like Claire herself. Claire's favourite had always been one of her earliest creations: Nova No-Show, a feisty rebel who operated on no one's schedule but her own. Seemed like she'd been sending them a message, even back then.

Paul took a single paper from the desk drawer, and held it out to her. It was a page ripped from a magazine.

"I found this down the back of her desk, about a year after she left," he said.

It was a profile of someone called Alvar Lundberg. He was once the owner of a medium-sized trucking firm, said the article's introduction, but now he ran a game development company called Defrost Digital...located in Lillavik, Sweden. She looked up at Paul.

"Do you think...?"

"Maybe. Look at the bottom."

There, in Claire's handwriting, was an address—a Lillavik address.

"I should have done something," he said. "But Sarah was so dead against any mention of looking for her..." He closed his eyes for a moment, years of *what ifs* cutting deep lines in his face.

"I remember her talking about this." Zoe thought back to the conversations she and Claire used to have. "She said the new Silicon Valley would be in the snow, not the sunshine."

He sighed. "I should have listened. I might have had a clue that she was planning something."

"It's not your fault," she insisted. "She made her own choice."

He just shook his head. "I know you don't want to go, but if you do, please see if you can find out anything more. When I found this, I should have tried to contact her." He pressed a hand over his eyes. "I just want them to make peace before Sarah dies."

"She's not going to die," Zoe said.

But he gave her a steady, wordless look. Right then, she knew she'd go to Lillavik—if by some miracle Alcina didn't choose her, she'd volunteer for the job. She nodded, and put the folded page in her pocket, and they closed the door behind them again.

Now she patted Denise's hand. "It's okay."

She sniffed and ran a finger under each eye, in case of eyeliner smudges. "But that's so sad."

"I know. But I think I can find her, or at least get on her trail. I should have done it before. It's been ten years, and soon it might be too late."

"And what will you say if you find her?"

"Yeah…good question."

It was exactly what she'd been wondering herself.

Chapter Three

Zoe pressed her forehead against the window as the train emerged from the wintry forest and slid into the snow-blanketed station at Lillavik. All she needed was a fluffy hat and some moustached guy to meet her, and it'd be a total Doctor Zhivago moment.

She'd been sleepy on the ride from Stockholm, but stepping out of the warm carriage into the chill snapped her awake. She looked at the clock above the platform. In England, one-tenth of this snow would have brought the entire railway network to a halt, but here, they arrived precisely on time.

From her spot towards the end of the raised platform, the scene in front of her was fairy-tale sweet. Stone buildings in shades of gold, cream and warm red stood low and snug along the street. It was just starting to get dark, and the road leading into the little town itself was strung with white lights. The blue-and-gold Swedish flag hung here and there, and next to the station, a frozen river wound through a snow-covered park. Everything was so pretty, she wanted to abandon her over-stuffed suitcase and make snow angels beneath the frost-kissed trees.

But her lungs hurt, and the metal of her earrings was starting to burn cold in her earlobes. She'd known it would be cold, but this? Brutal. Tucking her chin down into her scarf, she held a gloved hand in front of her mouth, hoping to take some of the ice out of the air before she breathed it in, but it made no difference. She pulled her woolly hat down further, and lifted her fur-trimmed hood (faux, of course) over the top. Unless she wanted Bengt Nilsson, wildlife conservationist, to collect a large block of ice from the railway station, she'd better wait inside. She pulled out the handle of her suitcase and headed for the doors.

"Zoe Bailey?"

She turned to see a tall, broad-shouldered man coming up the steps towards her. No moustache. And no hat or scarf either, she noticed, shivering as she nodded in reply.

"Yes."

"Wildlife volunteer?" A cloud of steam accompanied the words, and she half expected it to turn to ice and shatter on the ground.

"Yes," she said again, uncertainly. Unless her googling skills had failed her, she was pretty sure this wasn't Bengt Nilsson. All the pictures on his website had shown him as small, stocky and approachable-looking—pretty much the opposite of this man, who radiated impatience from a great height. "Sorry, you're...?"

"Here to collect you," he said. Then he took her suitcase, lifting it without flinching at the weight, and set off down the steps. "The car is this way."

She hesitated, watching him go. Was he kidding? Whoever he was, he was a) rude bordering on surly, and b) utterly watchable. Sweden was supposed to be safe, right? So maybe getting into a car with a strange man—who happened to be hot enough to melt the snow in a ten-foot radius—would be fine. In her mind's eye she imagined the snow and ice running away into rivulets as he walked, leaving only warm cobblestones in his wake.

He turned. "The Nilssons sent me."

She jolted to attention. "Oh, okay, sorry."

Gah, why was she apologising to him, when he was the one being so abrupt? Well, manners or not, she'd better get down there if she wanted to warm up some time this year.

She dashed down the steps to catch up, aware of his steady gaze on her. Down one, two, three…and then an icy patch…and then she was airborne. In the brief moment of suspension, as her legs flew out from under her, she had time to be embarrassed, and then afraid, as the ground loomed below.

The impact knocked the air out of her with a whoomp, and she heard herself emit an agonised grunt. Oh, it hurt. It really, seriously hurt.

He was there in a second, holding out a hand to help. But she shook her head. "I'm fine." Trying to catch her breath, the gulps of freezing cold air were cut glass in her chest. "I'm fine, really."

She forced herself to her feet, brushing snow off her coat sleeves, the side of her face, and her tender backside as she avoided his eye. Oh, very polished. Nice one.

He looked at her feet, clad in the black knee-high boots she'd splashed out on the winter before.

"Don't you have any other boots? You'll need something stronger than that." His tone made it clear that her inadequate footwear was a probable reflection of her suitability for the job ahead.

She bristled, even though she had her own doubts about what she'd signed up for. "I do. I have proper hiking boots. But I thought these would be okay for the trip." What qualified as non-slip in Selfridge's and on London pavements obviously wasn't non-slip enough for frozen Swedish winters.

"Good," he said. "Come on then."

He held out his arm, as though inviting her onto the dance floor at a ball, and she hesitated, then took it. The hesitation was only partly because she was still annoyed. Despite her aching butt, the thought of touching him gave her a rush that definitely took the chill off certain body parts. Then he smiled for the first time, just a little, and it went straight to her head. Uh-oh. This was *not* why she was here.

"I hope you can sit comfortably," he said. "We have to drive about twenty minutes."

She cringed inwardly at the indirect reference to her bottom, which was probably blossoming into a huge bruise about now. She took a icicle-laced breath, and gathered herself together. She was in PR, after all—and even a reluctant spin doctor like her should be able to turn a situation to her best advantage.

When they reached the car he opened the door for her, and she lowered herself gingerly into the seat, wincing a little as she touched down. Then, with her suitcase stowed in the back, they set off. Still hunched up from the cold, she looked at the dashboard display: eighteen degrees below zero. My God, no wonder she was frozen.

"It's really cold," she said redundantly.

He looked sideways at her. "It's winter. What were you expecting?"

"Um...cold. But I've never felt anything like this." It was reassuring to think of all the thermal underthings in her suitcase, most of which were deeply unsexy but practical.

"Try this." He flicked a switch, and pretty soon she felt the seat underneath her start to heat up.

"Oh, that's good. Thank you."

She pulled off her hat and unwound her scarf, and then struggled out of her coat. Finally feeling a more human temperature, she turned her attention to the view. They'd left the town behind, and although it was only late afternoon, the light was almost gone. He seemed to be driving very slowly—for safety, she supposed, or maybe the speed limit was low around here—but it gave her time to admire the houses they passed. Each one was a little oasis in the trees, light spilling into the snowy yards, and a surprising number of them had a flagpole in pride of place. She especially liked the houses painted in yellow or red or blue, trimmed with white. "It's so pretty here."

He just shrugged. "If you like that kind of thing."

She looked across at him. "Don't you think so? The houses are so gorgeous. I love the colours, and how they all have those steep roofs."

"They're steep so the snow won't pile up and break the roof and crush the house. Snow looks pretty, but it's heavy, and it's work. It's not only for snowmen and Instagram pictures."

It was only then that she realised two things about him (apart from what she'd already gathered—that he was hot, but grouchy). First, his English was really, really good. And second, was that a...Scottish accent? She was tired from the trip, and a ridiculously early start in London, but she was pretty sure there was more than Swedish in those deep, slightly husky tones.

"I'm not on Instagram," she said.

"Well then." He glanced in her direction, and there was a hint of amusement in his eyes. He wasn't entirely humourless then.

"I didn't catch your name," she said. Better late than never—and that accent had given her a clue.

"Jakob," he said, pronouncing it as though it started with a 'y'.

And there it was. In the background documents The Shark had given her, a Jakob Westermark was named as the researcher employed by the Scottish Wolf Reintroduction Society. Apparently he was finishing a PhD in endangered species management (specifically wolves), doing his own research here while providing information that could help the society's case in Scotland.

"Well, it's nice to meet you," she said. "Your English is so good. Have you lived somewhere else?"

"Yes," he replied. "And thank you."

She waited, but he didn't volunteer any more information. And she had to be careful—she didn't want to jump in with the wrong question and give herself away in the first hour. Small talk, then.

But her next comment was overtaken by a huge yawn— after the day's travelling, humming along the road in the warm car was lulling her into drowsiness. Really, she should be a better conversationalist. She could at least find out a bit more about him. She leaned back against the headrest, working to keep her eyes open. The last thing she wanted was to fall asleep and end up lolling and snoring in the passenger seat...

★

It was quiet. She jerked awake, suddenly aware that her mouth had been hanging open. Oh, great. She put a hand to her lips, but seemed all clear in the drool department. Small mercies.

Jakob sat in the driver's seat. How long had they been stopped? And where were they? For a moment she panicked, her sleep-fuddled mind convinced that he was, after all, a serial killer fit for a Scandinavian crime novel, and her once-warm behind would be found in the forest, half-eaten by wolves, come spring.

But then there were footsteps outside the car, and her door was pulled open.

"You are here!" boomed a hearty voice, much larger than the small man it was coming from. "Welcome! Come inside now, come on."

She smiled up at Bengt Nilsson, who did indeed look exactly like his website picture. Her journey was over, for now, but her mission was just beginning.

Chapter Four

Her footsteps crunched through the snow as she followed Bengt to the front door, noticing his slightly uneven gait. When they reached the steps, the door opened, and she recognised the other half of the Nilsson Vildmark Lodge team. According to Google, *vildmark* meant wilderness—and it seemed like the lodge was just a tiny pocket of habitation in the wilderness that surrounded it, part of which was a designated wildlife reserve. Greta wasn't dressed in the colourful blue and yellow traditional costume she wore on the lodge's website, but her friendly, welcoming face was unmistakable.

"Here she is, Greta," Bengt announced from the path, and his wife clapped her hands.

"Wonderful! Come in, come in," she said, waving them up the steps. "I have two girls who are excited to meet you."

"Really?" Zoe said, still feeling half asleep. "Thank you, it's lovely to be here."

Greta took her coat and hung it with her scarf and hat on a row of pegs by the door.

"Thank you, Jakob," she said, as he carried Zoe's suitcase into the warm house. Then she turned her attention back to Zoe. "Are you hungry?" she asked, looking concerned.

"Well…I am a bit."

The house smelled like all kinds of delicious things, and her stomach grumbled. She realised she was starving. It felt like ages since she ate at the railway station in Stockholm, just before getting on the train. Jakob said something to Bengt in Swedish, and they fell into conversation. The lilting, quick-fire staccato of their words was completely unfamiliar, even though she strained to recognise something from the Swedish language tutorials she'd been watching on YouTube.

Then Greta ushered her into the big kitchen, where a pine table was set with platters of meat and vegetables, bread rolls, pastries, fruit, and a giant pot of black coffee. Just the smell was enough to sharpen her up after her mobile nap.

Greta pulled out a chair for her. "I wanted to come and get you, but Malin needed a babysitter for her girls. And Bengt had the usual things to do here."

"Oh, that's okay, we were fine." She winced as she sat down with a bump, forgetting the hard landing she'd already had that day. "Ow."

"Are you all right?" Greta asked, pausing mid-pour with the coffee pot.

"Yes, I just…I fell over on the steps at the railway station."

"Oh, no. I'm so sorry. Were you hurt?"

Greta's English was just as good as her husband's, and Jakob's, and Zoe felt a pang of inadequacy at her lack of linguistic skills. Her French was almost passable, but the smattering of other languages she'd picked up as a kid, living with her parents in all kinds of places, had mostly faded away. Her brain still held a bunch of phrases in everything from Italian to Arabic, but this kind of fluency was something she'd never achieved.

"No, I wasn't hurt. Well, apart from my pride. And my bottom."

She rubbed it, shaking her head. Then she heard giggling from the doorway, and turned to see two little girls, each one as blonde and blue-eyed as the Nordic cliché.

"Hi," she said, giving them what she hoped was an encouraging smile.

The little one clutched the bigger one's arm and squeaked out a laugh, and her sister gave her a shove. Greta went over and steered them both in.

"This is Lena and Ebba," she said, pointing to each one in turn. "And this is Zoe. Can you say hello?" she asked them in slow, clear English.

But they just stared at Zoe, giggling behind their hands at this alien suddenly landed in their midst on a random Monday.

Greta looked encouragingly at the bigger sister. "Lena?"

Lena wound a strand of hair round and round her finger. "Hej," she whispered, pronouncing it *hay*, just as Zoe had heard online.

"Hej," she replied, and received endearing smiles from both little girls in return.

Greta gave them each a little bun with pearl sugar on top, and they went off happily back to the other room, whispering to each other.

"They're lovely girls," Greta said. "Malin waited a long time for them. Usually, she would never leave them overnight, but she has some appointments in another town. And I looked after her when she was little, so she trusts me."

"They're gorgeous," Zoe said. "If I was their mum I wouldn't like leaving them either."

Then Bengt came back in, rubbing his hands together. Zoe looked behind him, expecting to see Jakob's tall figure following.

"Is Jakob gone already? I never thanked him."

"He went back to his cabin," Bengt replied. "He's not very..." He hesitated, looking at Greta.

"Social," she provided for him. "He likes to be...private."

Zoe had started to figure that out herself. She didn't know what to make of him yet, but she did know this feeling creeping over her—disappointment.

"Oh, well....it was nice of him to come and get me.

Does he live near here?" She took the cup of coffee Greta offered, black as ink, and reached for the milk jug. "Thank you."

"Yes," Bengt said. "He's staying in one of our cabins."

"Oh, he didn't say that."

He hadn't said much of anything—if she didn't already have him in a file, she'd still be totally in the dark. Mind you, she hadn't exactly wowed him with her conversational skills either. Unless talking in your sleep counted for something. And although she already knew why he was here, she was interested to hear what the Nilssons would tell her.

Greta shook her head. "That's Jakob. He doesn't say much. He doesn't work for us officially. But Bengt had an operation a few months ago, and Jakob wanted somewhere to work on his projects. So he came back to help."

Bengt gave a wry smile, and pointed to his knee. "I needed a new one. Fine now."

"That's good," Zoe said. "It was lucky timing, that he could be here to help."

"*Ja*," Greta said, the agreement more like a little gasp than a word—sort of an affirmative intake of breath. Zoe had heard someone on the train do the same thing in conversation. "We like having him here," Greta continued. "And the volunteers seem to like him a lot."

Other than the obvious aesthetic reasons, she wondered what the volunteers found to like. But he couldn't be a complete grump, if he'd come to help Bengt and Greta when they needed it.

"Did he tell you he's studying the wolves?" Bengt asked.

"No, he didn't." She knew that already, of course, but now she'd met him, she found herself interested to hear more about Jakob Westermark. Purely a professional interest, of course. Nothing to do with those dark eyes, or the hint of smart humour she'd caught in his smile. Strictly business.

Bengt stole a miniature plaited bread roll from the table, and Greta handed him a plate. He took it obligingly, and sat down. "It's not a government programme, like our work," he said. "The county administrative board watches wolf numbers, but Jakob's work is funded by private investors in Scotland. He's doing his PhD at the same time. He loves his wolves...but they are not popular with everyone, you know."

"Are there quite a few near here then?" she asked.

He nodded. "Oh, yes. We are unusual, because we seem to be right where the territory of two wolf packs overlap. There has been a lot of activity this winter."

Zoe felt a chill run up the back of her neck. Of course she knew there were wolves here, but sitting in this house surrounded by forests and snow, talking about wolf packs, suddenly made it real. Just the idea of them was primal, wild—the unpredictable and the untamed.

Greta must have noticed her expression. "We don't see them close to the house. They would rather stay away from us."

She didn't want to seem like a complete rookie, even though she was. So she smiled. "They must be really interesting to study."

"Jakob seems very dedicated," Greta said. "It's good for him."

The way she said it piqued Zoe's curiosity, but it seemed too personal to ask why he might need something that was good for him. She took another sip of the coffee. It was potent stuff—she could feel a hum running through her veins already.

"And what about you?" asked Bengt. "You must also be very dedicated, to come up here in the middle of winter to help us."

She shifted in her chair a little. It wasn't dedication that had brought her here, but company politics and paying clients. She was interested in wildlife protection and conservation in principle, of course...just not interested enough to risk hypothermia. But, on the bright side, part of her role would apparently be to monitor the local golden eagle population, as captivating as any creature she'd ever seen on a David Attenborough documentary. Also, she'd always wanted to try a snowmobile, and she hadn't been ice-skating since she was a kid. And, for all his surliness, maybe it wouldn't be so bad working alongside tall, dark and Swedish Jakob...

And then, there was the other reason for her to come to Lillavik—Claire. She wouldn't share that with the Nilssons though, not yet.

"Oh, well," she replied. "This was the only time of year I could come."

That was actually true—according to The Shark, the volunteer places here were all taken from the coming spring until the following winter, and their clients wouldn't wait that long. Now that she thought of it, she wondered if that was really true. She wouldn't put it past Alcina to send her in the most frigid of months, just because she could.

"Well, we're grateful to have you," Greta said. "It must seem like a terrible climate, but we still have lots of visitors in the guesthouse. And Bengt is busy taking them skiing, now that his knee is better, or on safari with the snowmobiles. He doesn't have enough time to do everything else. And Jakob will have things for you to do, helping with his research."

Things to do...Zoe smothered the thoughts rising in her imagination. You're here on *business*, she reminded herself.

"A snowmobile safari sounds like fun." She was no skier, but she did have a secret fondness for high-powered vehicles that she never got to indulge, apart from watching replayed episodes of Top Gear. The Underground and London buses were her main form of transport, and neither of those made the grade.

"It is fun," Bengt said. "Maybe you'll join us one day."

"Yes, that would be great. Well, only if I have time," she added, remembering that she was supposed to be here to work. And in her spare time, she had a little Claire-related detective work to do too.

"Ah, well, tomorrow we can talk more about the work," Bengt said. "It's not difficult. For now, let's relax. You must be tired."

She had been, but the coffee had worked its dark magic.

She hadn't expected Sweden to be so...Italian with its coffee. Greta offered her more, but she shook her head.

"I'd better not, thank you. It's really good, but I won't sleep tonight if I have too much."

Greta nodded. "We love our coffee."

They ate dinner, the conversation flitting from English to Swedish and from topic to topic. When they asked about her work, she gave a loose description of her job in 'communications'. Then the subject of family came up, and under the gaze of the two little girls, she found herself telling the Nilssons about her own childhood. The edited version, anyway. First world problems, and all that. Yes, it was an amazing experience to travel the world as a child. Yes, her parents were very impressive. No, she hadn't seen them lately, but they were always very busy, so...

It was enough.

After dinner, Lena and Ebba went off to play while the adults sat by the fire and chatted. Soon though, they came back in, looking full of determination. Ebba nudged Lena forward towards Greta, and the little girl bit her lip, then asked something, bobbing hopefully up and down as she spoke.

Greta replied, then switched to English. "Maybe." She turned to Zoe. "The girls want us to take them ice-skating on the big lake tomorrow, but I don't think Malin will agree. They are in love with ice skating, but they usually skate on the rink in the village. Do you skate?"

"Not really. I mean, I did a few times as a kid. But I spent most of my time sitting on the ice, I think."

Bengt laughed. "I think you have sat on our ice enough already."

"I think so too." She grinned ruefully, and listened as Greta translated for the girls. They laughed too, then Lena said something to Greta, who smiled.

"Lena says she'll teach you to ice-skate."

"Oh, thank you!" Zoe said. "I mean, *tack*," she corrected herself, trying out her second Swedish word of the night.

Lena giggled, probably at the terrible pronunciation, but

it was nice to make a connection across the language barrier. She wished she'd had time to learn more before she came. Then little Ebba yawned, and Zoe caught it too—a huge yawn that made her jaw click and her eyes water.

Maybe that coffee wasn't as powerful as she'd first thought.

"You're tired," Greta said. "Bengt, we should let Zoe rest. And it's nearly bed time for you girls."

She looked at the little ones, and they must have recognised either the word 'bed', or Greta's meaningful expression, because they turned and scampered out of the room.

"Of course," Bengt said, getting to his feet. "Three girls to bed."

"They're so sweet and happy," Zoe said.

"They are," Greta agreed. "We're old, but we're not too boring, I hope."

Zoe laughed. "I don't think so."

"Come now, Zoe," Bengt said, with one firm clap that made her jump. "Come and see your Swedish home."

There were goodnights all round, then Zoe dug her sturdier boots out of her suitcase and put her coat back on. The offending slippery boots were stuffed into a plastic bag, probably never to see the light of day until she returned to London.

Bengt took the suitcase, and she followed him out of the house and along a path that ran though the trees. There was no need for a torch—the clouds had cleared enough to let the stars and moon illuminate the landscape, and the glow reflected back off the snow. Tiny lights lined the path as far as the turnoff to the guesthouse, which sat in a large clearing overlooking a frozen pond. Just like so many of the houses she and Jakob had passed on the way here, it was painted red, with white window and door frames. Smoke came from its two chimneys, and warm light spilled from the windows. It looked like a cosy place to be a guest.

"The cabins are this way," Bengt said, turning and leading her down a side path, until they came to another clearing. "The lake is about five minutes that way, and

Lillavik is around the coast a little way."

His voice was hushed in the cold night air, muffled by the snow that sat deep on the ground and softly dressed the branches of every tree. Then he pointed across to a little dwelling on the other side of the clearing. "That's where Jakob is staying. And this one is yours."

She turned to look. It was small but perfectly formed, a miniature version of the main guesthouse, but painted cornflower blue. There was a narrow trellis on each side of the front steps, and she imagined some tangly flowering vine framing the entranceway in spring. Candlesticks sat in the front windows, and on the door was a fat wreath, which she guessed was woven from willow. Bengt opened the door for her, and she touched the wreath as she went in.

"Greta leaves them there all year," he said. "At Christmas she adds mistletoe, and in the spring and summer she fills them with flowers and leaves."

"How gorgeous."

Inside, she took off her boots, hung her outerwear on the hook Bengt pointed out, then looked around. It was small, but it was much more than a cabin—with its comfortable-looking sofas, heavy curtains, perfectly appointed kitchen, and a wood-burner set into a full-sized stone fireplace, it was a cottage in miniature. On the other side of the main room she could see through to a bedroom, and next to that was a small bathroom. Everything was Scandinavian in the way that people aspired to in the UK, but never quite seemed to pull off. Pale wood furnishings were set off with traditional textiles, there were tons of cushions, woven rugs, and candles, and the tall, carved bookshelf in the corner was full of magazines, books, and antique trinkets.

"This is gorgeous. And it's so warm."

Bengt nodded. "I asked Jakob to light the fire for you before he went to bed."

"Thank you. This is so nice, just for volunteers to stay in." She walked over to the French doors on the other side of the room, and peered out. She could see the light from Jakob's cabin, but his curtains were drawn. "Is the other one as nice as this?"

"We think so." He came over and pulled the curtains across, blocking out her view of the snowy forest, and her mysterious neighbour. "We built them when Oscar was young, for his friends to stay in. He's in Australia now, so...the volunteers have somewhere nice to stay." He shrugged.

"Oscar is your son?"

"He is."

He bent down and opened the wood-burner door, and tossed in a new log. She waited as he shunted the wood around with a poker, but he didn't say anything more about Oscar.

"Well, this must have been a wonderful place to grow up."

He secured the latch, and turned back to her. "I'm glad you like it."

"I really do."

He smiled. "There's food in the kitchen for your breakfast. Sleep well now. *God natt.*"

"Thank you. Good night. Um, *god natt.*"

She saw him out, and closed the door. Then she opened it just a crack again, to see him stride back down the path and disappear between the trees. She looked across to the other cabin, not much more than a decent stone's throw away. The lights were still on. She wondered what Jakob was doing in there...and what he thought of her. He'd certainly made an impression on her. She just couldn't decide if it was a good one or not.

Then she shivered, and went back into the warmth. Bengt had left her suitcase on a rack in the bedroom. The bed looked squishy, and the comforter looked downy, and suddenly she was desperate to be lying down. She got changed into her pyjamas (unsexy but snug flannelette), cleaned her teeth and washed her face in the tiny but cleverly designed bathroom, and slipped into bed. Oh, bliss. Well, apart from the lingering ache in her bottom.

She closed her eyes. Bengt and Greta were so nice, she felt a twinge of guilt that she wasn't really here for the reason they thought. But she'd squash her qualms and help in the guesthouse, count golden eagle sightings, catalogue wolf poo or whatever, and be the model conservationist, while doing her undercover duty. Then she'd take what she found back to Vertex, and prove those snobs wrong about her.

And while she was here, she'd see what she could discover about Claire. Claire, who had made it perfectly plain that she never wanted to see Zoe again. Who had walked away from her home and family without looking back.

Zoe was the one who found the letter. In it, Claire spelled out exactly why she was leaving, and told them not to look for her. And because she was nineteen, officially an adult, the police had no interest in helping to search for her. Sarah and Paul—who'd become like Zoe's adoptive parents by then—were so broken by the whole thing that they seemed to simply let their daughter go. They didn't talk about her, at least not when anyone else was around. Zoe had tried, but they clammed up so completely at the very mention of Claire's name, it became pointless to keep on. After a while, she wondered whether they even thought about their daughter any more. Sometimes she had to remind herself that she'd had a best friend…a friend who'd become like a sister. And you don't just let a sister go, no matter what she might have written in the heat of anger. Well, Zoe couldn't, anyway.

And that, even more than her job, was why she was here—south of the Arctic, north of nowhere, in the middle of a white landscape and a not-so-white lie.

Chapter Five

T he snowmobile seemed to buck underneath them, and Zoe let go of the hand rails at the side and clutched onto Bengt's waist, possibly a little too tightly.

"Just a little bump," he called, over his shoulder. He sounded apologetic enough, but judging by the way his shoulders were shaking, she was sure he was laughing. That 'little bump' felt pretty big to her, and especially to her tender bottom.

In the warm safety of the barn that morning, the snowmobile had looked like a positively sedate mode of transport—padded seats, a broad, heavy front, and two ski blades sticking out at the front like a couple of mechanical clown feet. She hadn't expected it to move *this* fast. But as she started to get used to it, the excitement of the ride over-rode her nerves and the ache of her bruise.

"I'd love to try driving this myself," she yelled, over the roar of the engine.

"You can do it," he shouted back. "It's not difficult."

After their conversation the night before, Bengt had decided to give her a snowmobile tour of the property and surrounding country before showing her what was involved with the conservation work. To give her her bearings, he'd said, but when they struck out into the forest that surrounded the complex of buildings, she almost instantly lost track of where they were.

"Our land ends here," Bengt told her, crossing some line that only he could see. "From here to the lake, and right around to Lillavik, is government land."

"Okay," she called back, but she knew she'd never remember where that supposed boundary was. It was nothing but trees and snow as far as the eye could see, a beautiful trap for the unwary. Right then, she resolved to always take her phone with her when she went out. Assuming you could get any reception in this distant wild.

They took a sudden turn to the right, and she tightened her grip again as they powered up a slope. At the top, he stopped, letting the engine idle.

"There you are. The long lake, Långasjön."

She tried to pronounce it the way he did. "Long-i-shun? Long-uh-shurn?"

"Not too bad," he said. "But the most important thing is to admire it, not pronounce it."

She laughed. "I'll work on it."

She looked down at the lake, frozen and sparkling white in the bright morning sun. No wonder Lena and Ebba wanted to skate on it—it was almost hypnotically inviting, even to her, who knew she'd probably come to instant grief if she stepped out there on blades. Out from the shoreline, she could see someone on the ice. It looked like he or she was sitting in the shelter of a little tent.

"What's going on there?" she asked, pointing to the tiny figure.

"That's Hakon Halvarsson. He fishes on the lake all the time. He's retired, and he's not very strong any more. But his wife still makes him leave the house every day, and he can't think of anything else to do."

"Poor Hakon." She laughed. "Does he ever catch anything in that freezing water?"

"Oh, yes. There are lots of fish in there."

"Frozen fish?"

"Very strong Swedish fish," he said with a grin, flexing a bicep. "Sometimes he sells them at the Sunday market in

Lillavik." He gestured towards the other side of the lake.

"So Lillavik is in that direction?"

"Yes. At night you can see the lights."

She strained her eyes in the direction of the village, the only clue they had to Claire's whereabouts. It would have seemed an inexplicably random place, except for Defrost Digital, the software and app development company that had started there.

It made sense that Claire—an avid gamer, self-taught coder, and aspiring app designer—would end up at some super-techy place. Zoe just never imagined that place could be so very, very far from anything resembling Silicon Valley, despite Claire's prediction of a snowy tech future. But then she prided herself on doing exactly what people didn't expect of her. It was one of the things Zoe had liked so much about her.

Down by the lake, another snowmobile emerged from an opening in the forest. It stopped at a tree near the shore, and the driver got off and opened what looked like a box attached to the trunk. She squinted, but at this distance she couldn't be sure...

"Is that Jakob?" she asked Bengt.

He nodded. "He's checking a camera. Sometimes the cold affects them. The wolves are not usually in this area, but we heard them howling last week, so he put a camera there."

She felt that prickle on the back of her neck again. "So they're close."

"There is no danger," he said, reading her expression. "If we see them near, we'll tell everyone. But they don't want to see us, you know."

She was half relieved, but half disappointed too. There was something compelling about the idea of them, something elemental, roaming out here in the wild.

"Now we should go and talk about work," he said. "But let's take the long way, and give Jakob time to get back too." He revved the engine, betraying a little of the boy racer that she guessed he'd been in his youth.

She nodded and put her arms around his waist again. "Sounds good to me."

★

The snowmobile swooped to a stop behind the guesthouse, sending up an arc of snow, and Zoe whooped in exhilaration and delight. The ride back had been the most fun she'd had in ages, and her cheeks were tingling pink from the freezing cold air. At that moment she almost thought she could get used to the chill—on a crisply sunny day like this, you could probably call it invigorating, even. And Bengt really was great company. It made her wish she was here without complications, just for fun. And for conservation, of course.

"I think you're a bad influence on me," he told her, as they got off the snowmobile.

"Are you sure? I think it's the other way round," she laughed, her heart still beating fast.

He grinned. "My lovely wife would probably agree."

There was a line of other snowmobiles parked along the wall, ready for the lodge guests, and she itched to jump on one and have a go herself. But she dragged her gaze away—she was here to work, after all. Tucked against the side of the guesthouse was a tiny annexe, not much bigger than a playhouse and just as charming. Bengt led her up the steps. Under the steeply-roofed porch, a Swedish flag hung on the door, the gold and blue brilliant in the late morning sun.

"And this is the nervous centre of the operation," he announced grandly, as he opened the door for her.

She had to laugh. "Um…do you mean nerve centre, maybe?"

"Ah, yes, *nerve* centre," he agreed good-naturedly, and they went on into the warmth, a cheerfully companionable feeling between them.

All at once, nervous centre seemed an apt description after all. Inside the little office—which she now realised it was—two MacBooks sat on a long table, under a window that ran the length of one wall. And at one of the computers sat Jakob.

Her heart instantly returned to the same tumbling, racing pace brought on by the adrenaline-filled snowmobile ride.

Jakob turned to look at them, and nodded a curt greeting. "Good morning."

It would be a stretch in the extreme to say he looked pleased to see them. And yet, her heart continued at its *omg* gallop.

Which was annoying, actually. She'd never been keen on the dark-and-angsty type, and Jakob seemed like he could qualify as the poster boy for the breed. Or maybe it was just that famous Swedish reserve everyone in the office had warned her about before she left. She'd thought they were just rubbing it in, enjoying the chance to gloat about all the ways she'd be miserable here. But maybe they were right.

"Good morning," she replied, wondering if last night was the first and only smile she'd see from him. This office was going to feel very small if they had to spend much time in it together.

But Bengt—suffering from no Swedish reserve at all— was untroubled by Jakob's lack of enthusiasm. He was probably used to it, she guessed.

"Hej, hej," he said, giving Jakob a slap on the back. "I have company for you. Zoe is very keen to get started."

Jakob regarded her. Evidently, he was not at *all* keen for her to get started. "Okay."

At least he'd brought her heart to a halt. "Yes, I'm looking forward to it," she replied, with pointed good manners.

"Great," he said, and turned back to his computer screen.

Apparently their short and scintillating conversation was over.

Well, he'd have to talk to her eventually, considering that part of her role here was helping with his own conservation work. And part of *that* (the clandestine part) was finding, amongst his research, evidence that would count against the wolves and in favour of Vertex's clients in Scotland. So she'd *have* to get him talking, one way or another.

She suppressed the urge to poke her tongue out at his long, straight back, and avoided noticing how broad his shoulders were. And how his dark hair stuck up just a little there at the back, as though he'd pulled his sweater off and left it tousled. And how...ahem. She turned her attention to Bengt. "So what will I be doing for you?"

He pulled another chair over to the second computer and opened a fat red folder. "Everything you need to know is in here."

With Jakob's back still firmly turned, she and Bengt went through the guide for volunteer conservationists, her job for the next three weeks. It wasn't complicated. As well as assisting with the wolf project, helping Greta in the guesthouse as needed, and recording data from the weather station outside the office (to contribute to climate change monitoring), every day she would visit the golden eagle nesting site closest to the lodge. Bengt had already pointed it out on their tour that morning—an enormous construction of sticks high up in a birch tree.

At this time of year, towards the end of winter, the eagles could be starting to think about mating, he told her. On each visit, she was to make note of any birds she saw and the behaviour they were exhibiting, check the surrounding area, and take photos of anything unusual or interesting. If the birds chose to settle in—they would most often re-use an existing nest, rather than build a new one— Jakob would set up a webcam. Back at the office, all the data was entered into the computer, and any photos uploaded and labelled by date and location. Experts in the government's conservation department would take it from there.

She nodded. "So...I can take the snowmobile?"

"Yes, if you want to," Bengt said. "Some of our volunteers prefer to go on skis, but you can choose. And Greta can go with you for the first couple of days. But the snowmobile has a GPS, and the path is marked, so you can't get lost."

She considered it. "Well, I wouldn't get far on skis...but then I might never come back on the snowmobile! You'll have to show me how to use the GPS."

At that, she thought she heard Jakob laugh to himself, and she wondered if he was wishing she *would* get lost, so he could have the office to himself again.

Bengt waved a hand. "You'll be fine. Jakob will show you—he teaches all the volunteers to drive, when he's here."

Jakob looked up then. "Maybe you won't be the worst student I've had."

Really? She gave him her best PR faux-smile. "Maybe you won't be the worst teacher *I've* had."

There was a moment's silence as they regarded each other, then Jakob turned back to his work. This lesson would obviously be a laugh a minute.

Bengt chuckled. "Ah, joking already, that's good."

She couldn't tell whether he was oblivious to the tension in the room, or purposefully smoothing it over. Maybe Jakob was like this with every volunteer...although probably not, given Greta's comment about how they all liked him. She suppressed a sigh and looked out the window, where a small bird was hopping across the snow. What on earth could it be finding to eat in this snowbound landscape? Life obviously continued through the frozen days and nights, until spring came again.

Bengt seemed to read her thoughts.

"There isn't much to see in the winter months. But the government's rules for funding are very clear—the programme must be all year round. We're lucky to have people like you, who come and help. And it makes a big difference for Greta."

She blushed a little, guiltily aware that her motivations weren't as altruistic as he thought.

"Oh, well...thank you for having me."

He smiled. "You can start tomorrow. When the work is finished in the guesthouse too, you can do whatever you like each afternoon. Take the spare car into Lillavik, or ski, or ice-skate...but carefully."

He grinned at his own humour, and she laughed.

"I'll try, I promise."

She was keen to get back into Lillavik, and visit Defrost Digital, to see if she could find anything of Claire. If she had ever come here, she'd most likely gone again long ago. But with no other real leads, it was worth a try, and Paul would be waiting for news.

Bengt stood up. "Now I must go and look after our guests, so I'll leave you with the instructions," he said. "Jakob can tell you about his work. There's a coffee machine there, please help yourself. Then you can have your snowmobile lesson."

"Okay. Thank you."

"Take care of her, Jakob," Bengt told him as he left.

She stifled a snort. Sure.

But as the door closed, leaving them alone, Jakob turned and looked at her. "I think you can take care of yourself," he said.

It could have been a brush-off, or an insult, except that—for the briefest moment—he smiled.

And there was that speeding heart again, a surge of unexpected attraction. If he could shake off the surly, he might actually be good company. In that instant of a smile, the weight seemed to lift from his forehead, and his face cleared and became even more attractive. Maybe he wouldn't be teaching her to drive off the nearest cliff, after all.

Danger, her subconscious whispered. This is the man you're lying to. Just being here is a lie. Don't even think about it...

But she ignored it. She *could* take care of herself. She knew what she was doing. Get in, get the info, and get out, back to London to make her point. And a promotion, if she had her way. Well, why not? It was amazing how attempted humiliation could make you suddenly interested in your career. One moody but handsome man would *not* get in the way of wiping that sarky smile off The Shark's face.

Chapter Six

Throttle on the right, brake on the left. Feet in the slots. Lean with the machine as it corners. Jakob's instructions were fast and to the point, and she listened carefully, determined not to be his worst student so far. Next, the hand signals. Left arm up in an L—prepare to stop. Left arm waving up and down—pay attention. Pump the left arm: let's go.

Once she'd repeated everything to his satisfaction, he grabbed the starter cord of her snowmobile and pulled once, twice, putting the weight of his body behind the action. The engine sprang into life, and he stood back and indicated that she should get on.

She wasted no time. Astride the seat, the vibration ran through her body, charging her with energy. She took hold of the hand grips, and even through her gloves she could feel the warmth.

"Are they heated?" she asked him.

"Nothing but the best," he replied, but his tone was so dry she couldn't tell if he was being sarcastic or not. Well, whatever—the warmth was blissful.

He started his own snowmobile, and they drove slowly away from the lodge in single file, along a path that ran behind his cabin and towards the lake. She left a large gap between them, as instructed, and concentrated on getting a feel for the machine and how it handled the snow-covered terrain. It was surprisingly easy, and soon she wished they could go faster. But Jakob was riding safe and steady ahead, so she tamped down the urge to be a girl racer and focused on enjoying the scenery. He hadn't wanted to talk about his research, instead suggesting that they go for the lesson straight away, and now they were out in the bright crisp day she could see why.

They followed a well-defined path through woods and clearings, obviously in the tracks of earlier riders. She was able to relax and look around a little at the sapphire-and-diamond landscape of cool turquoise blue sky and sun-glittery snow. Peering into the trees, she wondered if she might see a deer, even though she knew the noise of the snowmobiles would surely scare them off.

They finally came down to the lake, at a different spot from where she and Bengt had seen him that morning. A tiny boathouse stood tucked into bare-branched trees by the shore, and a narrow jetty jutted out over the frozen water. It looked like a good place for swimming and fishing in the summer.

They turned off their engines, and the sudden quiet was so absolute that for a second she wondered if her ears were even working at all. Then a trill and chirp came from the trees behind them, breaking the spell. They both looked up as a little bird swooped down and past them, its red chest a vivid flash against the crystal landscape.

"Bullfinch," he said.

She looked at him as they got off the snowmobiles. "You must know this place really well."

He shrugged. "I do."

"I didn't have a chance to ask you much last night," she said. "Sorry I fell asleep."

"It's fine," he said. "You were tired."

He started towards the lake, his footsteps making a *crunch, crunch* sound as his boots broke through the firm top layer of snow.

"I was." She hesitated, then followed, lurching a bit as

she worked to keep her footing in the deeper spots. "So, are you from around here?"

He stopped and waited for her to catch up. "I am."

This was obviously going to be like blood from a stone, but she ploughed on. She was curious to know more about him. Just for research purposes, naturally.

"But you've been overseas, you said?" That much she already knew.

"I spend a lot of time in Scotland. In the north." His focus was on the horizon across the lake, as if trying to see all the way back to the Highlands.

Of course. But she couldn't give anything away. "I thought your accent was a bit different. Did you like it? It must be beautiful up there too."

Even though she'd been around the world as a kid, from Doha to Dallas, she hadn't been further north in the UK than Edinburgh. Family holidays were few and far between, but always somewhere warm—Anthony and Madeline (she hardly thought of them as 'Mum' and 'Dad') were believers in sand, sun and Bellinis on their rare breaks.

"It is beautiful," he said. "Cold too. You wouldn't like it."

She frowned, irritated at the implication in his words. "I'm not that soft. I'm just not used to it. London temperatures are nothing like this..."

Then she noticed the slightest glimmer in his eyes, and realised that he was teasing her, and wished she hadn't leapt so earnestly to her own defence. While she was still trying to decide whether she was more annoyed at being played than the insinuation that she was feeble, he turned away from the water, back towards the snowmobiles.

Already? She turned to follow him, cautiously picking her way through the snow. Then she stopped, looking at the boathouse. It would be a gorgeous place for a party in the summer. She could picture it strung with bunting and fairy lights, music playing, and people laughing and picnicking on the grass.

"Is there a boat in there?" she asked.

"No." He kept walking.

"Oh, it's empty then?"

"No."

The edge to his tone made her prick up her ears. "What's in there?"

"Nothing."

"But you just said it wasn't empty."

He narrowed his eyes as he looked at her, assessing her in some way she couldn't fathom, and she shifted under his gaze.

Then he seemed to come to a decision. He led her over to the boathouse, and reached up to retrieve a key from a nook just under the roof. It opened a creaky, narrow side door with a wrought iron handle. He gestured for her to go in, then ducked down to follow her through, and pulled the door closed behind him.

Inside it was hazy-dark, the light filtering through small windows dusted with ice on the outside and actual dust on the inside. The air was still, and smelled like the hay that was in bales along the back wall and sprinkled on the floor. As her eyes adjusted to the light, she realised that just as he'd said, the vehicle housed inside wasn't a boat. Instead, it was a sleigh. A sleigh beautiful enough to be Santa's ride in *The Night Before Christmas*, or an escape for a fairy-tale princess fleeing a cursed castle. The red paint on the woodwork was faded, but she ran her finger across the gold trim, and it glowed in the dim light. The black metal runners curved gracefully up and around at the front, and inside, the seats were pin-tucked and velvety.

"This is gorgeous," she breathed, feeling like anything more than a whisper would break some enchantment.

That self-contained, cautious measurement was still in his eyes. "It was my mother's. I don't know what to do with it now."

That first sentence, combined with his expression, told her everything. "You lost your mum," she said gently. "I'm sorry."

He nodded, and shrugged, and busied himself pulling wisps of hay from the floor of the sleigh.

She took his cue, and didn't ask any more. "It seems a

shame for it to be in here, when it's so beautiful," she said, wiping dust from the runner. "It needs to be out in the sunlight, pulled by a reindeer."

He smiled at that, and his expression made her feel like she'd passed the test, whatever it was. He pointed to the harness hanging at the back of the shed. "She had Icelandic horses. Smaller than reindeer, but strong."

"Icelandic horses are almost as romantic as reindeer."

As soon as she said it, she blushed. Would he think she was trying to force some kind of romantic moment? Because she wasn't. Even though in the half-dark, now with his usual guard down, he was undeniably gorgeous. Not the pale-blond Scandinavian kind of good-looking, the sort that featured in Volvo ads and modelled Norwegian knitwear. There was something more unexpected about him, a kind of complicated, compelling attractiveness that she couldn't pin down. It seemed appropriate, given that she couldn't pin *him* down either.

He shook his head. "Reindeer are not romantic. They taste good though."

"Oh, no. Tell me you don't."

"Oh yes," he replied. "We do."

She grimaced. "Christmas will never be the same again."

"We have worse things. Rotten herring, goose-blood soup..."

Well, if there had been even the briefest danger of a romantic moment, it was gone. She held up a hand. "I'm only here for three weeks, so I'm happy to say I probably won't have time to try those."

He smiled, and his teeth flashed white in the dusky light. "Someone could arrange it."

"Is that a promise or a threat?"

"Whatever you think."

She turned her attention back to the sleigh. "I think your mum would probably really like this to be back out on the snow one day."

His face sobered again. "I think so too." Then he held out a hand, inviting her up onto the seat. "After you."

She put her gloved hand into his, and stepped up. There was less room than she thought there'd be. When he sat down next to her, she felt the sleigh dip to his side, and the angle of the seat made her tilt towards him. He smelled surprisingly good for a guy who spent his days tramping around in the wilderness. Oh, it was tempting to just let herself slip a little to the left, just a little, and see what happened next.

But she looked up at him, and his expression was unreadable, his brow heavy again. There was nothing to show that he felt any romance in this moment, with or without reindeer or ponies or princesses. Oh heck, he was probably thinking of his mother. How inappropriate was it for her to be veering into sexy thoughts, when he'd just shared something so sad and beautiful?

Three weeks, she reminded herself. That was all. Do what she'd come for, then back to London.

The length of his body pressed against hers from shoulder to knee, and despite her thick pants and puffy jacket, she was aware of his warmth. He took off his gloves, and she found herself looking at his bare hands, their fingers long and agile-looking. In the quiet, she hesitated, then peeled off her own suede gloves. It felt weirdly intimate, each of them dressed in the most impenetrable items of clothing, exposing just the body parts that could reach out to one another and...

Even in this chill, her imagination knew what to do with a tempting man, in a sleigh, in a boathouse by a lake.

She kept quiet, not wanting to give away her train of thought, but not wanting to disrupt the moment either. His right hand lay on his right knee, *this close* to her left hand, hesitating on her left leg. He looked down, and she held her breath. All he had to do was stretch his little finger across, and the connection would be made...

"You must be cold," he said.

She looked again at her own hands, and saw that her fingernails had turned an unattractive shade of purple, while the tips of her fingers were mortuary-mottled blue and white. She stuffed her hands in her pockets.

"No, no, I'm fine." So much for that romantic little scenario she had going in her own mind. Served her right. Stick to why you're here, she told herself. Then she regrouped, changing the subject.

"So…you're studying the wolves?"

"Yes."

"Bengt said you're doing a PhD, but some other work too." Here was a chance to get his own description of what she already knew. "Is that for the university, or…?"

He shook his head. "No, it's a group of people in Scotland who have created their own organisation. They believe that the native animals should still be welcome in their own country." He turned towards her a little more, making the sleigh creak, and a new energy was in his voice as he continued. "They want to let the wolves come back to Scotland, and I'm helping them."

It sounded utopian, she had to admit…but possibly not super practical. Who would really want wolves running around their property? She could see both sides, but it was easy enough to understand the Scottish landholders' point of view.

"It must be really interesting," she said, staying neutral. "But why are you here in Sweden, instead of there?"

"It's still only a plan. A dream for them. Right now, they're writing proposals and trying to convince the government, and the people. And the information from Sweden will be very helpful. It's not all positive, but sometimes the negative things teach you more."

Her ears pricked up. "What kind of negative things?"

"Nothing so bad." He waved it away. "The wolves do attack farm animals sometimes. But my information is helping them to make a good argument. And if they are successful, they need someone like me to help monitor the programme there."

Finally, they were having an actual conversation. After his attitude in the office, she hadn't been sure he'd talk to her at all—about anything. It was going so well, she hated to be a downer, especially when he was talking in that ridiculously charming and musical Swedish-Scottish

English. But she was here for a reason, and she had to ask.

"Do you really think it's a good idea though? Wouldn't it cause trouble?"

"Honestly? Yes, I think there would be conflict between the wolves and the people, especially the farmers. We can see it in Sweden. But they really believe it should happen."

"Do you?"

He looked at her, his dark eyes seeming to deepen in intensity. "There's something special about the wolves. When you see them, you know they're meant to be."

"When you say it like that, I believe you." And right then, she did.

"Maybe you'll see them yourself, while you're here."

She didn't want to admit that the thought made her nervous in the extreme. "Maybe."

Suddenly he looked at his watch. "We'd better go. I have a Skype meeting soon."

He got up and stepped out of the sleigh, then turned to her. She took the hand he offered, and got down as gracefully as she could.

"Thanks for showing me this. It's beautiful. I'd love to see it out on the snow one day."

There was a pause. As they stood on the hay-strewn floor, dust mote stars floated between them in the pale strip of light coming from the window. Then she realised that her hand was still in his, politely resting in his grasp, but very obviously *still there*. They both looked down at the point of connection, and all at once she wanted to tangle her fingers in his, pull him in close, and uncover all the other overly-clothed parts of him...

She looked back up, but when he met her gaze, there was nothing to be discerned from his expression. Was the air extra thin up here, making her light-headed? The angsty, handsome loner, with a sleigh in a boathouse by a lake, the dark charm of his wolves, and a moving story about his mother. It was good, she'd give him that, and so tempting. It was cold, he was hot, and would it be so terrible to throw in a little pleasure with the business?

But no. She couldn't let herself be distracted. Three

weeks, in and out...and not *that* kind of in and out. She laughed out loud, and took her hand back. He gave her a quizzical look, but she shook her head.

"Nothing." She pulled her gloves back on. "Let's go."

He put the key back in its hiding place, then strode over to her snowmobile, starting it with two mighty pulls on the cord. Then he went to his own machine, and started it up too.

As he pumped his left arm, the signal for them to go, she remembered what Greta had said the night before. *The volunteers do seem to like him a lot.* She was starting to see why. She liked him a bit too much herself.

Chapter Seven

U p, up, up in the bare branches of the towering birch
tree sat the nest, a huge, twiggy mass so big that Zoe
wondered how the branches held it, let alone the added
weight of the eagles once they settled in.

"Amazing, isn't it?" Greta smiled with pride, as though
she'd overseen the construction herself. "They used this one
last year, and the year before."

"It is amazing," she agreed. "Will they use it again this
year, do you think?"

"We'll have to wait and see."

Zoe turned in place, scanning the forest and sky around
them. "I wish we could see them now."

"I wish you could too. They are very impressive.
Pictures don't compare with the real thing."

It was another out-of-the-box day, the sun shining and
the snow achingly white in the cold air. Jakob hadn't been
in the little volunteer office when Zoe got there after
breakfast that morning, so she'd entered the weather data
into the computer—minus fifteen, positively balmy—and
then gone to help Greta with a few jobs in the guesthouse.
Wolfy stuff would have to wait until he turned up, she
supposed. Alongside Greta, she helped to confirm
bookings, plan the following week's guest activities, and

peel potatoes for the night's dinner. But it was obvious that Greta was as keen to get out on the snowmobiles as she was. Before long, she threw up her hands.

"That's enough! I'll do the rest later. Let's get outside."

And Zoe was happy to agree.

Now, with the nest still empty, they did a quick survey of the surrounding area for animal prints or droppings, or anything out of the ordinary. Zoe paced a methodical route around her side of the nest area, as Greta had instructed, glad of her sunglasses in the pristine brightness. There was nothing to see but pillowy snow and sugar-dusted trees, a tantalising landscape that beckoned her to come, come further in. She paused for a minute and peered into the woods, where the tree trunks and whiteness stretched into a gauzy distance. If this was a fairy tale—and coming from the concrete streets of London, she totally felt like it was— she would step forth into the forest's enchantment, only to find herself face to face with...what? A troll? A wolf? On second thoughts, maybe the woods weren't that inviting after all. And she knew that there were even bears in Sweden, although they'd all be tucked up asleep at this time of year, she supposed.

"Zoe!"

Greta's voice rang through the clear air, breaking the almost-spell. She turned and headed back to the tree with the unoccupied nest. Just on the other side, Greta was taking photos of the snow. Or, as she could see when she got closer, of prints in the snow.

"Jakob is going to be so excited," Greta said, leaning carefully in for a close-up of a single print. "I don't think we've had prints so close to home before."

Zoe crouched down and looked at them, tracked in straight lines through the snow. They were almost big enough to put her hand into, and she could clearly see the claw marks on each one.

"Wow," she said. "How...amazing."

Did she sound enthusiastic enough? Because yes, part of her was excited—but part of her found it flat-out freaky that she was standing where wolves had passed, what...a few hours before? Or less, even?

Greta must have heard the uncertainty in her voice, because she smiled reassuringly.

"Don't worry. You know, they are scared of us more than we are scared of them."

Zoe pursed her lips. "Mmm. I think you're thinking of spiders."

Greta laughed. "Okay, maybe they're not very scared. But they would rather avoid us, honestly. They have their territory, and they just want to live. It's sad that the government is allowing them to be killed."

She'd read about this in her briefing notes—it would be good to get some on-the-ground perspective. "Why is it happening?"

"Well, they call it 'managing' the population." Greta frowned as she made air quotes. "They say they have calculated how many wolves are needed, so they don't become endangered, and they decide how many can be killed each year. But some farmers want them to be completely gone, and some wildlife fighters think they should be free to breed. I don't think there will ever be an agreement." She shook her head.

"But you said they're not dangerous?" Zoe asked, as they walked back to the snowmobiles.

"No human has ever been killed by a wolf in Sweden, since they came back in the country. But farm animals...yes."

Hearing that, she felt herself leaning to team wolf. Surely it wasn't their fault that farmers were leaving animals out in their territory, when they had to eat to survive. But something else had caught her attention. "Since they came back?"

Greta leaned against the seat of her snowmobile, her expression sombre.

"At one time, it was legal to kill wolves—so people did. Until there were almost none left at all. Then in the 1960s they became protected, and only the government could...what do you call it? Cull them?" Zoe nodded, and she continued. "But now hunters can shoot them in the winter, a certain number every year. This year the European Commission is arguing that Sweden does not have good enough reasons to kill any wolves, so everyone is in court to argue about it."

"Is anyone hunting them here?"

"No one from Lillavik, because they know they would have to deal with Bengt. And me." She pounded a fist into her opposite palm, parodying toughness. But there was a steel in her eyes that showed how serious she really was.

"And Jakob," Zoe said.

"Yes, and Jakob, as long as he's here. He stays so quiet, but I think if anything happened to his wolves, that would be the thing to set him on fire." She reached for the snowmobile's starter cord. "What do they say, about some people...something about deep water..."

"Still waters run deep?"

"That's it. That's Jakob." She pulled once on the cord, and again, and the snowmobile started, the sudden sound of the engine jarring in the wild space.

"I sort of got that impression," Zoe replied, over the noise, and Greta nodded.

They set off, Zoe hoping that the ruckus they made would be enough to scare off any lingering wolves. At the same time, she hoped that they stayed around, for their own sakes—because they were obviously safer here, on the Nilssons' turf.

And for Jakob's sake, too, even if he was an unpredictable (but annoyingly attractive) grump. Because didn't everyone need that one thing that meant something? The thing that lit your fire, made you want to get up in the morning?

She hadn't managed to find the thing that lit *her* fire yet. PR was her job, but not her passion, like it was for some of her colleagues. Sometimes she wondered how she'd carried on for so long, putting in so many hours at work that she didn't have time to think about what her thing might really be. Her parents had found it in their work, Claire had found it in her coding, and it was obvious that the Nilssons lived theirs every day of the year.

And she'd seen it in Jakob's eyes when he talked about the wolves.

Anyway, best not to think about him and his sleigh and his come-hither-grouchy eyes, wherever he was. This afternoon she was working on her other mission—to find Claire.

Whether Claire wanted to be found was another question.

★

The road was clear of snow between the lodge and Lillavik, but Zoe drove like a nana anyway. She might strike a patch of ice, she reasoned, and even though there were winter tyres on the lodge's spare car, she was used to driving on the left, not the right. Also, those moose signs on the side of the road weren't exactly reassuring.

Elk, she corrected herself, remembering that Greta had called them that before she left. But not the same as an American elk, she had explained, which was a different animal entirely, so there it would be a moose, although on the other hand an elk in England *was* an elk...at that point, Zoe's eyes had started to glaze over, but she'd got the message. Moose, elk, whatever—if she drove into one, Greta said, there would be no winner. Whatever you called them, even airbags were no match for the arrival of a fully-grown animal through your windscreen. And being squashed behind the wheel of a Volvo by seven hundred pounds of Scandinavian ungulate was *not* the way she'd choose to go. Far too comical to be truly tragic.

So, careful driving it was.

After barely twenty minutes, she was approaching Lillavik. Despite its name, which translated as 'small bay', it wasn't actually by the lakeside. Instead, it sat on elevated land above, at the edge of the forest. She'd seen a little of it the night she arrived, of course, but she was keen to see it in daylight. Now she slowed even more, from nana to great-grandmother speed, so that she could take it in.

The requisite red houses were interspersed with blue or yellow ones, all with the traditional white trim. On the outskirts they were set back from the road, but as she came into the centre of the village, they sat right on the narrow cobbled street. If she got out and walked, she'd be able to press her nose against the windowpanes as she waved to the occupants.

She emerged into an unexpectedly wide square, and bumped slowly around the perimeter, taking care not to veer into the empty market stands that sat in one corner. On each side, low buildings lined the square, giving it a snug feeling. Nothing was more than one storey high, and in the centre a flagpole stood tall. There were a few shops— amongst them she spotted a bakery, some kind of eatery, and maybe a pharmacy. Outside an unassuming-looking premises, she recognised the word *Systembolaget*. Apparently the government-controlled outlet was the only place Swedes could legally buy alcohol, other than bars and restaurants. Good that she'd found it—she might be heading straight back there if her visit to Defrost Digital didn't go well.

There were no other vehicles driving in the square, so she let the car idle while she gathered her thoughts. According to the Google maps navigation, the Defrost offices should be down a street on the other side. Would she discover anything of Claire there? She tried to ignore the churning in her stomach as the words in Claire's letter ran through her head, heart-wrenching despite the tinge of teenage melodrama. She'd re-read it before she came, and it even now it still hit her right between the ribs.

This life is suffocating me. I don't need you any more, and you obviously don't need me. You had a daughter, but I wasn't enough. Now you have a good girl you can be proud of. I hope you're all happy together. I don't want to see any of you ever again.

She'd never forget standing in Claire's room, the note in her hand, nausea welling up as she realised that this was what Claire really thought of her. How could she have been so blind, to not see the truth?

While Sarah shut her daughter out of her heart and mind, and Paul reluctantly stood by her decision, Zoe had veered between anger at the abandonment, to aching sadness, to a hideous embarrassment. Embarrassment that she'd thought everything was fine, still confiding in Claire, sharing what she thought were reciprocal sisterly moments. All that time, had Claire been playing along, listening with sympathy to Zoe's stories and secrets and doubts, while despising her for intruding on her life?

She didn't want to see them ever again, Claire had said. But *ever again* was an awfully long time. Even if she mostly felt like a kid playing at a grown-up life, a decade of water under the bridge had given Zoe some perspective—wouldn't Claire be the same?

This was her friend and sister—the person who'd been her anchor, and given her a taste of the normal life she'd never have experienced with her own parents. She'd never tried to push in front of Claire, even if she was the 'good girl' to Claire's self-assured rebel.

And now, after years of press releases, positioning, trend analysis, advertorials and crisis management, schmoozing clients and accounting for every minute of her long days, all while smiling through gritted teeth...this 'good girl' was teetering on the edge of a pre-thirties rebellion. She'd never really been one for 'spin' in the first place, and now she was all spun out, with no clue where her true heart lay. Having spent her childhood here, there and everywhere, and her adulthood hopping from flat to flat, and job to job, always with an exit in the back of her mind...maybe she'd never figure it out.

Claire the bold would never have gone along with the career choice of her parents (if she happened to have those sorts of parents, which she didn't). She would've raised one finger to it all as she made her exit, off to conquer the world.

Which was pretty much exactly what she'd done, except the raised finger was aimed at the people who loved her.

And now, if Zoe could find her, she had to tell Claire that her mother was in hospital, struck almost senseless by a stroke, while her father was at a complete and lonely loss. Before it was too late, she wanted to give Claire the chance to heal the family she left in pieces. The family that had also become Zoe's, whether Claire liked it or not.

She took a deep breath in and out, and turned the car towards Defrost Digital, and her past.

Chapter Eight

A fter the luxury of the heated car seat, it was a shock to emerge into the chilled air. Zoe slammed the door and hustled to the entrance of the Defrost Digital building as fast as she could, without risking another tumble.

But on the doorstep, she hesitated. She'd never let herself think about what would happen if, once face-to-face, Claire told her to get lost. Probably in stronger language than that, knowing her. Now though, thoughts of rejection came second to the need to let her know about her mum.

She pushed her shoulders back, pulled the heavy glass door open, and went in.

The reception area was empty, the desk unattended. She stood at the counter for a while, wondering if someone would be back shortly. The décor was everything a ground-breaking tech company should be—lots of chrome and sleek surfaces, with the furniture in cool colours, and one wall inset with tiny bulbs that switched on and off to create the outline of the company's double D logo. In the corner was an elegant tree, its leaves made entirely of green computer chips. She had to smile. This was Claire all over.

Still no one had come, so she called out a tentative hello. The door behind reception, which presumably lead to the offices, was closed, and she couldn't see anything through its narrow glass panel without going behind the desk. Obviously, short of yelling, no one would hear her. She cleared her throat, and eyed the bell on the countertop. It always seemed sort of officious to ring a bell, but she couldn't stand here any longer, putting off the moment. She reached for it.

At that exact second, the main door swung open behind her. She turned to see a tall, blond man—yes, Norwegian knitwear material—coming in with a brown paper lunch bag.

He stopped in his tracks when he saw her, and smiled. "Hej."

She smiled back. "Hi. I mean, hej."

"English," he said, switching languages effortlessly. "You're a long way from home."

"Yes, I suppose I am." If she could call it home. But that was a whole story that didn't need to be shared.

He put the bag down on the counter and unwound his scarf. "How can I help you?"

How could he help her...? She bit her lip, while he looked at her expectantly. Really, the only thing to do was dive in.

"I'm actually looking for a friend of mine...I think she might have come here."

He tipped his head. "She? I'm afraid we don't have any women working here right now. Just the usual computer geeks, all men."

"Well, I'm not sure if she actually worked here. And it might have been some time ago...about ten years ago. Do you know of anyone called Claire Evans? She worked with computers... coding, and apps, and..."

She wasn't really a hundred per cent sure how to describe what Claire did. She was reasonably tech-savvy herself, but Claire was at a whole other level—talking about JavaScript and Python, coming up with concepts for games and apps, fiddling around with websites. Inside the internet, as her dad Paul used to say. It was his usual call when she wouldn't come down for dinner: *Get out from inside the internet and join us in the real world.* Well, now Claire *was* in the real world—if only Zoe could find her.

But the man in front of her shook his head, making a lock of blond hair fall across his forehead. "No, I'm sorry. I've been here for about ten years, so I would have met her."

"Oh. Damn. Are you sure?"

She peered past him, trying to see through the glass panel in the door again, but he stepped slightly to the side, obscuring her view.

"Yes, I'm sure."

"Oh…okay."

Without any more leads, this was about as far as she could go. She stood there in reception, suddenly at a complete loss about what to do next.

Her uncertainty must have been obvious, because he held out his hand.

"I'm sorry, I should have introduced myself. I'm Fredrik."

She took his hand. Or rather he took *her* hand, as his seemed to be about twice as big. One firm shake, one big grin, and one wink, and suddenly she knew she was being flirted with.

"Hi," she said. "I'm Zoe."

"*Very* nice to meet you," he said, with a decided emphasis on the *very*.

"You too." She paused. If this was where he was going, she'd take the chance to press a bit further. "The only thing is, I think Claire might have been in touch with Alvar Lundberg, and she might have come here to…"

His eyebrows shot up, but he quickly got them back under control.

"You look surprised," she said.

"No, not at all," he replied. "Alvar is…a ladies' man. He has been *in touch* with all kinds of women."

"Oh…" She screwed up her nose. "I see."

Well, she could imagine. Older man, wealthy, running a company that an aspiring young coder would die to work at, even if it was in the middle of nowhere. After all, everyone knew that Minecraft, Candy Crush and Spotify had all come from developers in Sweden, and Angry Birds from just across the border in Finland. And Defrost Digital had joined the big names with their game Dynamite Defrost, which Zoe had never played, but everyone else had seemed to be hooked on for ages. Although it was still a fledgling company then, would Claire have been seduced by the attraction of his business, and the man himself, if she'd come here? Zoe would have guessed not...but you never know.

"Don't tell him I said that," Fredrik added. "I want to keep my job."

He made a faux-scared face, and she had to laugh.

"I'm sorry I can't help you find your friend."

"That's okay. Thanks anyway." Her mind was already working, working, trying to imagine where Claire might have gone if she hadn't come here.

He nodded towards the sofas in the reception area. "Would you like to have a coffee? I could tell you about the new games we're developing." He said it as though it would surely be impossible for her to resist. "And we have *kanelbullar*," he added.

She knew now that kanelbullar were the little cinnamon rolls topped with pearl sugar that Greta had given the girls that first night. And she knew they were good. But she really wanted some time to think, and figure out where to look for Claire now. The thought of bringing her back together with her parents, when they needed her most—and maybe before it was too late—added a new urgency to the task.

And she didn't want to be rude, but she wasn't particularly interested in gaming stuff, even when explained to her by someone tall, blond, and cheek-boned enough to be a lost Skarsgård brother.

"Thank you, but I won't today."

"Okay," he said. "If I told you our company secrets I'd have to kill you, so probably better not anyway." He laughed. "But maybe another time? How long are you staying in Lillavik?"

"About two and a half more weeks," she told him. "I'm

volunteering at the Nilssons' wildlife lodge."

"Ah. Beautiful *and* environmentally friendly," he said.

"Yes, it really is," she agreed.

But he shook his head. "I was talking about you."

Oh, too much. And yet—gah!—she felt her cheeks warm with a blush. Surely she wasn't such a sucker as to fall for that kind of shamelessness. "Ha! Well...thanks."

He grinned, obviously satisfied to see proof of his flirting's effect. "If you're staying, I'm sure I'll see you around. It's a small place, you can't avoid anyone."

"All right then." She turned to go. "Enjoy your lunch."

"I will."

He opened the main door for her, and waited until she'd made it to her car before finally letting it close.

She leaned back in the seat. He was...sort of weird, although friendly enough. A bit *too* friendly, maybe. Then again, she wasn't going to be offended by a flirty compliment, cheekily offered. One of those a day would keep the doctor away, and was more fun than an apple.

Anyway, the point was, Claire wasn't here and apparently never had been, despite the attraction of Alvar's business. Judging by his picture in the magazine article, he was way too old for her. Still, charisma did count for a lot, she accepted that. And power, and money. God knows, she'd seen it in her own world in London. The most jowly, gnarled and obnoxious men had the youngest, most beautiful trophy wives, acquired once they'd risen so far in the business world that income and prestige tipped the scales in their favour. It was an old tale. More than one of the women she'd worked with in PR had ended up married to a guy who could have been their great-uncle. And every one of them was better than that, and cleverer. They didn't need a man to leverage themselves up in their careers, or in life. Neither did Claire.

And neither do I, she reminded herself. Which was lucky, given that she currently had no man at all. Oh well, her room in the Bayswater flat was so small, she couldn't fit one in anyway. She laughed to herself, and started the engine.

Now what?

Well, she had a job to do here...if she could make any progress at all with Jakob. He didn't seem in desperate need for help with his own research—he hadn't shown up at all that morning. She'd better make herself useful, and fast. She was only here for three weeks, and she had no intention of sneaking through his papers and his computer.

On the other hand—ethics aside—maybe it would be the safer option. He was...distracting, and she couldn't let herself be distracted. She was getting what she came for, and then going back to London, to stick it to The Shark and her sneery colleagues.

As for Claire, she'd have to dig around a bit more online, and see if she could find anything. It was unbelievable how a person could disappear so thoroughly, in this age of Google, when you were supposed to have an indelible digital footprint. Either Zoe wasn't tech-smart enough to figure out how to find Claire—apart from the usual Google/social media search trail—or Claire was so clued-up in the ways of the digital world that she was able to erase all obvious references to herself. Maybe it was a bit of both.

Her stomach rumbled, and she realised she hadn't eaten since early that morning, before starting work. Thinking of the bakery she'd seen, she turned the car back in the direction of the square.

As she parked the car in what she hoped was a more-or-less legal spot—there were no painted lines, but other cars were parked here and there in the centre of the square—she saw Greta and a blonde woman with Lena and Ebba, each one of them carrying a white bag. She pulled her gloves back on, then got out of the car and waved in their direction. They saw her and waved back.

"Hej," she said as she reached them. "What are you ladies doing?"

"Hej," said Lena, and both the girls broke down in giggles, still tipped into hilarity every time Zoe attempted the simplest Swedish.

She laughed too. It was pretty contagious, even if she

was basically joining them in laughing at herself.

"We're going ice skating at the rink," Greta said. "Oh, and this is Malin."

"Hej, Zoe," Malin said, holding out her hand. "Nice to meet you."

Ah. Another tall, elegant Swede with immaculate grooming and perfect bone structure, her hair was the palest blonde Zoe had ever seen. Although Lena and Ebba had darker blonde hair, Malin looked like the blueprint from which those two sweet little facsimiles had been made. If her adorable kids were anything to go by, along with the warm smile she offered now, their mother must be as nice as she was beautiful.

Zoe took her hand. "It's lovely to meet you too," she said, and meant it.

Then Lena tugged on her mother's hand, saying something in Swedish.

"Okay," Malin told her. Then she turned back to Zoe. "Lena wants me to ask if you can ice skate with us."

"Oh, thank you, but I'd better not," Zoe said, tucking her still-cold hands under her armpits. "I don't have any skates. And I've decided to do all my falling over in private from now on."

Greta laughed. "Zoe slipped on the ice, on her first night here."

"Oh no," Malin said. "But ice skating is fun. Are you sure?"

As Zoe hesitated, Lena said something to Greta, who nodded.

"Lena says she'll teach you, remember? You can use my skates if you like."

Zoe looked at the little girl. Her hopeful face reminded her of herself as a kid, when they'd stayed with the Evans family. Hopeful that she could hang out with Claire, just because she liked being in her company. Some people just make you feel that way.

"Okay." She smiled as she saw the spark of excitement in Lena's eyes. "That would be lovely. Thank you so much, Lena. *Tack så mycket*."

An afternoon of being a kid again, with someone who wanted her company? That actually sounded pretty good.

Chapter Nine

W hen light finally started to dawn the next morning, it was overcast, and Zoe hoped the clouds might bring snow. The clear blue days since her snowy arrival at the train station had been gorgeous, but she was longing for some more actual snowflakes. If it was going to be this damn cold, she might as well have the full experience.

She made a coffee and had breakfast in her cabin. Breakfast here was way heartier than at home, where she had a bowl of cereal at best, or one of those cardboardy wrapped breakfast bars at worst. No, actually, worst was stopping for an emergency raspberry and white chocolate muffin and a takeaway hot chocolate at the café on the corner. But here...wedges of Greta's tasty, almost chewy, homemade bread. Slices of cheese and ham, and all kinds of toppings. Most different of all was the slightly gluggy *filmjölk*, from a carton, on top of cereal and fruit. It had a weird consistency and flavour—not really yoghurt, but definitely not milk either, although Greta had called it fermented milk when she'd tried to explain what it was. Either way, it was surprisingly good.

She ate as quickly as she could, then put the breakfast things away and went up to the volunteer office in the almost-light to grab the camera. No sign of Jakob, yet again. Well, it was still early, she told herself. He'd turn up eventually.

For the first time, she did a solo run to the eagle nest. With markers set along the path, she actually had no need of the GPS, and she made it there and back safely without seeing any sign of wolfish activity. And there was still no sign of the eagles either—they seemed to be proving as elusive as Claire.

Parking the snowmobile back by the office, she realised that although she'd been holding her breath before every turn in the path, she was a little disappointed not to find any evidence of the wolves. It would have been nice to know that some of them at least were safe here in Nilsson territory. And…it would have made Jakob happy.

She blew puffs of steam as she checked the weather station before going into the office. It seemed impossible to make them cigar-ring shaped, but she'd keep practising. With stinging cheeks, she went inside, trying to ignore the little zing in her tummy that had started at the thought of seeing Jakob.

He wasn't there.

She looked at the clock on the wall. He didn't seem the type to keep gentleman's hours…he was probably out in the forest somewhere, doing his Scandinavian Bear Grylls thing. She eyed his computer. How the hell was she going to make any progress with her Vertex assignment if he was never around?

Willing the heavy sky to produce something magical, she went into the guesthouse to see how she could help out. Greta asked her to start by tidying the guest rooms, and gave her brief instructions. The guests were out with Bengt, so she went into each of the comfortable rooms in turn, straightening beds and replacing towels. Most of the rooms held bunks or single beds, and shared the two bathrooms in the long upstairs corridor. But two were furnished with wide, rustic four-posters, and had en suite bathrooms with big bathtubs. She paused by the window in one of the luxury rooms, drinking in the view—across the frozen pond in front, to the snow-blanketed fields and woods, and the mountains far beyond. With a fire burning in the stone fireplace behind her, and the right company, this would make a dreamy romantic getaway.

Finding the right company was always the tricky part in those scenarios. She hadn't done particularly well in that department so far. Guys had come and gone, in and out of her bed and her life, but there'd been no one she'd found too hard to let go.

She shook herself back to reality and finished the rest of the rooms in record time. Then she reported back to Greta's office near the entrance.

"I'm finished."

Greta looked up from her computer. "Already? I think you are the most efficient volunteer we've ever had."

She shrugged. "I'm used to accounting for every minute of my time, so it can be charged out to clients. Nothing goes unpaid-for. It's soul-destroying, but it does make you more focused."

Greta looked doubtful. "I feel like we should be paying you."

"God, no," Zoe said hurriedly. "What you're doing for me is better than any salary."

It was true. Since she'd got here, despite the uncomfortable awareness of her subterfuge, she'd felt the knots slowly, gradually, start to unravel. In her tensed-up shoulders, and in her head, which had felt permanently taut with the relentless need to be slicker than she really was. Even the setback in finding Claire hadn't fazed her as much as she thought it would.

"It's doing me good to just get away, especially somewhere so beautiful," she added.

Greta smiled. "I have something else that might be good for you."

"That sounds interesting. Better than ice skating?"

The girls-only afternoon on the rink had been fun. The two little ones had set off like extras from Disney on Ice, twirling and swooping and generally looking remarkably effortless for such little kids. Malin had followed them, pushing off from the side without a moment's hesitation, gliding swan-like after her cygnets.

Zoe, on the other hand, had slid and shuffled onto the ice in Greta's slightly-too-big skates, then tentatively inched her way around the edge of the rink, holding onto the railing. By the time she'd done one circuit, Lena and Ebba had done, ooh, a hundred? It made her feel about a hundred herself. But soon she'd started to find her feet, and after a while she was cautiously striking out from the safety of the side. Like a nervous swimmer in a pool, she first tried cutting across the corners, then graduated to crossing the rink from side to side. The *short* side, admittedly, but it was something. Amazingly, she only fell twice, but the second time she was able to grab the railing and stop herself crashing to the ice. No one was going to be tapping her for a bit part in an Ice Capades reboot, but all up, she counted it as a success. And afterwards, hot chocolate and *prinsesstårta* in Lillavik's bakery was a fitting treat for two little princesses and their attendants. The princess cake was a heavenly confection—layers of sponge and pastry cream, topped with a dome of whipped cream, and then a layer of green marzipan, topped off with a delicate pink marzipan rose. In short, it was the absolute opposite of Jakob's threatened rotten herrings.

Now Greta nodded. "Yes, I think this will be better for you, even though your skating was not so bad. Shall we *fika*? And then I'll tell you."

"Fika?" She tried to pronounce it the same way as Greta had: fee-ka.

Greta laughed. "Good try. But you must know *how* to fika if you're going to be a real Swede."

"I'm not sure three weeks will turn me into a real Swede..."

"Ah, you never know." She stood up and pushed in her chair. "It's a start. Come on."

Soon they were sitting at the table in the big guesthouse kitchen, with mugs of coffee and a selection of baked goods. Zoe breathed in the aroma of her coffee—hot, strong, and reviving—and sighed. "So good."

Greta offered her a plate. "So. Fika is not just eating

and drinking. It's to slow down, take some time. Life is so busy, you must stop and enjoy the moment."

She chose a sugar-topped kanelbulle. "That sounds very civilised."

"It is." Greta took a bun for herself. "But...maybe we don't have to be civilised all the time. Sometimes we can be a little bit wild too."

Zoe paused halfway to taking a bite. "Okay, now you have my attention."

She smiled. "I have a party for you to go to."

"Oh, that would be fun." A bead of pearl sugar fell onto the plate, and she popped it into her mouth. "Maybe my Swedish will improve with a few drinks."

"It usually works that way." Greta laughed. "Malin asked me to invite you. It's her birthday, but her husband isn't here, so she decided to have a party for herself."

"Oh, good on her," Zoe said. She'd enjoyed spending time with Malin and her sweet girls yesterday. Malin seemed like someone who might be fun to have a few drinks with.

"I'm going to babysit the girls for the night, so I won't go." She didn't look sad to miss out, just pleased at the prospect of playing grandma again, with Malin's own mother apparently too far away. "I'll go and get them this afternoon, so Malin can get everything ready."

"It's tonight? Is it okay for me to take the car then?"

She shook her head. "No, Jakob will drive you. I already asked him. You can't drink anything at all if you want to drive, and we want you to have a good time."

Zoe wasn't sure that being accompanied to a party by a stone-cold sober Jakob would equal a good time, but she appreciated the thought. She hadn't seen him since the visit to the sleigh, and she was starting to wonder if he was avoiding her...

Truthfully, she was half-and-half on whether she wanted to see him or not. The hopeful half kept thinking about those dark eyes, and how they'd sat so close in the sleigh, she could feel him breathe. But then the other half piped up with reasons to not let her mind go there. Judging by Greta's comment, she was probably just one in a long line of female volunteers with crushes on him. Plus there was the whole angsty-and-brooding thing, which was usually guaranteed to make her roll her eyes. She didn't suppose he'd be any better in the company of vodka-infused party people. She, on the other hand, would love that company, so maybe she'd just let him angst and brood to his heart's content.

"If he doesn't mind, that would be good."

"Of course he doesn't mind. I told him he didn't." Greta grinned. "He doesn't like driving in bad weather, but there won't be snow tonight."

Ah. Hearing that, Zoe was pretty sure he did mind...but *she* didn't mind that he did. A party would be a lot of fun, and maybe a chance for her to crack that reserve of his. The days were counting down, and she was determined to go back to The Shark with a result. To do that, she needed Jakob to let her in.

★

Later, she ate an early dinner with Bengt and Greta and the girls. They usually had whatever Greta had prepared for the guests, but ate comfortably in the guesthouse kitchen while the visitors dined in the high-ceilinged dining room. Tonight it was Swedish meatballs—a meal so cliché that Zoe had half expected it to be a myth. Cliché or not, they were delicious, accompanied with sweet-tart lingonberry sauce, and Lena and Ebba tucked in with glee alongside the adults.

After dinner, Zoe helped clean up, then went to get ready while Greta and Bengt took the little ones back to the house for bed. Walking back to her cabin, she laughed as she repeated the Swedish words Lena had taught her after dinner, puffing each one out in a miniature cloud.

Hej då. Banan. Tuggummi. Bajs. Goodbye. Banana. Bubble-gum. Poo.

Maybe she'd better get some grown-up input on her

vocabulary.

The contents of her suitcase didn't hold much party-wear, but she found skinny jeans and a glittery silver jumper. She'd thrown it in at Denise's insistence, in case she met a 'hot Swede'. At the time, she'd rolled her eyes, but now she was pleased she had—even though she wasn't supposed to be getting entangled with any Swede, no matter how hot. The one guy who had caught her eye definitely qualified as that, but—probably luckily—her secret admiration seemed to be an entirely one-sided thing. Even so, she put on some makeup, and decided to risk the slippery London boots, for the sake of vanity. It was a party, after all.

By the time Jakob knocked, she was ready.

"Hej," he said, when she opened the door. And smiled.

And there went her heart again.

Chapter Ten

As they walked from the cabins up to the garages by the house, Zoe felt a single snowflake land on her cheek. She reached up with a gloved finger and dotted it away, waiting for another one to land. Maybe Greta was wrong, and there would be snow tonight after all. But that was it. She looked over at Jakob, whose face was as austere as the sky again, giving nothing away. But, like the one snowflake, that smile had hinted at something more. Maybe, maybe, he wasn't completely immune to her either. It was a satisfying thought.

"Maybe it'll snow tonight after all," she said to him.

But he frowned. "No. No snow tonight." It sounded more like a dictate to the weather gods than disagreeing with her suggestion.

"No?" She shrugged. "Well, you know, the weather forecasters get it wrong something like sixty-two per cent of the time."

He was unconvinced. "Where did you hear that?"

"On the internet, of course."

"Well, if the *internet* says so…" He opened the car door for her, and she laughed as she got in.

"We'll see," she said. That one snowflake just might be a sign.

Malin's place was on the outskirts of Lillavik, a two-storey, golden-yellow house worthy of Pippi Longstocking. Zoe smiled as they pulled up—it was nice to know that Lena and Ebba had such a charming home.

Judging by the music and voices as they went up the steps, the party was in full swing already. They added their boots to the pile in the entranceway, and went into the living room. And with just one glance, she could see that the vibe was the polar opposite of that supposed Swedish reserve. She felt herself relax, a smile spreading across her face. Seriously, she didn't go to enough parties.

The room was lit with fairy lights and soft lamps, and candles sat in snowball-shaped glass holders on the coffee table. There were more candles on each of the deep windowsills, and the flickering light reflected in the glass. The music was loud enough that people were leaning close to talk to each other, or conversing loudly. Even though Zoe didn't understand the snippets of conversation she caught, she did recognise a familiar word or two. Anyway, she'd spent large parts of her youth having people talk around and over her in a foreign language. It didn't bother her. It was much the same as letting the PR-speak of her colleagues swirl around her head when she tuned them out.

The living room opened onto a dining area, where a table was set up so prettily that she wanted to take a photo of it. Small Swedish flags stood between vases of winter twigs entwined with white ribbon, the cutlery was chunky silver, and crystal glasses glittered in the warm light. Since she'd been here, she'd started to wish she was on Instagram after all, so she could share the gorgeousness she came across every day. Apart from the stunning scenery, there seemed to be an effortless style evident in everything, from Greta's wreath on the cabin door, to the way the women were so smooth-complexioned and high-cheekboned. With her uncooperative sort-of-red hair, and her neither elegant nor willowy figure, it all made her feel positively clunky, and she thought back to her chaotic London flat with shame.

To be fair though, with six of them elbowing their way

around in what had originally been a three-bedroom flat, that place was never going to be in the running for a design magazine feature. With some creative and probably illegal construction work by the landlord, her own room had been carved out of a quarter of the living room and a slice of dining room. Anyway, as nice as it would be, she was hardly ever home to think about painting her floorboards, or stencilling a blanket box, or arranging snowball candles. The closest she got to Scandinavian style was the occasional trip to Ikea...maybe that counted for something?

Next to her, Jakob sighed, bringing her back to the moment. For a second she almost felt guilty that Greta had made him bring her. But then it passed. Wouldn't it do him good to get out and relax, after all? Okay, he couldn't have a drink—the Swedish drinking laws were brutally strict, Greta had explained—but a dose of good food and good company, and apparently good music too, might loosen that reserve a little. He spent too much time by himself—that couldn't be healthy for anyone. Maybe there hadn't been any romance that afternoon in the boathouse, but they had made a crack in the ice between them...surely she could break through a little more.

"Come on," she told him. "Let's find Malin and say hello."

"Okay," he said.

By his tone, you'd think she'd suggested they go for a tooth extraction, but she kept going, and he followed. She said hello to Stina, the cheerful girl who did housekeeping at the lodge, and then she saw Malin emerge from the kitchen carrying a platter of food.

"Malin, hi. Happy birthday!"

"Oh, hej, Zoe!" she said. "Thank you. I'm glad you could come." She nodded at Jakob, and he nodded back.

"Thank you for inviting me," Zoe said.

"You're welcome." She put the platter on the table. Finely sliced salmon sat with thin crispbread, sprigs of dill, and a dish of creamy sauce.

"That looks so good." And stylish.

Malin nodded. "*Gravad lax.* Something Swedish for you."

"Yum." She gestured towards the kitchen. "Can I help with anything?"

"No, just relax, and eat," she said, adjusting one of the Swedish flags on the table so that it hung exactly the same way as the others. "The girls had so much fun yesterday. They talk about you all the time."

"They're so sweet and funny." She looked around. "This looks amazing. I'm sorry your man isn't here to celebrate your birthday."

She waved a hand, her nose crinkled. "Pah. More fun without him, probably."

"Oh, well then..." That was awkward. Maybe he wasn't the kind of husband she wanted around at all.

But then Malin laughed. "It's okay, he's not so bad. His name is Anton. He'll be back in a few weeks. With a big present, I hope."

"Ah, you can't go wrong with a big present."

Over Malin's shoulder, she noticed Fredrik from Defrost Digital, talking animatedly to a couple of people in the corner. He turned and saw her, and immediately came over. Without a word, Jakob turned on his heel and headed for the drinks table. Fredrik watched him go, then turned his attention to Zoe.

"Is my sister making you eat her terrible cooking?"

Malin rolled her eyes, and he grinned. This was obviously a well-practised routine.

"Oh, I didn't realise you were related!" Zoe looked from one to the other. With the two of them side by side now, the resemblance was obvious.

"Yes, poor me." Malin stuck out her tongue. "Imagine growing up with this baboon. And he lives next door now. It never ends."

"Well, I'm an only child," Zoe replied. "Any sibling looks good to me, human or ape."

They laughed, but she was glad they didn't know how much she meant it.

"So you're saying I look good." Fredrik took a step in Zoe's direction, one eyebrow raised, and Malin rolled her eyes again.

"Good luck with that," she told Zoe. "There are bananas in the kitchen, if you want to shove one in his mouth to make him shut up." She went off to talk to someone else.

Fredrik took a sip from his almost-empty glass and grinned again. "Sisters. You're better without them."

She knew otherwise. "Maybe."

"Brothers, though..." He slipped his free arm around her back, and rested his fingers on her spine, ever so gently. Then he leaned closer, his breath laced with sweet whiskey fumes. "Being *with* brothers is better. Didn't you ever have a crush on a friend's big brother?"

Wow. That was...right out there.

Maybe Denise had been right. She was quite the internationalist—in the man department anyway. And when she'd first heard Zoe was going to Sweden, she'd tiptoed into the office shared by several of the firm's consultants, a conspiratorial look on her face.

"Here are those clips, Zoe," she said in an over-loud voice.

"Thank you," Zoe replied, taking the folder with a heavy heart. This client was breaking records for bad press, and being spectacularly unhelpful in crisis management. She added the file of clippings to the pile on her desk. Then she looked up. Denise was still hovering. "Was there something else?"

Denise threw a glance over her shoulder, waiting until the other consultant had left the room. Then she perched her generously-rounded bottom on the corner of Zoe's desk.

"I can't believe you have to go."

Zoe grimaced. "I know. But everyone knew it would be me."

Denise checked the door again, then leaned in. "But, Swedish men," she said in a low voice, followed by a meaningful nod.

"Um...what about them?"

She tilted her head, raising one on-point eyebrow. "You know what they say."

"What Swedish men say?" Zoe couldn't resist messing

with her.

"No, what they say *about* Swedish men! Seriously, they're all proper and haughty, like 'how do you do' and 'you must wear a seatbelt in my Volvo', and then when they have a few drinks...holy shit." She blew out a lusty breath. "Let's just say things *change*. For the *bet-ter*."

She laughed. "Well, I'm only going for three weeks, so..."

She thought back to the last time she'd slept with anyone. She'd finally given in and gone home with one of the guys from IT, after Friday night drinks. Ack, such a cliché. But it had felt like an eternity since she'd had any kind of fooling around. Unfortunately, Jason's competence at fixing computer glitches hadn't translated into competence in other areas. And the few drinks he'd had—actually, the many drinks—definitely hadn't helped him for the better. There was nothing Swedish about *him*, obviously, just a London lad who really should have had a curry and gone home alone.

Denise leaned further over the desk, her cleavage threatening to spill out of her snugly tailored suit jacket. "It only takes one night. And you'll have twenty-one of those. I expect regular reports."

Well, she was probably going to be disappointed. Not that Zoe was on the prowl, but she was up to the fourth night already, and so far Fredrik was the only one who'd shown an interest, which she totally didn't feel like reciprocating. Jakob, on the other hand...well, drinks or not, it didn't seem like he was in any hurry to loosen up.

Then she realised that, with perfect/imperfect timing, Jakob had come back just in time to hear Fredrik's shamelessly blatant question about crushes on big brothers. She took a breath, trying not to look at him as he stopped next to her—out of the corner of her eye, she could practically see the light from all the glowering he was doing—and gave Fredrik a level smile.

"No," she said. "No crushes."

"You should try it," he said, steadfastly ignoring Jakob. "I'm always available." Then he held up his empty glass.

"Can I get you something to drink?"

By now the heat from Jakob's glower was threatening to scald her cheek. He stepped forward and passed her one of the pretty crystal glasses.

"No need," he told Fredrik.

Watching them, she thought it was going to be pistols at dawn, the atmosphere between them was so charged. They regarded each other with barely concealed venom, and she held her breath, her fingertips growing chilled from the cold liquid in her glass. Then Fredrik shrugged, laughed, and walked away into the other room.

Zoe looked at Jakob. There was a flush in his cheeks, and she could literally see a vein throbbing in the side of his neck. She thought that only happened in movies, but there it was.

"What's the story with you two?"

"No story." He looked at her glass. "Try it. It's *akvavit*."

Hmm. Definitely a story. But she decided to leave it alone for now. Maybe she could subtly try to get some info from Greta. She looked at the liquid in the glass, admiring the pretty light gold colour, then smelled it. At the first hit to her nostrils, she ducked her head back.

"Whoa."

He smiled for the first time since they arrived. "Yeah. About 40 per cent."

"Huh. Aquavit, did you say?"

"Ak-*va*-vit."

She took another sip. Behind the fire it tasted sort of spicy, in a weird way, with a flavour she couldn't quite pin down. A clear, almost outdoorsy flavour, like the forest distilled into a glass. Another sip, bigger this time. "It's...not bad. I *might* like it."

"You get used to it," he said. "Really you should just..." He mimed throwing a drink back in one hit.

"Ah. Okay." She swallowed the rest as one shot, shuddering as the alcohol hit the bottom, making her eyes water. "Whew."

Just then Stina came and grabbed her arm. "Zoe, come on. I want you to meet some people!"

She hesitated. Really, she should stay with Jakob, seeing as he'd brought her here as a favour and was obviously not having the time of his life. Or she *would* have hesitated, if she'd been physically able to, but Stina was propelling her with determined force towards the other room. She looked back over her shoulder, but Jakob just raised a hand, part farewell, part *go*.

"Everyone is talking about the new volunteer at the lodge," Stina was saying. "Karl-Olof texted me to ask who is the redhead he saw in town yesterday...I knew he must mean you. Now, introductions..."

From there on, it was party mode. Zoe met a dozen or so people whose names she repeated carefully, but would surely never remember. She ate and drank, and drank a little more. Then quite a lot more. Whoever she talked to directly would speak English, but otherwise the conversation swirled around her in Swedish. Every now and then someone would yell "English! English for Zoe!" and there would be a burst of her own language before everyone forgot again and slipped back into Swedish. That was fine with her. She was warm, well-fed, and comfortably tipsy, joining in with toasts of *skål!* and clinking her glass with whoever offered. It was a welcome distraction from thinking about where the hell Claire could be, and how she'd get any Shark-busting info out of Jakob. She sent a photo of the akvavit bottle on the prettily-dressed table to Denise, who replied *Whatever, where's the man?* She was tempted to sneak a shot of Jakob, but sent back emojis of a drink, a thumbs up, and a winky face instead. That'd keep her guessing.

Then the singing started—drinking songs that they all apparently knew by heart. Although she had the *skål* mastered, she thought there was no hope of joining in with the songs. But after the fifth-sixth-seventh-whateverth time, she started to get the hang of the lyrics, even if she had no clue what the words meant.

Helan går, sjung hopp faderallan lallan lej...

Denise was right about one thing—there was nothing proper or haughty about this crowd once the drinks were flowing. No one seemed to care that it was a Wednesday, and they'd have to get up and go to work in the morning. Jakob was the only one not in full swing/sing, but then he was the only sober one. Ah, Jakob. She considered him from across the room in what she hoped was a surreptitious manner, but probably wasn't. Damn, he was hot. But so bloody earnest. If he was any closer she would have given him a squeeze. Probably lucky he wasn't though—that brief moment of hand-holding in the barn hadn't exactly been a success. She laughed to herself and threw back another drink, feeling at one with the world, or with this part of it anyway.

Some time later (she'd lost a grip on the minutes somewhere back around the time Malin brought out the bottle of Absolut), she was standing between Jakob and Stina, listening to a bunch of guys having a spirited argument that seemed to have something to do with ice hockey, when an older man came in. Immediately, she felt Jakob tense up next to her. And was it her imagination, or did a number of people glance in his direction? She looked at him, then at the new arrival. Older than everyone else here, was her first thought. Followed by her second thought: but still kind of attractive, in an off-beat way. Sort of had a look about him. Something familiar. Her akvavit-fuzzy brain struggled to get hold of it...

Then it struck her. He looked like Jakob. She turned to say something to Jakob, but he'd disappeared. Weird. Also, turning like that made her head spin. She went over to the sofa and sat down, leaning back against the cool leather. The room was so warm, you'd never guess it was minus-iceberg outside. She closed her eyes for a second, stretching her legs out in front of her. God that felt good—how long had she been standing up? And when she opened her eyes again, the older man was sitting next to her.

"*Trevlig fest*," he said, smiling in her direction.

"Oh," she said. "I don't actually..." She waved a hand and tried to remember the phrase Greta had taught her. "Jag talar inte svenska." *I don't speak Swedish.*

"It seems like you speak *some* Swedish," he replied, in

beautifully accented British English.

That was one funny thing she'd noticed. Most of the younger people she'd met spoke English with an American accent—apart from Jakob with his melodic Scottish-Swedish—while the older people spoke English so well-enunciated it was verging on plummy. It was the same everywhere, probably, around the world—the inexorable spread of American TV and movies and internet celebs and...everythingness. Even way back when, as a kid, she'd seen it in her international schools. Despite the teachers coming from every imaginable English-speaking country—Australia, Canada, New Zealand, England itself—the kids were determined to sound as California as possible. She didn't care either way, herself, and her own accent was a gentle kind of trans-continental blend. She didn't claim anywhere as home, and neither did her vowels.

She looked more closely at the man next to her. Yes, he looked like Jakob. They *must* be related. But there was something else too...

"I should have introduced myself," he said, holding out his hand. "I'm Alvar."

She squinted at him, trying to figure it out. "Alvar?" Then, mid-handshake, she clicked. The torn-out magazine article from Claire's room. "Oh! *Alvar.*"

Alvar Lundberg. The provincial trucking operator who'd morphed into a tech entrepreneur, thanks to a team of whip-smart young coders. The very team that Claire had aspired to join.

Chapter Eleven

Here sat the person from Defrost Digital she should have asked about Claire in the first place. Maybe she had contacted him, but he'd never mentioned it to Fredrik. And maybe he'd suggested other places to work, that she might have gone. It was worth a try.

He was looking gratified at her recognition. "Have we met?"

"Uh, no. Well, I was at your offices today, but no. I'm Zoe Bailey." Get your head straight, she told herself. Forty per cent now felt like the approximate operating level of her brain, as well as the akvavit's alcohol content.

"I'm sorry I missed you," he said. "Why did you come to visit? Are you a game developer?"

She snorted. "I'm not even a game *player*."

Seeing his bemused expression, she continued. "I was looking for a friend who was a game developer. Or who wanted to be one."

"Really? What is his name?"

"*Her* name. Her name was—her name *is*—Claire Evans. But Fredrik said she hadn't been there, not since he started working for you. Do you know of her?"

She watched him for some sign of recognition, but he just laughed. "We don't see many women in our offices. I wish we did."

"Claire talked about Defrost Digital. She dreamed about working for a company like yours. Except she didn't just dream about it, she was studying and working towards it, practising all the time. Did she contact you?"

"A lot of people want to work for me, Zoe." His voice suddenly became very...*patient*. "They want me to look at their badly-coded games, or they want a job, or they want to know how to make millions with their app. I probably don't remember half the people who have contacted me."

That sounded reasonable, even if she wasn't in love with his mansplainy tone. She sighed, suddenly feeling tired. "I can see that."

At that moment, Jakob came over, wearing his coat and carrying hers. The look he gave her was impossible to misread. They were leaving. Without a word to Alvar, he passed over her coat.

"I'll see you at the car."

"Um, okay." But she said it to his back, as he was already walking away.

She got to her feet, swaying slightly, and started to put the coat on. The fur-trimmed hood got caught inside the back, and she twisted around trying to reach over her own shoulder and pull it out. She hadn't done nearly enough yoga to flex that far, and she was aware of Alvar watching her struggle. But then she felt hands on her arms, holding her steady, and realised that Fredrik was turning her around. He pulled the hood out and lifted it onto her head.

Then he looked behind her. "Alvar, you could have helped her. Too lazy to get up." He shook his head.

She heard Alvar laugh, but avoided his eye. "I have to go," she said, feeling like a mouse between two cats. "I'll just say thanks to Malin."

"Okay. I'll see you again."

Fredrik leaned in, but with a reflex so quick she surprised her tipsy self, she twisted around to avoid his kiss. His lips landed somewhere in the fur of her hood, and she made her escape.

"Lovely to see you," she trilled over her shoulder, the

sentiment as faux as the fur he was picking from his mouth. God, he must have been going for an open-mouther. Maybe the prized akvavit had actually sharpened her self-preservation skills.

She called out goodbye to Stina and the room in general, then went and found Malin in the kitchen.

"Thanks for a great night," she said. "It was so much fun." Fun enough that she needed a slight squint to get Malin in focus, not so fun that she was falling down. Perfect.

Malin frowned. "You're going already?"

"Well, Jakob is leaving, so..."

"Ah." She pursed her lips. "Well. His father..."

"Alvar is his father? I thought they looked similar."

"Yes."

So they *were* related—as related as you can get, even if they didn't share the same surname. Maybe that fact revealed something about their relationship, or lack of. "They don't seem very, um...friendly."

"No." For a second, it looked like she might say something more, but then she tucked another plate in the dishwasher, and closed the door with a firm push. "Well, thank you for coming!"

Zoe debated whether to ask what the deal between them was. There seemed to be more people in Lillavik Jakob wasn't speaking to, than people he was. But there were other people in the kitchen, and also, she didn't know if Malin was the person to pursue that conversation with. Better not. She plastered on a smile.

"Okay, well, happy birthday!"

"*Grattis på födelsedag!*" called out someone in the corner, raising a glass, and then the others in the room echoed him. "Grattis på födelsedag!"

With jollity restored, Zoe waved and made her exit.

Outside, the cold air stopped her in her tracks. Hell, it was freezing. Actually though, given that freezing point was officially zero degrees centigrade, that wasn't anywhere near an accurate description of the temperature, way down in the negatives. Above, the clouds had cleared to reveal the wide northern sky. So much for her snowflake.

She saw Jakob waiting by the car, and set off to join him. As she went, she plunged her hands into her coat pockets, looking for her gloves, but they weren't there. For a brief moment, she considered going back in to find them, but then she looked at Jakob, standing in the dark with the car running. Jeez, why didn't he just get in, if he was so impatient? It practically gave her frostbite just looking at him.

She reached the car, and he opened the door for her. Oh. She'd automatically thought he was standing by the driver's door waiting for her, but with the car being right-hand drive, he was standing on the passenger side. She got in and sat on the heated seat, and realised—he'd had the engine running so it would be warm for her.

For someone so surly, he had surprisingly nice manners.

He got in his own side, and they set off. Within a minute they were out amongst the trees and fields. The road was empty of other cars, but she tried to keep alert, watching for moose/elk/anything on four legs. Her squinting technique got tiring after a while though, and he drove like a granddad to her nana, so she started to relax.

"What does grattis på födelsedag mean? Happy birthday?"

She knew she must have mangled the words, but he understood her enough, and nodded.

"Yes."

She leaned back against the headrest. "We sang all those other songs, but we never did Happy Birthday." Then something occurred to her. "Do you sing the happy birthday song here? You know, *Happy birthday to you…*"

She let her discordant solo fade away. The akvavit might have sharpened her kiss-dodging skills, but it hadn't helped one bit with her tuneless singing voice. At least at the party her bung notes were drowned out by everyone else, who actually knew the words.

"No. We have our own birthday song."

She might as well have implied they didn't have their

own prime minister, judging by his tone. Or was his pained expression because of her singing? She hoped for the first.

"Well, yes, of course you have your own song. That makes sense." She changed tack. "When's *your* birthday?"

He sighed. "December. The twenty-fifth."

"You're a Christmas baby? But that's so...festive." And he was so...not.

He looked sideways at her. Oops.

"I mean, how fun! Although not so great sharing your birthday with the Christmas celebrations, maybe."

He shrugged. "Actually, we open Christmas presents on Christmas Eve, so it wasn't so bad."

"Really? Is that a Swedish thing, or just your family?"

"A Swedish thing. But Christmas isn't a big thing with my family. Not since my mother..."

"Oh. Of course. I'm sorry."

Given his reaction to his father, which was frostier than hell frozen over, she guessed they didn't enjoy heart-warming family Christmases together. What had happened between them? She couldn't stop herself.

"And your father? He seems..."

Well, now she couldn't come up with an adjective at all. Irritating? Superior?

"Like a prick," he supplied for her.

She snorted with laughter, inappropriate but involuntary. "I didn't think a Swede would know that word."

"I met a few in Scotland."

"Ah." She bit her lip.

She considered asking more, but they were arriving back at the lodge. It would keep. He parked the car in the big triple garage, then waited until she was out before hitting the switch to close the door. It was quiet at Bengt and Greta's house—the little girls would be fast asleep—but as they walked down the path past the guesthouse, music and voices drifted from the big front room. The current batch of guests was from a university outdoors club, and they knew how to have a good time, day or night.

Down the tree-lined path towards their own cabins, it

was quiet again. She walked slightly ahead on the narrow way, the moonlight shining on the snow in front of her. The path glittered at her feet, tiny sparks of light echoing the pinpoints of stars above.

As they came into the clearing, she paused. Sitting snug in the snow, the two cabins were twin refuges in the wilderness. She tipped her head back, letting her hood slip off, and looked up. If they raised their branches, the snow-kissed trees could surely reach that starry expanse of sky.

She wanted to stay there, turning a slow circle in the snow, breathing out white puffs of air, and soak in the pale magic. But the tip of her nose was starting to numb, and although her puffy coat was warm, her bare fingers were becoming icicles in the pockets. She shivered, and they went on to her cabin. On the first low step, she stopped and turned back to him, their eyes almost level. Over his shoulder, the scene looked more like a painting than real life.

Maybe it was the akvavit, but she felt a wave of emotion rise in her chest. "So pretty." She waved a hand at the moon-drenched view, unable to come up with a better way to say it.

But he didn't turn to look at the trees, or the stars, or the moon. He was looking at her.

"So pretty," he repeated.

She looked to the sky over his shoulder, then back at him.

"Not the stars," he said, his voice low.

Oh. Not the stars.

For a moment, everything hung in the balance as she looked at him, seeing possibility in his eyes. Was this going to happen, really? She searched in her foggy brain for a reason why not, and came up blank. Well, then. She leaned forward, only the barest millimetre...but it told him enough. He put one arm around her and pulled her close. It must be like embracing a huge doughnut, she thought vaguely...but then all thoughts were gone. His other hand cradled the back of her head, his fingers tangled in her hair, his dark eyes intense. That long-forgotten, about-to-be-kissed sensation washed over her—racing heart, heavy eyelids, heat rising...

She wouldn't be dodging *this* kiss.

His cheeks were cold too, but his lips on hers were warm. Their breath mingled, creating a tiny hot zone between them that spread through her body, igniting parts of her that had been neglected for way too long. Oh, lord. Who knew that the poster boy for Scandinavian angst would be such a good kisser? On her step, she leaned further into him, hating the squashy barrier of their coats. He crushed her closer, obviously frustrated too, and she felt a laugh bubble up. This kind of angst was seriously sexy.

Then a sound cut through the frigid air, and he pulled suddenly away, snapped to razor-sharp attention. The sound repeated, something so raw and primitive that she felt an instant, prickly-necked chill of fear.

Wolves.

The howling came again, from nearer the lake, and was echoed by a wolf somewhere in the trees on the other side of the cabins.

He let her go, and turned to scan the surrounding forest.

"I might just go inside," she said, her voice casual but her heart pounding—not just from the kiss. She tried not to think about the next morning's eagle run, when she'd be heading in exactly the direction of the answering howl.

He turned back, but she was already halfway through the door.

"Sorry," he said. "I saw the tracks you and Greta found, but I've never heard them so close to the lodge."

"That's okay." For a second, she hesitated, the kiss still resonating in her body. She could invite him in. For...coffee. Or something else. Maybe. Even though she probably shouldn't. "Unless you'd like to...?"

He looked at her. The last unspoken words were a taut thread running between them. He only needed to follow them those few steps to the doorway, gathering them up as he went. She held her breath.

But then the howl rang in the night again, and he looked over his shoulder, and she knew the wolves had won.

"I should—" he started.

"Okay, well, I'll leave you to it," she said, keeping her voice in polite mode. "Thanks for taking me to the party, it was brilliant. Thanks so much. Goodnight."

Was that a hint of regret she saw in his face as she closed the door? She leaned against it on the other side. He *should* regret it. Maybe she was just another volunteer who liked him too much—but he wouldn't be getting that chance again. She was here for business, not pleasure.

But a little voice crept into her head. That kiss hadn't felt like she was just another person. It felt like...*something*. She clunked her forehead against the door, wishing she hadn't even gone there.

"It was just the akvavit," she told the voice firmly, loud enough to banish it.

On the other side of the door, she heard footsteps walking away. Oh, hell. He must have been standing right there.

Was he about to knock on the door and...what?

Maybe *she* wouldn't be getting another chance either—whether she wanted it or not.

Chapter Twelve

.

U gh. Akvavit.

Zoe raised herself on one elbow and gave her head a tentative shake. Yep, it ached. She sat up slowly. It wasn't pretty...but then again, it wasn't the brain-rattler of a hangover she'd expected, considering how much she'd had to drink. Maybe she was making progress towards becoming a Swede after all.

As the events of the night came back to her, though, she started to feel less positive. No luck with Alvar on the Claire question. And then just enough luck with Jakob— oh, that kiss—to leave her let down, when he basically turned her down.

Stupid scary wolves.

She waited until it was almost completely light before walking up to the lodge, one cautious eye on the landscape around her, at the same time trying not to look in the direction of Jakob's cabin. She hadn't figured out what she'd say when she saw him. Her fingers were freezing, and she wished she'd brought more than one pair of gloves. Maybe there were spares at the guesthouse.

She took her boots off in the wet room and went in search of Greta. She was in the office, in a state of excitement. She and Bengt hadn't heard the wolves the night before, but Jakob had already been in and told her about it.

"I'll come with you this morning and look for more tracks," she said, getting her camera from her desk drawer. "It's lucky there was no snow last night."

Jakob and the weather man had been right after all. Zoe felt a wave of relief at the thought of having Greta's company out in the forest, but kept her voice casual. "Okay." The noisy snowmobile would most likely scare any wolves off, but it would be nice to have someone there, all the same.

"Let's do the other jobs later," Greta added. "I think Stina will be late this morning, after the party. Did you enjoy it?"

"I did, thank you."

"And did Jakob take care of you?"

Her cheeks suddenly felt hot, and she bent to adjust her jeans where they were tucked into her thick socks. "Yes, it was all good. Fine. Good."

She stood back up, tucking a strand of hair behind her ear as Greta looked at her.

"That's good," she said. The phone started to ring, and Zoe caught a sort of knowing in her smile before she turned to answer it. "Have a coffee if you like, then we'll go."

She'd already had coffee this morning, but she scuttled out of the office, along to the big guesthouse kitchen. As she poured a cup of Greta's muscular brew, she shook her head. What kind of PR person was she if she couldn't keep a neutral expression while answering the simplest questions? Her mother would be shaking her head if she knew.

She added milk, and stirred thoughtfully. Well, she never had fit into that world anyway, and honestly, she probably never would. She put the carton of milk back into the fridge, alongside the filmjölk. The slightly zingy stuff was supposedly an acquired taste—which she seemed to have acquired already. Between the filmjölk, akvavit, snowmobile driving, ice skating, and her new fika skills, she was making impressive progress towards Swedish-ness. Out of all the places she'd been in the world, she felt surprisingly at home up here.

Ironic, considering that this was the one place she couldn't stay.

The sun was over the trees by the time Greta led the way through on her snowmobile, breaking the morning quiet. Zoe followed on her own machine, wearing borrowed gloves, confident now in her driving after the days of practice she'd had. She still itched to run riot, and have some high-powered fun, but she stuck to the straight and narrow...and slow.

Every so often, Greta held up her arm, then stopped and scanned the snowy ground, but there was no evidence of wolf tracks along the route they took. And at the nest site, there was still no sign of the golden eagles setting up house. Zoe was relieved about the first, but disappointed at the second.

"Do you think they'll come soon?" she asked Greta, as they got back on the snowmobiles.

"I hope so," she replied. "But they might not use one of these nests. Maybe home is somewhere else this year."

The words resonated in her head. *Maybe home is somewhere else this year.*

She'd lived that way herself, but could never get the hang of it.

"I don't feel like I'm being very helpful, though, if there's nothing to do with the birds."

"You *are*." Greta reached for the starter cord. "And anyway, I like your company."

"Oh! Thank you. The feeling is totally mutual."

Greta grinned in reply, and threw her leg over her snowmobile, as nimble as a woman half her age. Zoe followed her lead, and they headed back.

Outside the volunteer office, she hesitated, knowing that Jakob might be there...but he wasn't. Seesawing between relief and disappointment, she entered the weather data and noted the non-appearance of the eagles, then went to help Greta with the other jobs. By the time she'd also helped a headachy and droopily tragic Stina clean the rooms, she was feeling wrecked herself. So after lunch, she decided to go back to her cabin and try—again—to find any trace of Claire online. And maybe have a nap. She pushed aside the nagging knowledge that she hadn't done anything about the undercover Vertex mission yet. But there was plenty of time. Plenty.

She glanced at Jakob's cabin as she went up the steps to her own. He was probably out scouring the woods for wolfish evidence. Inside, she tucked the gloves in her pockets, pulled off her coat and boots, and padded towards the bedroom, yawning. It would have to be sleep first. After that, with a clear head, she could start on Claire. So far, she'd been playing as hard to get as the eagles. It was warm enough inside the cabin that she pulled off her jumper and got into bed in leggings and a t-shirt. Bliss...

Hazy sleep had only just claimed her when there was a knock on the door. She jolted upright, disoriented.

The visitor knocked again, firm and steady.

Oh hell...was it Jakob? She jumped out of bed, ran her fingers through her hair, swiped under each eye in case her mascara had smudged, and straightened her t-shirt. That would have to do. She'd probably looked just as rumpled by the end of last night anyway. She opened the door.

"Hej, Zoe."

Oh. Not Jakob.

"Hi, Fredrik."

If she looked disappointed, he didn't let it faze him. "I brought your gloves back," he said, holding them up triumphantly.

"Oh, okay..." He came all the way for that? As she took them, she kept a safe distance—she wouldn't risk a repeat of last night's near miss. All the same, she tried to look suitably grateful. "Thank you."

"You're welcome."

"So...I was just having a nap." She maintained a neutral expression, not wanting to seem rude, but hoping he'd take the extremely large hint and go.

He didn't.

Instead, he peered past her into the cabin. "Ah. Did you enjoy the party?" he asked.

"Yes, I did." Small talk, small talk. She dredged up some more manners. "It was lovely thanks. What about you?"

"Yes, *I* enjoyed it. I'm sorry you had to leave so early."

He managed to imply that he, Fredrik, was the hippest guy in Lillavik, while Jakob in comparison was a drag and a party pooper. It made her suddenly compelled to defend him.

"Well, it wasn't really *early*. It was after midnight."

He shrugged. "Was it?" Then he looked over her shoulder into the cabin again.

Oh, God. Fine. She gave in. "Would you like to come in?"

"Okay, yes, thank you," he said, apparently terrifically surprised.

His acting was terrible. She stood to the side and let him come in.

"Coffee?"

He hung his coat on the hook by the door. "Excellent."

The cabin felt small with six-foot-plus Fredrik inside. She sat cross-legged at one end of the sofa clutching her mug, while he relaxed with his arm across the sofa back, resting his coffee on his knee and chatting. Today, he was charming and pleasant instead of pushy and creepy, but her mind kept wandering...thinking about someone less convivial, but more compelling.

While Fredrik was in the middle of a story about robots and wombats and power-ups and experience points—all to do with the latest game they were developing—there was another knock at the door. It came as a relief. To be fair, she *had* asked him how his work was going, but since both he and Alvar had told her Claire had never worked there, she'd lost a bit of interest in Defrost Digital's workings.

"Excuse me." She stood up and put her mug on the coffee table, and went to open the door.

Jakob was standing on the porch, holding a pair of white ice skates.

"Hej," he said. "I heard you might need these."

"Oh...yes. I do."

Such an out-of-the-blue gesture took her completely by surprise. She smiled at him. As they looked at each other, she had the feeling she wasn't the only one thinking about last night's kiss. The skates hung between them, a token of unspoken possibility.

Then he looked over her shoulder, and his face changed. She turned to see Fredrik standing behind her in a proprietorial way. Oh, shit. She'd forgotten he was there. She wrapped her arms around herself, suddenly feeling the chill in her t-shirt.

All three of them stood in silence for what seemed like forever.

Hell, this was awkward. And *cold*. She wasn't dressed for a showdown at the Iceberg Corral.

Finally, Fredrik spoke, but only to her. "Did you find your friend? Claire, was it? Claire Evans?"

She'd intended to keep her search for Claire a secret, as much as she could. Not because it was incriminating in any way, but because it seemed better to appear entirely focused on the volunteering. Also, it was probably safer not to put out any more personal information than necessary.

"That's right," she replied cautiously, aware that Jakob was suddenly intently focused on her.

"Yes, Claire Evans," he said, nodding. "I thought so. No luck?"

She glanced at Jakob. She couldn't exactly read his expression, but he wasn't looking pleased.

"No, no luck," she said.

Fredrik shook his head. "I'm sorry. I'm sure your friend Claire would want to see you."

God, why wouldn't he shut up about it? "It doesn't matter really," she said, even though it did.

Before he had the chance to say anything else, she decided to put an end to it—to that topic, and his visit.

"Well, I'm freezing." She turned to Fredrik, who was looking smug. Instead of slapping him around the back of the head, as her fingers itched to do, she smiled ever so politely. "Thank you for coming and returning my gloves, Fredrik. I'll see you again soon, I'm sure." She stood back, pointedly leaving room for him to go out.

He took his coat from the hook. But then he had to pass by Jakob, who suddenly seemed as immovable as one of the trees in the surrounding forest. They eyed each other like boxers about to go a round, then Fredrik looked back to Zoe.

"Yes. See you soon," he said. Quick as a flash, he stepped closer and kissed her on the cheek, then turned and went down the steps and back up the path towards the lodge. Even from behind, there was a certain spring in his step that suggested he was pleased with himself.

Jakob narrowed his eyes as he watched him go. Then he passed her the skates.

"I hope you can use them. Greta said they were the right size."

She started to say something, but he was already turning to go. Curse Fredrik for his crappy timing and his point-scoring kissing.

"Jakob, thank you so much. That's really sweet." *Don't go.*

At the bottom of the steps, he shrugged. "You're welcome."

Then he walked away, back to his own cabin. For such a big guy, he had a stride as easy as one of his wolves, and he traversed the short distance in no time. The sound of his closing door echoed in the clearing.

She was left standing in her doorway with the ice skates, and a dose of goose-bumps and uncertainty. There went the second chance she wasn't sure she'd get.

But…maybe it was for the best. After all, he had no idea why she was really here. She was almost starting to forget why herself. But this was her chance to prove something to The Shark, and to everyone else…and okay, to herself. And she didn't want to mislead him any more than she had to. She liked him too much.

Third chances might be lucky, but the reality was, she'd be wiser to cut her losses and get her mind back on the job right now. She went inside, shutting her own door firmly behind her.

Chapter Thirteen

That night, she had dinner with Greta and Bengt. They'd promised her something special, something *mycket svenskt*—very Swedish. Remembering Jakob's threats about rotten herring and goose-blood soup, she took her place at the table with trepidation. But as always, there were little touches that made her smile. Cloth napkins in heavy silver napkin rings, tealight candles in the ever-present glass snowballs, and ornate cutlery that Greta said had belonged to her grandmother.

They had mastered the art of making everyday things a little bit special.

Greta's voice came from the kitchen. "Are you ready? Are you sitting down?"

"I'm ready," she called back.

She and Bengt emerged from the kitchen, each one bearing a platter. Bengt set his down on the table with a flourish.

"*Var så god!*" he said.

Var så god, she now knew, meant to go ahead, help yourself, or you're welcome. But what was she helping herself to? She looked at the dark, succulent roast meat. In true style, it had a small paper Swedish flag stuck in the top, as though a tiny mountain climber had claimed it for the kingdom of Lillavik.

"It looks very good," she said. "What is it?"

"*Ren*," he said, beaming.

"Ren?"

"Reindeer. My friend Svante hunted it a long way north of here."

An image of Svante, dressed in camouflage gear and stalking Santa's stables, flashed into her head. But Bengt looked so proud of his offering, she made an effort not to screw up her nose.

"Oh...reindeer."

"You must try it," Bengt insisted.

She arranged her face into a smile, and picked up her knife and fork.

Of course, it was delicious—rich, wild, and perfectly set off by Greta's lingonberry sauce. Greta passed her a glass of red wine, and she sent a silent apology towards the north as she settled into her helping of Prancer, or Vixen, or one of their less fortunate cousins.

★

"So," Greta said later as they washed the dishes. "Jakob came to ask me about something this morning."

Zoe plunged the silverware into the sink. "Was it the ice skates?"

"So he *did* give them to you."

"He did. Well, just to borrow, I'm sure. It was really nice of him." She didn't want to mention what had transpired between him and Fredrik.

Greta was smiling. "Did he tell you who the skates belonged to?"

"No."

"They were his mother's."

"Oh...wow."

His mother's skates. His mother's sleigh.

"Yes. Brigitta. When she was young, she was a successful...what do you call it? Art skater?"

"Figure skater?" Zoe suggested.

"Yes, that's it. She was amazing. She went to live in Stockholm for her training, and Alvar would go and visit her there. We were all surprised when she came back...until we found out she was expecting Jakob."

Zoe thought back to the softness of the leather skates, and the elegance of their design. She'd thought they seemed especially nice—that explained it. Surely Jakob wouldn't lend them lightly. She had to ask. "Does he usually lend them to people?"

Greta smiled again. "No. He does not. I think he likes you." She gave a meaningful look, then went back to drying the cutlery, while Zoe blushed over the suds.

"Oh, I don't know about that. Anyway, I shouldn't get distracted. I'm supposed to be working." Doing what, she couldn't tell Greta, but it was more than the volunteer work stopping her from going there with Jakob.

"Are you thinking we would disapprove about the sex?"

Zoe burst out in shocked laughter. "The...oh, no. I..." She wanted to dive under the bubbles and disappear. Of course, that was *exactly* what she'd been thinking about lately. Well, not the disapproval, but the sex part.

Greta laughed mischievously, obviously having fun stirring things up. "You know, we are realistic in Sweden. If you like each other, you're allowed to do it."

"Well...I don't think..." She scrubbed at a stubborn spot on one of the pots, the heat in her cheeks matching the scalding dishwater. How embarrassing.

Greta shrugged. "Okay. But you're in a liberal country now."

Zoe could only nod wordlessly. After a moment, she asked, "What happened to her? Jakob's mother?"

"Brigitta?" She shook her head. "Cancer. It was a terrible time. Jakob was only a teenager."

"Oh, God. How awful."

Her relationship with her own mother wasn't exactly close. They were far apart in miles now, but they'd never been much of a close-knit family, despite only having each other as they trooped around the world. It was just the way it was. Zoe had always felt like an item for her mother to tick off her to-do list. Education—check. Marriage—check. Career—check. Child—check. Despite that, the idea of her mum being so sick, and dying...it didn't bear thinking about. Facing that prospect with Sarah, her 'other mother', probably felt close to what losing her own mother might feel like, but she had no idea what Jakob must have gone through.

"And what about Alvar?"

"Pssht." Greta waved a dismissive hand. "She left him before Jakob was even born. It was a good thing. That man..." She shook her head, her lips pressed together.

"I met him at the party," Zoe said.

"That's bad luck for you," Greta replied. She sighed. "Jakob deserves a better father."

"What's he like?"

She paused with a handful of knives and forks, considering. "He has that business, and expensive cars, and a big house—Hofsvik, it's called. But really, he's alone."

It looked like she might have more to say, but then she put the last of the silverware into a velvet-lined box, and hung the tea towel on the oven door.

"Come now. Leave the rest. Let's see about coffee."

Zoe followed her, grateful that she hadn't asked anything else about Jakob. After last night's kiss, and then the episode with Fredrik this morning, she knew her attraction to him couldn't be entirely one-sided. And his mother's skates...well. Maybe *that* told her something.

But—and wasn't there always a but?—she should be making sure nothing more happened. Because if he tended to be surly now, she could only imagine what he'd be like if he found out she was secretly trying to find a way to sabotage his Scottish wolves. The thought made her queasy.

Later, she went back to her cabin and started googling again, trying to find any hint or shadow of Claire. But every result was from before she left home—school prizegivings, sports teams, that time she was in the paper for winning a coding contest for girls. And there were a million and one other random people called Claire Evans.

Disheartened, she hesitated...then entered another name in the search bar. Jakob Westermark. Scrolling through the results, she felt a bit stalkerish—but she clicked on them anyway.

He obviously wasn't one for social media, as his Instagram comment had suggested. But there he was on a research trip with a university group, somewhere in the wilds of Scotland. His name on an academic paper published in an environmental journal. And his profile picture on the Scottish Wolf Reintroduction Society website. She lingered over the image. Just a half smile, enough to hint at the dimple that lurked on each cheek. Serious eyes. His hair caught by the wind on whatever hillside he was standing on.

And then, there he was on a YouTube video, talking in rapid-fire Swedish about wolves, pointing out evidence of a den where pups had been raised. That's what the caption said he was talking about, anyway—she listened to his deep, rolling voice with no idea what the words were, just watching the expression on his face as he spoke. It was like seeing a different person, someone she'd only seen flashes of in the days she'd been here. Serious, but none of the angst—a person lit up by the fire of his heart's pursuit.

Intrigued, she found herself drawn into a YouTube click trail, watching one wolf-related video after another.

Finally, with a yawn, she forced herself to quit and shut down the laptop. Slipping under the covers, she thought of Jakob, probably in his bed just a few lopes across the clearing. What was he thinking about over there? The rugged, distant hills maybe, and freedom on the wind, and the piercing eyes of a Swedish grey wolf.

At that moment, as if in answer to her thoughts, she heard a howl rise in the night, a single, keening call that spoke of the ancient wild—the ancient wild that lay outside her four small walls.

The inevitable chill that went up her spine was tempered by something else now. It belonged to them, she thought as she fell asleep. It *belongs* to them.

Chapter Fourteen

The next morning, after doing another uneventful nest run and collecting the weather data, she cornered Jakob in the office. Well, not literally, but the set of his back when she came in was like a man braced for attack. At least he was there. It was a start.

"Thank you again for lending me the skates," she began, talking to his broad, silent back. "I'm looking forward to using them."

He nodded, focused on his screen. "You're welcome."

In the drawn-out pause that followed, punctuated only by the sound of his fingers on the keyboard, she imagined grabbing hold of the back of his office chair, spinning him around, and telling him that Fredrik was an idiot, and in fact she was stupidly, prematurely crazy about him, Jakob, and heaven help her but she had to know, was he ever going to kiss her again?

Instead, she reminded herself of her complicated reality, and assumed a business-like tone.

"So...how can I help you with your work? That's kind of why I'm here."

Totally why, in truth. If other reasons had unexpectedly appeared to make her want to stay...she'd just have to keep them reined in.

He shut the folder next to him, keeping his eyes on the screen. "I don't need help."

She stifled a sigh. "I'm sure there must be something? It's so interesting, I'd love to know more."

He turned and looked at her, maybe hearing something genuine in her voice. And it *was* genuine. All those videos, and Greta's explanation of the wolf's plight, and his own passion for their fight...it had all combined to ignite something in her, too.

"Did you hear it last night?" he asked.

She knew what he meant. "I did. It sounded really close."

He nodded. "He's one of the tagged wolves. His name is Brynjar. Look."

He went to a website, and showed her a page with photos of all the wolves being tracked by the Swedish wildlife authorities. Brynjar was a young, pale grey wolf, who had apparently travelled a zig-zag route from much further north.

"Bryn-yar," Zoe repeated, the name rich and evocative on her lips. "Brynjar. He's beautiful."

Jakob smiled. "He is. His name is from the old words for armour and warrior. He left his pack a few months ago, and we've been following his journey."

"Why did he leave?"

"It was just time to go. He's old enough to look for a mate. He hasn't found love yet though."

The reference to love was enough to make her blush like a schoolgirl. She looked away, ducking her head and rubbing the back of her neck as though she had a sudden itch. Hopefully he hadn't noticed. With the worst of the heat out of her cheeks, she turned back. "So...what can I do?"

"You could go through these tracking reports and update my map. I'm using it to build a picture of where the wolves are travelling, and how far they go."

Finally. "Okay." She took the folder and sat at the other computer. "So this data will be on the website?"

"No," he said. "That would be giving directions to

anyone who wants to hunt the wolves."

"Oh, heck. I didn't think of that."

He nodded. "Everything used to be public, but now...we have to keep them safe."

"Of course."

As he leaned over her shoulder and explained how to enter the data so it showed on the map, she felt a version of the wolfish prickle run up her spine and tingle in her neck. But it wasn't a cold chill this time...it was the teasing fingers of temptation.

He went back to his own seat, and she sat still for a minute, letting her million agitated nerve endings settle. Oh, this was trouble.

When she heard him start typing again, she snuck a look across. He might be a difficult character, but he had a passion, and a place in the world. She didn't just fancy him—she envied him. With an effort, she turned back to the computer and started work.

★

Later that afternoon, she went back to the cabin and called Paul. She hated having to report that her visit to Defrost Digital and her talk with Alvar hadn't uncovered anything of Claire, especially when she heard the disappointment in his voice.

"Don't worry," he said. "It was a long shot. Now you can get on with your work."

"I suppose so."

Somehow, being here was beginning to dampen her drive to show Vertex what she was made of. Maybe it was too much fresh air and outdoorsiness...and the growing sense of being just one tiny part of a great big world. She looked at the ice skates in the corner. Not to mention a certain distraction.

"I'll keep looking online though," she promised. "How's Sarah?"

"Oh, well..." He paused. "You know. Hanging in there."

What he didn't say spoke volumes. "I'm sorry. I'll come and visit as soon as I get back."

"That would be nice. Sarah would like that, I'm sure."

She forced a bright tone into her voice. "Yes."

They both knew full well that unless things changed, Sarah would probably have no idea she was there.

"Off you go then," he said. "Keep warm."

"Thanks, I will. Lots of love."

"Right back," he said, the way he always did.

As she hung up, her heart ached. Everyone said life was a roller coaster, but sometimes it seemed more like a seesaw. And right now, Paul was stuck at the bottom end, loaded down with troubles, and none of the good stuff at the other end to tip the balance and raise him up.

She tapped her finger on the arm of the chair, twitchy, restless. Then she got up, pulled on her boots, coat and gloves, and set off up to the lodge. The sky was dark and heavy with the promise—or threat—of snow. But she itched to be out, moving, in the elemental open. Bengt was away for the afternoon with Jakob, checking fences on the other side of the property, but she knew he wouldn't mind her using the snowmobile.

With the ease of practice, she started it up, and set off along the path towards the lake. It was just as cold as when she arrived. She couldn't say she was used to it, exactly, but it wasn't as shocking as it had been at first. As she travelled the sugar-dusted track, and breathed the clear air, the tension in her chest started to dissipate. For the first time, maybe in her whole life, being somewhere that wasn't home felt like exactly what she needed.

She paused at the top of a rise, where she could see the lake. It was a smooth, white expanse of ice, embraced by frosted trees, but the sky above and beyond was dense with smothering grey clouds. How different it was to *see* the weather, good or bad, instead of peering up at it between London's high-rises. With one final look, she turned the snowmobile and set off to circle back around to the lodge.

As she powered through the forest, the light was starting to fade, but she wasn't worried—the GPS was no longer a mystery. She shouldn't need it anyway.

Just on the lodge side of the still-empty golden eagle nest, something off the track caught her eye. She stopped and peered into the trees, the dying light making it hard to see. Yes, something was definitely moving in there. She kept a tight hold of the snowmobile's hand grip, her pulse racing, ready to hit the accelerator if she needed to. Then the clouds shifted, letting the last of the sunlight through, and she saw it—a whisper-grey wolf, lying at the foot of a tree, its sides rapidly moving in and out. A collar was easily visible against its pale fur.

Could it be Brynjar? It looked like him.

Heart pounding, she debated whether to take a closer look. Something must be wrong if her presence and the noise of the snowmobile hadn't scared him off. With every nerve in her body on alert, she turned off the engine, and picked her way down off the track towards the wolf. She stopped some distance away, and the animal lifted his head and looked right at her—*into* her, it seemed—silent resignation and vulnerability in his eyes.

"Brynjar," she whispered. "You need help."

At the sound of her words, he lowered his elegant head to the snow. For a second longer, she stood, mesmerised—and then she sprang into action. She didn't have Jakob's mobile number, but she called Greta, who deciphered her hurried words and promised to find him.

"I'll be back," she told the wolf. "I promise."

She'd been wanting to kick up some horsepower on the snowmobile, but she hadn't imagined it would be on a lupine mercy mission. Now she pushed it as fast as she dared, hurrying to meet Jakob and lead him back to the right spot.

When she reached the lodge, he and Bengt were by the garages, hitching a small open sled to a snowmobile.

"We use this to carry supplies on safari," Bengt explained, making sure the coupling was secure. "But when Oscar was small, the children rode on it. It should be okay for a wolf."

"Let's go," Jakob said to her, slinging a gun over his

body and getting on the snowmobile.

She stared at the weapon. "You're not going to...?"

"Tranquiliser," he said.

"Oh, okay. For a second there, you looked dangerous."

"It *is* dangerous," he told her. "The amount it takes to make a wolf sleep can be enough to stop a human's heart. That's why we always carry an antidote too." Then he pointed at her machine. "Get on."

Chastened, she did as he said and set off, knowing he'd be right behind her. As they entered the woods, he turned on his vehicle's headlight, and she did the same.

Before long they reached the spot where she'd found the wolf. He was still there, looking just as fragile. Jakob was off his snowmobile in a second, down the slope and on his knees, assessing the situation, checking the animal's vital signs. She stood back, amazed at his cool fearlessness. Then he gathered the wolf in his arms, and started back up to the path. It was much bigger than she'd realised, the long legs and heavy head making an ungainly load, but he covered the ground without difficulty. There was obviously no need for the tranquiliser gun.

"Is it Brynjar?" she asked quietly, as he lifted the wolf's slack body into the sled.

He nodded. "I think so."

Hold on, she silently implored the wolf. *Please hold on.*

Once he was secure, they set off again without a word, the precious cargo all that mattered in that moment. She only hoped they'd found him in time.

Chapter Fifteen

Zoe pushed the bell at the door of the vet clinic, jigging up and down in the freezing air. They were in the countryside beyond the northern outskirts of Lillavik, where fields met the forested wild again. As Jakob had driven them there—still slowly, despite the urgency of their mission—darkness had properly fallen. Now he waited by the four-wheel drive, not wanting to bring the unconscious Brynjar into the cold until the last possible moment. He'd phoned ahead, and Emil the vet had promised to be ready for them.

The door opened to reveal a tattooed, spike-haired, black-eyelinered second cousin of Lisbeth Salander, wearing a medical tunic and pants. Zoe hesitated, but the girl smiled. Then she looked over Zoe's shoulder, and her face lit up.

"Jakob!"

"Hej, Vera," he replied, then switched into English for Zoe's benefit. "This is Zoe. We need some help."

"Emil told me." She came down a few steps and looked into the truck. When she saw the wolf, limp and heavy, her smile faded and she immediately sprang into action, going back and holding the door open for them. "Bring him in."

Jakob gathered Brynjar in his arms and carried him

carefully up the steps, through the waiting room, and into the treatment room, where Emil was holding the door. The vet nodded to Zoe, but his focus was on his patient—she could see him assessing the situation as Jakob went past bearing Brynjar, four legs dangling, his paws enormous. As she wondered whether to go in or not, the door shut behind them.

"I'll wait here," she told the cats of various breeds on the poster stuck to the door.

Vera closed the outer door, then gestured for Zoe to sit on the little padded window seat tucked under the front window. She took off her coat and sat down, feeling worried about Brynjar, but relieved to have made it to medical help.

Vera took her own seat behind the desk, and gave Zoe a cautious, testing smile.

"You are from England?"

Zoe considered the question. She didn't feel like she was, really, but it was a good enough assumption. "Yes."

"And you and Jakob...how do you know each other?" Her accent was heavier than his, but the words were clear and crisp.

"We don't know each other, really," she replied. It was true. "I'm volunteering at the Nilssons' lodge."

It seemed to be a satisfactory answer. Vera nodded. "Oh. Okay. That's nice."

"It is. I'm helping him a little bit with his work."

"Ah. Jakob is so smart. He knows more about the wolves than any person around here."

The admiration in her voice was obvious, her eyes dreamy-bright below her eyebrow piercings. Zoe smiled. She recognised that feeling—when you have to talk about someone, to hear his name on your own lips, just to make him more a part of you.

"Yes, he is smart."

And mysterious, and frustrating...and under her skin, unfortunately. She obviously wasn't the only one. They both looked towards the closed door, where the muffled voices of the men could just be heard. Then Vera sighed.

"So terrible though. He was not the same, after the accident..."

Zoe frowned. "Accident? I thought his mother had cancer?"

"His mother? Yes...she did."

They looked at each other, both realising at the same moment that they were talking about different things. Vera pressed her lips together, clearly intending to close the subject, but Zoe wanted to know more.

"There was an accident?"

Vera picked up a random piece of paper from the desk, then put it down and picked up a folder instead. "I'm sorry. I must go and help."

"Wait," Zoe said, but she was already disappearing through the treatment room door.

Well. An accident? Something that changed him, so that he was never the same...and on top of his mother's death. What had happened? She suspected he wouldn't be in a hurry to tell her himself, and Vera obviously wasn't going to...but maybe Greta would. His story must have more layers than she knew.

Then again, didn't everyone's?

She could hear activity in the treatment room, and wondered how Brynjar was faring. It was some kind of luck that she'd found him—surely he was meant to make it.

The phone on the reception desk rang a couple of times, but Vera must have been answering it on another line behind the scenes. No one else knocked to come in, and when she looked out the window, she could see why—it had started to snow heavily. Under the street light just outside the clinic, Jakob's truck was slowly accumulating a white topping. It was warm inside, but she shivered at the sight. She remembered Greta saying that Jakob didn't like to drive in bad weather. It could be a difficult trip back to the lodge if that kept up.

After a while, she took off her boots, swung her legs up onto the window seat, and leaned back on the cushions sitting against the side wall. In the warmth and quiet, drowsiness started to creep over her. Maybe she could read to pass the time. She got out her phone, pulled her coat over her legs, and settled in to wait.

★

Several chapters later, she jumped, suddenly aware that Jakob was standing right next to her seat. He looked world-weary. It suited him.

He raised his hand in a half-wave. "Hej."

"Oh! Hej." She looked around. "How did it go?"

"Okay, I think. Emil is finished for now. Vera went home."

She tucked her phone in her back pocket and shifted her legs to make room, and he sat next to her on the window seat. The strain showed on his face as he ran his fingers though his hair.

"And Brynjar—will he be okay?"

He leaned back. "We don't know yet. Emil will sleep here and check him in the night."

"Oh, God. I hope he'll make it through. Do you know what's wrong with him?"

His expression became even darker. "We think maybe it was poison."

"Wait. Do you mean he ate something poisonous, or someone poisoned him?"

Emil came in just in time to hear her question.

"Someone poisoned him," he said. "I'm doing tests, but the symptoms are there."

"Who would do that?"

He rubbed his head, looking tired too. "A lot of people."

Jakob nodded in agreement.

She thought back to what Greta had told her. Wolves were hunted in Sweden, but no one would shoot a wolf on the Nilssons' land. No local person, anyway. Leaving poison, though, was a quiet and efficient way to get the job done. There were people who didn't want the wolves around, and would do anything to stop them. Hell, she was working for a bunch of them herself. A wave of guilt went through her, and she bit her lip.

She looked out the window, where the snow had formed a small drift against one side of Jakob's truck. "The weather is getting worse."

Jakob nodded. "It is."

"You can drive," Emil told him. "It's not so bad."

He hesitated. "Maybe."

"You have winter tyres?"

"Yes, but..." He cleared his throat. "I'd rather stay here. Until he's out of danger."

"I can send you a message," Emil said. Then light dawned on his face, as he seemed to realise something. "But the cabin is there, of course, if you want to stay."

Jakob looked at her. "Would you mind?"

Suddenly her heart picked up speed, and a little part of her whispered that it might be more than snow and wolf that made him want to stay. But she brushed the thought away. He was a dedicated wildlife ecologist, and clearly a sensible outdoorsman—it wasn't about her. But...staying the night in a cabin with him would be tempting a fate she was trying to avoid. Not that she had much choice at this point—she could hardly take his truck and go, even if she felt confident about navigating snowy roads at night. Which she totally did not.

"Oh, no, that's fine," she said, her voice betraying none of her thoughts. "I don't mind."

Emil rummaged in one of the reception desk draws and pulled out a key. "There's some food in there, so please help yourself. See you in the morning."

He gave Jakob the key, then went back into the treatment room, leaving them alone. Alone, with each other.

Chapter Sixteen

They left the truck parked outside the clinic and walked across to the cabin. It was only a short distance, but the snow was gusting around them, and the chill was vicious on her bare cheeks. She was grateful to make it to the porch, and out of the wind.

Jakob unlocked the door and stepped back for her to go in. They took off their boots by the door, then she looked around. It was more basic than her little retreat at the Nilssons' place, but the layout was almost the same. And just like her own cabin, the bedroom at the back had only one big bed.

She took a breath. "This is nice."

He nodded as he hung their coats on a stand in the corner. Was he thinking the same thing as her: where would they sleep? Well, if he wasn't mentioning it, she wouldn't either. It obviously wasn't any kind of big deal to him...so it shouldn't be to her either. She smoothed her ponytail and straightened her woolly jumper. In this state she was about as alluring as a llama anyway, so there was no danger of tempting him. Which was good.

No, really, it was.

Just don't think about that porch kiss.

As he turned up the heating, she looked around in

hopes of a distraction. Coffee, maybe. In the kitchen alcove she opened a cupboard, in search of mugs, and discovered a treasure trove. Vodka, gin, wine, whiskey, akvavit…it was enough to warm the cockles of the most frozen traveller.

"Wow."

He came in, and smiled when he saw the array of bottles. "Still the same. We used to have some big parties here."

In the small room, she was hyper-aware of his height, the breadth of his shoulders, and his *nearness*. She wanted to find a reason to step closer—pick an imaginary thread off his jumper? pretend she was suddenly hard of hearing? feign a heart attack?—but instead she made herself lean against the counter.

"Who does the cabin belong to?"

"Emil's family. There's a lake behind here. We used to come out from town every summer. And sometimes in the winter."

"But now he lives here?"

He nodded. "Yes, he bought some land next door. He specialises in large animals, and he's interested in the wolves too." Mentioning the wolves seemed to jolt him out of his reminiscences, and he frowned. "He said he'll text if there's any news."

"That's good."

"I told Bengt where we are too."

"Okay. Thanks." She was glad they wouldn't be worrying… although this would give Greta some great ammunition over the next batch of dishes. That would make her happy.

She watched as he went back out to the living area and pulled out his phone. He set it on the coffee table and sat in an armchair, elbows on his knees, waiting. She was tempted to open one of the bottles in the cupboard and have a little something to settle her own edginess. A night in here with him was going to be one long exercise in self-restraint.

"Can I get you anything?" she asked. "Coffee? Something to eat?"

"No thanks." He eyed the phone.

"Okay." She came out and sat on the sofa, then tucked her sock-clad feet under her. Might as well get comfy. It could be a long wait.

He looked over. "I didn't say thank you for what you did."

She shrugged. "I didn't do anything. It was sheer chance that I found him."

"Well…thank you."

His voice was suddenly low, and it sent a hum through her body. She swallowed. "You're welcome."

All at once, the distance between them seemed very small—just a few feet from armchair to sofa, bridged by one long look between them. She thought back to the moment in the boathouse, and glanced down at his hands. Which were now sitting in his lap. Which meant that she was actually glancing in the direction of his…she ripped her eyes away. Oh, classy.

When she met his eyes again, there was something new there—a knowing, and a sort of assessment, as though he was trying to get the measure of her. If she hadn't given herself away with the hundred and one times she'd stolen surreptitious glances at him, before and after that single post-party kiss on her doorstep, she definitely had now. That night, she'd closed the door on him…but now he knew that, actually, she'd left it the tiniest bit ajar.

Outside, the snow fell, but inside, it was definitely getting warmer…

Then his phone beeped, and they both jumped. Her chest tightened, and she saw the worry reclaim his face. He stood up as he picked up the phone, and she did too. It seemed the right thing to do, to learn the fate of such an amazing creature. She came closer, wanting to read the screen, but of course it was in Swedish, a collection of letters scattered with double dots and little circles that made no sense at all.

But one look at him told her what the message conveyed. Every bit of weight seemed lifted from his shoulders, and from his expression.

"He's okay," he said, his face clear with relief. "He's awake, and drinking some water."

Her hands went to her mouth, and she let out the breath she'd been holding. "That was fast. Thank God."

"We can't be completely sure yet," he said. "And we have to wait for the test results. But it's a good start."

"Do you want to go over and see him?"

"I do," he said. "But Emil wants to keep everything quiet, so Brynjar can rest while the medication starts to work."

"That makes sense, I suppose," she said. "Doctor's orders."

"Exactly." He texted back, then threw the phone onto the sofa. "Let's have that drink now."

She hesitated. "I thought maybe you didn't drink."

"I don't drink and *drive*."

"Oh...okay."

What she really meant was, uh-oh. Already, she was teetering on the brink...if they started drinking together, she knew her wafer-thin shred of resolve would crumble. As it was, she was fighting the urge to fling herself across the space between them and hope for the best. It wasn't like anything that happened here would last—she'd be back in London, or wherever, and he'd be here, or in Scotland. And when she got back to Vertex, she'd make sure they never crossed paths from opposite sides of the wolf campaign. But the thought of him knowing, after the event, that she had lied so thoroughly...

He went into the kitchen, and she heard bottles clinking, then he emerged with a three-quarters full bottle of Absolut Kurant and a couple of small glasses.

"There's nothing to mix with it. You'll have to drink Swedish style."

She straightened her shoulders. "I can do that."

For the first time, she saw him grin. It transformed his face with a flash of dimples, making him look younger, and freer, and yes, even a little wolfish. Or maybe that was her imagination. Her imagination was becoming pretty damn creative lately.

"I believe you," he said, filling the glasses. "I saw you win against the akvavit."

"I don't know if I *won*," she said, taking the drink he offered. "But it was a good night."

"Not *that* good," he said.

She paused, the glass almost at her lips. He was looking at her, a level challenge that made her blush as she remembered the kiss, and the night's end. Then he smiled.

"*Skål*," he said, and threw back the shot.

"*Skål*," she echoed. Her own shot burned on the way down, but not as much as her cheeks.

They sat down again, and he poured them each another glass.

Time to change the subject. "How long have you been studying the wolves?" she asked.

"A long time," he said. "After school, I left to go travelling. I needed to…get away for a while. You know. So I started university late. But I studied zoology, and when I had a choice I wrote about wolves. Then I did a master's degree in wildlife ecology, in Scotland. And now the PhD."

She tried to calculate how old he must be, but without knowing his age when he started university, she couldn't guess. Getting to PhD level was pretty impressive though. "That's a lot of studying."

"It is. But there's practical work too, fieldwork. You're not in a classroom all the time."

"You wouldn't like that."

He shook his head. "I would not."

It was hard to imagine him trooping into a lecture theatre, confining his long legs behind a desk, submitting to exams and assessments. Looking at him now, filling the armchair, legs stretched out in front of him, was like observing a piece of the wild brought indoors. You could put four walls around him, but he'd always belong out there.

She should be asking him more about the research, trying to find out things that had gone wrong with the Swedish wolves. But while the conversation was flowing for once, she decided to take a chance. "And your family…?"

He curled a lip, suddenly darkening again. "Nothing to tell. You already know about my mother." She started to say something, but he waved a hand, cutting her off. "The rest is not worth talking about."

He downed his shot. The subject was closed.

"I don't know *you* very well," he said. "Tell me something."

"Um...okay." No problem. There was plenty she could tell without giving anything away. "Well, I grew up in eight different countries. No, wait—nine, if you count England."

"That's a lot. Was it fun?"

She shrugged. "Depends how you define fun."

"That sounds like a no."

She picked up the bottle and refilled her glass, then leaned across to fill his, but a splosh of vodka spilled onto the table. Huh. The glasses must be shrinking. She hadn't had *that* many shots.

He got up and came to sit next to her on the sofa, then put his glass next to hers.

"Try again."

Having him right next to her was *not* going to help. She sat forward, concentrating on keeping her arm steady, and managed to fill the glass. When she sat back, she sank into the sofa, tipping towards him where his weight deepened the seat cushion.

"Oops," she said. "Sorry." Even though she wasn't. At that moment, though, she knew what The Shark would say if she could see this scene. Regretfully, she levered herself away towards her own side of the sofa.

"Tell me about your job," he said.

Ack. Could he read her mind? She reeled off the speech she'd been giving anyone who asked. "I work for a communications company in London. Publicity, social media, branding."

Upon hearing that, most people glazed over. But he didn't.

"So is that marketing, or more like public relations?"

Oh, hell. Why was *he* the one person who wanted to know more? And damn his excellent English. "Uh...public relations. It's not saving the world, but it's okay." She tossed back the shot, and reached for the bottle again.

"Public relations…" he mused. "Do you work for a good company?"

Why had she said public relations? She could have said anything at all. This was getting too close for comfort.

"Depends how you define good," she said, and laughed. To her own ears, it sounded way too much like a nervous giggle. Please don't let him notice, she chanted in her head. Please don't let him notice.

"I mean not un…what's the word? Unethical?"

"Yes. Unethical. I mean, that's how you say it. I don't mean *they're* unethical."

But they were. She was. It was the truth. She'd always thought she was better than the rest of them, but here she was, searching for ways to spin her story, misleading a perfectly decent person. And not even for some greater good, or for something she believed in. Only to prove a point.

"What's the company called?"

Alarm bells started up in her head. Abort, abort.

She did the only thing she could think of. She put her hand on his thigh, leaned in, and kissed him.

And he kissed her back, a heady, blackcurrant-laced kiss. Well, what did she think he'd do? Oh lord, this was one distraction technique she *liked*. She turned and kneeled up slightly—he was so tall—and in one effortless movement he picked her up and brought her to him, so that she was straddling his legs. He wasn't asking questions now—apart from the unspoken one that was growing between them as rapidly as his obvious desire. How far were they going to go?

In the back of her mind, a tiny memory remained, a niggling reminder that she was the unethical one. But the other ninety-nine point nine nine per cent of her was focused on only one thing—the man under her. And specifically, what that man had started to do with his lips, and his hands. This is what she should have done after the party, if she'd had any sense. Or no sense at all.

Then he pulled away, leaving her more than a little breathless.

"You kissed me," she said.

He raised an eyebrow. "You kissed *me*."

"Yes, but...before. After the party."

"I did."

"Why?"

He laughed. "Because I wanted to. And I thought you wanted me to. And now I think I was right."

He ran one hand slowly, gently, around the back of her neck, and her head fell to the side, her eyes closing for a moment. Oh God, the luxury of being touched by this man, feeling his heat and hardness underneath her, knowing what was possible...

She looked over his shoulder towards the bedroom. He followed her gaze, then looked back at her. Neither of them needed to say anything, in English or in Swedish—their next step was sealed. She got off his lap, and he stood up and took her hand.

But at the bedroom door, he stopped, a question in his eyes. Was she sure? In that moment, faced with his good manners, every reason to stop right here crowded into her head. It was bad enough that she was here like some kind of secret agent—how much worse would it be to do this, and then be found out? Because now she knew what his work meant to him, and what a betrayal would mean. No, she definitely shouldn't go any further.

But she wanted wanted *wanted* it, and the driving ache was impossible to resist with him right in front of her. She glanced down. With the proof of his own wanting right in front of her too. She might be unethical, but hell, she was only human.

"I'm sure," she said, and led him into the room.

By the bed, he pulled off her jumper, revealing the tight white thermal top she was wearing underneath. Oh no— from llama to granny. She'd forgotten about that frumpy thing. At least she was wearing a matching bra and panties underneath. Because now he was going to see every item of her underwear...and more.

She tried to cover the thermal with her arms, wishing they'd turned off the light in the main room. "Ugh, this is *so* not sexy."

He took her hands and pulled them away from her body. "Yes it is." He ran his hands down her sides, dipping into her curve of her waist and back out again at her hips. "Look at you."

But she could only look at *him*, lit from behind in a broad-shouldered silhouette. Then she grabbed the hem of the thermal and tore it over her head, letting it fall to the floor. He let out a breath, and pulled off his own jumper (not Norwegian knitwear, thank God). She tugged his t-shirt out of his jeans, then slipped her hands under the soft cotton fabric. His skin was warm at her fingertips, and she let them run up his back, then around his sides to his flat stomach. She could feel the breaths he was taking, shallower and faster, just the same as her own. In one impatient movement, he had the t-shirt off, and a flush of heat ran through her as they pressed together, only the lace of her bra between his bare chest and her hardening nipples.

He reached around and released her hair from its ponytail, so that it fell down her back and around her shoulders, silky against her skin.

"Like sunset," he murmured, running his fingers through the coppery lengths, and she shivered.

Then he stepped forwards, and she let herself fall to the bed, wriggling backwards as he followed. Propped up on his arms above her, his dark hair fell over his forehead, and his face was serious again. The rough-spun blanket covering the bed was scratchy against her bare back and arms, a contrast to his smooth skin as she explored the foreign country of his body. Soft skin, hard muscle, hot under her fingertips. An involuntary sound of appreciation escaped her lips, and he smiled, then lowered himself to kiss her, the length of his body against hers.

But she pushed him away, and reached for his belt buckle. "You're overdressed."

He stood up and undid the belt, shucked off his jeans, and was back in an instant.

"Now," he said, and kissed her with the most restrained urgency, a starving man at a feast still remembering his manners, making her squirm and hunger for him even more.

Where had this man *come* from? Maybe she could have guessed there'd be something sultry beneath the surly—all that suppressed angst had to boil over some time. She wrapped her legs around him and let her last thoughts slip away, sinking into the irresistible spell of his lips and hands, of shuddery breaths and small moans and whispered exclamations. And the one blazing central point where their bodies met, separated only by the thinnest layers of cotton and lace.

But then, through the lust-haze, a sliver of reality intruded. "Do you have any protection?" she whispered. "You know, a condom?"

He shook his head. "No. Do you?"

"No."

He rested his forehead against hers. "Shit."

"Yeah." She felt like crying, or possibly screaming.

They stayed like that for a few seconds, then he pulled back and looked at her, wicked determination in his eyes. "Don't move."

Slowly, steadily, he traced a trail of kisses from her lips, down the side of her neck, and between her breasts, only pausing at the deepest point of her cleavage. Then she felt the warmth of his tongue against her skin, and the heat of his breath, and her body arched underneath him. With a quiet laugh, he continued down, stopping to circle her belly button, and she hardly remembered to worry about the appendectomy scar there, or the fact that her stomach wasn't flat enough for her liking. Between lips, tongue, and the occasional scrape of stubble, she hardly remembered her own name, and by the time he reached the edge of her panties, there was nothing in the world but his mouth.

And then he paused. She twisted upwards in blissful frustration, his lips so close to where she wanted him to be, his breath warming the one spot that had taken over her entire body. Why why why had he stopped?

Oh. Her blurry mind slowly became aware of a sound…a phone ringing. *Her* phone ringing, in the pocket of her jeans, abandoned on the bedroom floor. Well, not ringing, but playing the theme from Jaws—da-da, da-da, da-da-da-da-da-da—that she'd selected for Alcina. It had been hilarious at the time, Jaws and The Shark. Not so much now.

She lifted her head, and he was looking at her, bemused, his dark hair rumpled, his eyes heavy with heat and promise. She wasn't interrupting *that* for anything. She shook her head in desperation, and then, mercifully, the phone went silent.

He ducked his head again, and she sank back, one hand tangled in her hair, the other pressed against her belly, every shameless millimetre of her longing to rise up and meet his teasing mouth. Patience, patience…

Then Jaws rang out again, and he pushed himself up on his hands.

"Do you need to answer?"

She looked at his shoulders, the muscles extra defined as they held his body weight. Then at his broad chest, the abs sketched upon his stomach, the impressive fullness straining the front of his boxer briefs, and then back to the tempting curves of his lips.

"No. *Definitely* not."

He grinned, and returned to his task. Finally, finally, his tongue met that sweet, aching spot that had been waiting for him. And as the waves rose in her body in answer to his tender, unrelenting strokes, she knew she was in the worst, best, most addictive kind of trouble.

Chapter Seventeen

For a creature so untamed, Brynjar seemed remarkably relaxed in his little room with the glass front. Maybe he knew that being there was actually a good thing. Through the glass, his dark eyes regarded Zoe steadily, a window into another world. Did he remember her, or understand that she had been responsible for his rescue? As they looked at each other, she felt like he must.

"He's amazing," she whispered to Jakob, as Emil measured out a serving of dog food.

He nodded. "They all are."

Emil went in and set down the bowl, and she held her breath.

"Is it safe?"

"Yes," Jakob replied. "He's not at full strength, anyway."

She looked again, and saw that one of the wolf's legs had a small shaved patch, where a drip was still inserted, bandaged to hold it steady. "Oh. Poor thing."

"If he was poisoned, it should help him process it faster."

He put a hand at the small of her back. It felt like a combination of reassurance, and pride that she seemed to care so much. She might be secretly on the opposing team, but you'd have to have a heart of stone to not be affected by this denizen of the wild, first suffering at the hands of humans, and then being saved by them. She sighed. It was a crazy world.

Just then, Vera came in, wearing regular clothes instead of her tunic, and Zoe remembered that it was Saturday.

"Oh," Vera said, her eyes going from Zoe, to Jakob, then back again. "I just wanted to check on the wolf."

Zoe shifted under her scrutiny, acutely aware she was wearing the same clothes, and that Jakob's hand was still at her back. He didn't take it away though, and she liked it there. She liked it a lot. She snuck a glance at him, but he didn't seem at all self-conscious.

Last night, after her own climax—powerful enough that she was sure she'd thawed the snow on the roof above—she'd been jelly. But within a few minutes, she'd itched to return the favour, aroused all over again at the thought. She rolled over towards him, but he just lay a kiss on the side of her neck.

"Go to sleep," he whispered. "It's late."

"But what about you?" she said, reaching for him in the dark.

"No." He grabbed her hand and tangled his fingers in hers. "We have time."

Not enough time, she wanted to say. Her first week was almost over already.

But they'd drifted off together, and she had the kind of dreamless, sated sleep that only came after such a release. She woke up to the sound of him in the shower, and blushed as the night before replayed in her head.

And she blushed again now, as Vera narrowed her eyes and came to exactly the right conclusion.

But Jakob wasn't blushing. When Emil came back out, they fell into a discussion in Swedish, and Vera joined in. Zoe found a chair and sat down, pleased at least that Brynjar seemed to be stable. She leaned her chin in her hands, and watched him finish his small portion of food. Apparently you could be wild, and yet tame enough to take what you need. She glanced back at Jakob. He was human proof of that.

And what *she* needed was more of him. In the (literally) cold light of day, with two unanswered messages and three unread texts from The Shark waiting on her phone, she knew she shouldn't. But she and Jakob had unfinished business now. She owed him. And she intended to pay him back…preferably with substantial interest.

★

Jakob stopped the car in the garage, and switched off the engine. They turned to look at each other. With Brynjar out of immediate danger, the tension had lifted, and their mood was cheerful—not surprising, she thought, after the activities of the night before. In the sudden silence, she couldn't help laughing, and he smiled.

"That was…something."

She nodded. "It was."

They undid their seatbelts, but no one was going anywhere.

"Would you like something *else*?" she asked.

He leaned closer. "I think I would."

"I wonder what that something might be…" She lay one finger on his lips, then began to trail it down, down, down, over his chin, in a wavering path down his chest, closer and closer to—

They both jumped as Bengt flung open the door on the driver's side.

"Hej!" he said, holding a snow shovel like a soldier on duty. "The heroes are back. How is the patient?"

"Good," Jakob replied, as she whipped her hand back and gathered her composure.

"Excellent." Bengt looked across to her. "Good work, Zoe."

"I didn't really do anything," she said. "But thank you. I'm just happy he's recovering."

She and Jakob got out, and they all went out of the garage into the biting cold. The new snow had covered the driveway and left deep pillowy piles against the house, and she could see where Bengt had started clearing it away.

"We need a few more days to be sure," Jakob reminded her. "And if he was poisoned, I want to know who did it."

"Yes," Bengt said, his usually cheerful face grim. "We will find them."

Jakob reached out and took the shovel. "I'll help you."

"*Tack*, Jakob," Bengt said. "And you go inside, Zoe. Someone came to see you."

"Oh! Okay."

She took one last look at Jakob, already wielding the shovel like an expert. Snow is work, he'd said to her when they first met. She would have loved to stay and watch him work, flexing his muscles, especially now she knew what those muscles looked like. But instead she smiled, hugging the knowledge to herself, and went to see who was waiting for her inside.

Four little arms embraced her as she came in the door.

"Hej!" she said, gathering Lena and Ebba into a triple bear hug. She looked over their heads, through to the living room, and saw Malin smiling. "Hi! Thanks again for the party."

"It was fun," she replied. "But we didn't get much time to talk. The girls wanted us all to get together." She said something to them, and they nodded, smiling at Zoe, then milled around her as she went in and sat down.

"That's so lovely," she said.

Like everyone, she'd heard the cliché of the cold, distant Swede—but so far, most people had been perfectly nice. Certainly no worse than your average English person, anyway. Or the people in any of the countries she'd lived in as a kid. In fact, it felt like she'd got to know people here faster than in any other place.

One person in particular…

"So we thought we would come and have morning tea with you," Malin was saying.

"Ah. Fika?" Zoe gave the girls a wink, and Lena winked back—the cutest six-year-old version of a wink, with both little blue eyes closed.

Greta came in, beaming. "Listen to that. I *said* you'd be a real Swede."

"Maybe." She laughed. "But is it okay? I haven't done my jobs yet."

"I did them," Greta said. "You were *busy*." Her eyes caught Zoe's, a sparkle of mischief evident.

She was so busted. "Thank you."

Greta just nodded, obviously enjoying the tease.

"Well it's nice to have everyone here, together." She turned to Malin. "So your car is okay now?"

Malin rolled her eyes. "Ugh. I think so. Sometimes it won't start," she explained for Zoe.

"I'm amazed that anything starts in this weather," Zoe said.

Greta tutted. "You should buy a new car."

"I know," Malin said. "When Anton gets back he can help me choose."

"Good," said Greta, satisfied. Then she turned to the girls. "Okay. *Ska vi fika?* Come and help me." They went off to the kitchen.

"So when will Anton be back?" Zoe asked.

Malin screwed up her nose. "Not until spring. He works on an oil rig, in the North Atlantic sea."

"Wow. You must miss him."

She shrugged. "It's okay. But we get used to being without him, then when he comes back all our routines are broken. It's hard to make him...fit in again."

"Oh, I hadn't thought of that."

"But they pay him well, so I can be home with the girls."

"Well, that's one good thing. They're so gorgeous."

She looked pleased. "Thank you. Honestly, I don't know what I'd do without them."

"I can imagine."

"What about you—are you having fun here?"

"I am." After last night, the fun had definitely stepped up a notch. His promise lingered in her mind—*we have time*. She couldn't help it—she was very *interested* in her conflict of interest. She tried not to laugh, the Jakob high still lingering. "It's *interesting* work."

Malin pursed her lips. "Hmm. And working with Jakob—is that okay?"

Remain neutral, she told herself. "Yes, it's fine. I don't see him an awful lot, but he seems very dedicated to his work."

"He is. And what do you think about the wolves? Should we have them so close to humans?"

Even after only a short time in Lillavik, the issue didn't seem at all clear. "That's a hard question. I can see both sides, I suppose."

Judging by Malin's face, she was unconvinced. Fair enough. Zoe herself was only just able to hear a wolf's howl without freaking out.

"Did Greta tell you about the wolf I found? He might have been poisoned."

"Yes, she told me. She was upset about it, but she didn't want the girls to see. You were in the right place at the right time."

"I was."

At that moment, the girls came back in. Each of them proudly carried a plate, Lena with the kanelbullar Zoe had come to love, and Ebba with gingerbread biscuits. Greta followed with a tray of mugs, glasses, juice and a coffee pot, and they settled in for fika and chat.

With the little ones having a wonderful time, it was the sweetest tea party Zoe had ever been to. And if she had to stifle a yawn every now and then, after her 'interesting' night, she made sure not to show it.

★

That afternoon, after changing into fresh clothes, she went to help Greta and Stina over at the guesthouse, making up for missing her morning's tasks. They were down in the basement, having a sort out.

Greta sighed as she surveyed the mess, kneeling in the middle of dusty boxes, broken pieces of furniture, bags of old-fashioned linen, and ancient skis…the kind of assorted debris that isn't needed any more, but can't seem to be thrown away either.

"I don't know why I kept all this. Who's going to sort it out when I'm gone?"

Stina shushed her. "You're not going anywhere." She rummaged in a box, and pulled out a child's drawing. "Look at this! So sweet."

Stick figure people with balloon heads stood waving between zig-zaggy trees, under a huge, smiling sun. A wobbly blue circle off to one side looked like it might represent the pond, or maybe even the lake.

"Oh, cute. Is it Oscar's?" Zoe asked.

Stina pulled out another drawing, and an old school book. "You can't throw this stuff away."

But Greta's face closed over. "Just leave that box," she instructed.

Stina glanced at Zoe, but put everything back in and closed the box again.

"You must miss those days," Zoe said.

Greta occupied herself with a pile of old magazines. "Hmm."

The girls looked at each other, and Stina shrugged.

Then Greta stood up, vigorously dusting herself off. "Let's leave this for now. The university group is going tomorrow, and then we have a few days with no guests. It's a good chance to do a big clean of each room."

"No," Stina said. "It's a chance for you to have a holiday."

"Uff, no," Greta said. "We can't just leave. Who would look after everything?"

"We could do it," Zoe said.

Stina nodded. "Yes! And Jakob would help. You and Bengt never go away together. It would be *romantic*."

"Oh, I don't think so," Greta said. "There's no time to plan. Where would we go?"

But she was smiling to herself, and Zoe could see that the seed of an idea had been planted. She liked the idea herself, especially if Jakob was part of the plan. Stina clapped her hands silently behind Greta's back, and gave Zoe a double thumbs up.

Over dinner that night in the kitchen, once the guests were settled to their own meals in the big guesthouse dining room, Zoe couldn't help but ask about Jakob. He never seemed to eat with them, at any meal, and she wondered what he was doing. Or maybe she just wanted to hear his name on her lips, like Vera.

"He went back to see the wolf," Bengt said.

She shuffled her food on the plate. "Oh…I would have liked to go too."

"Maybe he'll take you tomorrow," Greta said, giving Bengt a look.

"Yes, I'm sure he will," he agreed.

"I'm just worried about the wolf," Zoe said.

Greta nodded. "Of course."

There was a moment's silence.

"I really am. I feel sort of…invested, since I found him."

Greta and Bengt glanced at each other. "Do you want me to phone him and check?" Bengt asked.

"Oh no," she said hurriedly. "No, that's okay." What kind of lovestruck teenager must she seem? She changed the subject. "This dinner is amazing—I should get the recipe. What's it called?"

Greta sat up a little straighter. "Thank you! Not everyone likes it. It's *Janssons frestelse*. We always have it at Christmas, but I wanted you to try it, so I made it for everyone."

She started to talk about the ingredients, and the difference between Swedish anchovies (actually sprats) and true anchovies (called something-or-other else in Swedish). It seemed to be the fishy equivalent of the elk/moose complication, and Zoe tried to concentrate, but felt her mind wandering to other things…

Later, Janssons frestelse recipe in hand, she walked back down to the cabin. After last night's snowfall, the sky had cleared, and the million-and-one stars were bright above her. At her little blue retreat, she stopped on the step, taking it in. It would be hard to leave, when the time came. But she couldn't be a volunteer forever. London called, and work, and her second family, and the need to find Claire before it was too late. Her own parents were in Singapore on assignment—a place about as different from here as she could imagine. Maybe she should Skype them, show them how beautiful it was. If they cared to know.

She sighed and went inside. It wasn't very late, even though it was so dark. She looked up the time difference, but it was the middle of the night in Singapore. Oh well. Instead, she decided to send Denise a photo of her view. Not bothering to pull her coat and boots back on, she opened the door...and gasped with surprise. Jakob was standing on the porch.

He held up a pair of black ice skates. "Someone said you might need skating lessons?"

Her mood went from wistful to wonderful in the blink of an eye.

"I do."

Chapter Eighteen

They rode double on his snowmobile on the way to the lake, her arms around his waist, her legs each side of his. She didn't *need* to sit so close, but he wasn't complaining. From behind him, she watched the shadowy landscape go by, wondering where the wolves were tonight and if they had noticed Brynjar's absence.

At the lake shore by the boathouse, he brushed the snow off a wooden bench, and they sat in the moonlight to put their ice skates on.

"How was Brynjar this afternoon?" she asked, as she took off one boot and slipped her foot quickly into the first white skate.

He was already tying his laces with swift efficiency. "Okay. Not great, but steady."

"Cross fingers he'll start to improve."

He stood up. "Hold your thumbs."

"Hold my thumbs?"

"*Hålla tummarna.*" He tucked each thumb inside closed fingers on the same hand. "For luck. Fingers don't work here. Thumbs make the magic happen instead."

She laughed, thinking about the magic his fingers had worked the night before. "If you say so."

With both laces now tied in firm bows, she wiggled her

toes in the skates. They fit her perfectly, the soft leather snug, but her ankles went this way and that as she tried to balance on her feet. The wide open space of the lake stretched away in the moonlight. No railings to cling onto out there.

She bit her lip. "I'm not very good."

"You'll be okay," he said.

He held out his hand, and she hung onto it as she tottered alongside him to the lake's edge. There was no point trying to impress him now—the most she could do was try not to fall on her butt in front of him again. There was no sign of Hakon Halvarsson, but she had a moment's terror as she imagined skating right into one of his fishing holes. Then she realised that they would surely have frozen over again by now. She made herself breathe. No panic necessary. Not hole-related panic, anyway.

Jakob stepped confidently onto the ice, and she shuffled after him. Instantly, her feet went out from under her, and she landed on her side with a splat and an *oof*. Oh God, not again...and right in front of him.

He was there instantly, helping her back up and holding her steady. "Are you okay?"

Okay was a relative term. She rubbed her hip. She wasn't hurt (apart from possibly getting a bruise to match the fading one on her butt cheek), but the heat of her embarrassment could melt a hole big enough for Hakon to pull a whale through.

"I'm fine," she said, forcing herself to smile. "I'll get there."

"Okay." He took her hand, and started to push off again. "Try it like this."

"Whoa..." As her feet threatened to head in opposite directions, she grabbed his upper arm with her other hand, clinging on for dear life. "Sorry."

He laughed. "Very graceful."

She rolled her eyes. "Someone needs to install hand rails out here."

They made their way out towards the centre, going at her slow and careful pace. If she could manage on the ice rink in Lillavik, she could do it here. At first, she was still shaky on her legs, but then she started to get more confident, tentatively pushing off with one foot, then the other.

She wasn't planning to let go of his hand though.

As she found her feet, she relaxed, and the beauty of their surroundings started to come into focus. Soft moonlight, the wide sprinkle of stars, the forest coming down to hug the lake. The slight glow of Lillavik's lights in the distance. The sound of their blades on the ice. And Jakob, tall and steady, someone to hold onto on the slippery surface. It was a scene from a movie, she had a starring role, and her leading man was totally big-screen-worthy. If she'd been on solid ground, she would have pinched herself, but she couldn't risk any false moves. She settled for a quiet smile.

But then, there was something else, too.

"Wait." She tugged at his arm, and he paused. She wobbled to a stop beside him, their hands still linked. "What's that noise?"

Otherworldly sounds were emanating from the lake, a strange orchestration of pings and twangs and weirdly beautiful warps. "I've never...it's like the lake is singing. It wasn't doing that when we were here last time."

He looked out over the moonlit icescape. "The ice shifts. That's the sound of it moving."

"So the sound is sort of resonating through it, like music? It's amazing."

He squeezed her hand. "It is amazing."

"I'm glad I got to hear it."

They stood for a moment, listening, hands linked, and she wished she could stop time, here in this perfect, cinematic dreamscape.

Then a sudden sharp crack echoed in the cold air, and she froze—as much as she could while her feet were still threatening to scoot out from underneath her. "What was *that*?"

"A crack," he said, letting go of her hand and skating away.

"A crack?" she squeaked, her throat barely able to let the words pass. It was a long, long way to shore—and he was going *further out*. What the hell? "Come back," she whispered, not daring to raise her voice in case she caused some kind of major fissure and disappeared into the frigid depths. "Come *back*."

But he circled smoothly around her, just out of reach, teasing.

"This is not funny," she said, through gritted teeth. Beneath her unsteady feet, the ice suddenly seemed alive, an unknown quantity. "*Seriously*."

Maybe hearing the fear in her voice, he glided back. "It's okay. It's normal. There are inches of ice."

"Oh." Now she was embarrassed to have got so panicky. But still mad. And relieved. "Okay, then. Thanks for the fright."

He laughed. "Come on. Let's skate."

He held out a hand, a peace offering, and she considered it. After the adrenaline rush of her panic, she felt more like slapping him. But it was a long way back to shore, and he was matinee-idol handsome in the starlit night...and she remembered the last time she'd seen him in the half-dark. There was no holding grudges against a man with *that* kind of talent.

The lake, and temptation, called. She took his hand.

★

Déjà vu. She stood on the first step, and he stood on the path. Across the clearing, his cabin waited in the snow. Behind her, her own cabin beckoned, with the fireplace, and the warm bed...

"Here we are again," she said.

He nodded. "Here we are."

"Thank you for the skating lesson."

"You're welcome."

She knew full well she was going to ask him in, but there was something too irresistible in the anticipation.

She glanced across at his cabin. "Do you have anything you need to do now?"

"Yes, I do."

Oh. Maybe it really was déjà vu. "Do you need to check on Brynjar?" That was important, of course...but she tried not to let any disappointment show in her voice.

"No. I'll wait until tomorrow."

"Something else, then?"

"Yes."

At the expression in his eyes, a little spark flared inside her. "Something *else*..."

"Yes."

Just like last time, she leaned forward, and he did too. But this time, there was no sudden exit. Their kiss held all the frustration of what they'd missed the previous night, and all the promise of how they intended to make up for it. She pulled him up the steps, keeping their lips together, gloved hands fumbling with coat fastenings, laughing and swearing. Finally in the door, they shucked off their winter layers—but the cabin was cold.

"Maybe it should be warmer," he suggested.

"Yes, I think so."

She knew she could turn the electric heating on, but when he knelt on the hearth to light a fire, she didn't stop him. A blazing fire in a cabin in the snowy woods...a tall, dark and handsome man...sometimes a cliché was the best thing ever. She sat on the sofa with her legs tucked under her and watched him work, building a fire with the ease of years of practice.

Soon the flames were burning brightly, and he closed the wood-burner door. He lit a couple of candles on the mantelpiece too, then turned to her. She looked up at him, and he reached down and pulled her to her feet.

"We have something else to do, remember?" As if to clarify, he bent his head and dotted feather-light kisses in a cluster just beneath her ear, in exactly the right place to send a shiver through her body. A *hot* shiver. Damn, he was good.

But she lay her palm against his chest, holding him off.

"Wait. Just tell me you have something now. You know."

He reached for his coat, where he'd thrown it over the armchair, and took a small box from the inside pocket. "I have something now."

"A whole box? You're pretty confident, wilderness boy." She thought she might make *him* blush for once, but he met her teasing eyes directly.

"I am."

A delicious impatience sped through her, and she laughed. "Well, that's big talk...let's see some action."

She pulled off her jumper. She'd made sure to get rid of the thermal, just in case, and now she was wearing a tight t-shirt with a plunging neckline. She smiled as his eyes fell to her cleavage, intending to taunt him a little longer, but when he looked back up, the hunger in his eyes triggered a sudden desperation in her. All at once they were tearing off clothes, each others' and their own, half-laughing, half serious, lost in the urgent need to feel skin on skin.

And then, with every item of clothing discarded, they stood facing each other, firelight playing on their naked bodies. He took her face in his hands, and her hurried breathing slowed and steadied, until she was nearly holding her breath. With the fire's heat warming her left side, and the heat of desire warming the rest of her from the inside out, she waited.

She'd never known anyone like this man. Undomesticated, yet so civilised—a dangerous, intoxicating combination. Who would have thought that surly guy who met her at the station would turn out to be such an irresistible diversion?

Finally, he lowered his head to kiss her, and when their lips met, her body's reaction was as though she'd been waiting one year, not one day. Warm breath, seeking tongues, wandering hands...the rush filled her veins and ignited every secret part of her. He kissed her with expert thoroughness, a promise of the pleasures ahead. And this time, she knew, they could take any pleasure they wanted. And she wanted them *all*.

By the time they paused for breath, her knees were

wobbly, her heart was pounding, and all she wanted was to get him horizontal, and get serious.

"God, this is good," she said, pressed against him, feeling his arousal insistent against her belly.

He ran his hands down her back, crushing her closer. "Do you want to stay here, or...?"

She looked around. The whole lovemaking-in-front-of-the-fire thing always sounded good, but the rug was kind of knobbly, and the hearth was of sharp-edged stone, and there wasn't much room.

"The bedroom?"

She'd barely got the words out before he had her hand, and was on his way. She laughed as he scooped her up in the doorway, and deposited her on the bed.

"Wait," he said. He went back out to the living room, but before she had a chance to ask what he was doing, he was back, carrying a candle and triumphantly holding up the box. "Very important."

But she wasn't looking at the box. In the candlelight, he was sculpted, golden, and utterly enticing. She crooked her finger at him, and he tossed the box on the bedside table, put the candle down more carefully, and obeyed.

In the warm, shifting light, they lay side by side. His fingers travelled over her skin, caressing the curves and dips of her body, while she let her hands and eyes explore his lean, strong physique. A fine scar ran down the length of his thigh, evidence of something major in his past. He saw her noticing it, and answered her unspoken question. "I have a pin in my leg."

She remembered what Vera had said about an accident—maybe it was the result of that. But she wasn't going to risk ruining the moment by asking him about it now.

"Iron man, huh?" she murmured, tracing her finger gently down the scar. Then she followed it back up to the top of his thigh, and higher again, until her fingers closed around the steely-warm hardness that awaited there. "Iron man."

His only response was a swift intake of breath as she

began moving her hand in firm, confident strokes. It was intoxicating to hold him captive this way—seeing his taut muscles tense, hearing his ragged breathing, feeling him move at the mercy of her hands—and an insistent, answering heat grew between her own thighs.

Then he gathered himself, giving a low, frustrated rumble as he forced himself back from the edge. With a determined look in his eye, he flipped her over, so that she was underneath him.

"Not so fast," he said. "I have some things to do to *you*. I want to do it properly, the first time."

His words triggered a rush of desire, and she wrapped her legs around him.

No, it definitely wasn't the time for questions.

It was time for something else.

Chapter Nineteen

Zoe turned and tipped her head back, letting the hot water run over her head and down her back. This morning-after feeling was so heavenly—a tired body, but a lingering, deliciously decadent haziness. They hadn't got through that whole box, but they'd made a damn good dent in it. She smiled as she soaped herself all over, all the places where his lips and hands had been…which was everywhere.

Her phone rang in the bedroom—da-da, da-da, da-da-da-da-da—but she turned her face into the stream of water, ignoring it. Right now, she really, really didn't want to think about the massive conflict of interest she'd leapt into. Because it had been the best bad decision of her life. Best, as in hottest.

As she wrapped a towel around herself, she heard a man's voice calling her name from outside. She stopped still to listen, but it wasn't Jakob. He'd gone already, needing to get some things done, but had promised to see her later.

"Zoe!"

The shout came again, and she tugged on her clothes. "Just a minute!"

With her hair still dripping, she dashed to the door. Malin and Fredrik were outside, looking like they'd skied out of a Fjällräven ad. Both of them were wearing puffer jackets and reflective sunglasses, and leaning casually on their ski poles. Malin had a backpack too, which she imagined was holding extremely healthy snacks.

"Hej, Zoe," Fredrik called, and Malin gave her a wave.

"Hej," she said, drying the ends of her hair with her towel. It was way too cold to be out here, damp and barefoot. "You're out early."

It was lucky Jakob had already left—she didn't feel like a repeat of the last time he and Fredrik had met on her doorstep.

"We're getting some Sunday exercise," Malin said. "Family tradition. Sorry to disturb you."

"That's okay." She hesitated. "Um...would you like to come in?"

Immediately, Fredrik pushed off towards the steps. "Yes, thank you."

Damn it. She'd really thought they'd say no. Malin was nice, but after all the awkward attention from Fredrik, she wasn't thrilled about spending time with him. It was rapidly bringing her back down to earth from her Jakob-induced high.

Fredrik had his skis off and was coming up the steps, but Malin was fiddling with her ski boots. "I won't be long," she said.

"Let's go in," Fredrik said. "You must be cold." He took off his ski boots and came inside in his socks, shutting the door on his sister.

He hadn't taken much convincing. Zoe excused herself to pull on some thick socks and a jumper and comb her hair, then put the kettle on. She didn't have anything yummy to offer as fika, but she could make coffee at least. She'd probably need a few to get through the day anyway, after the late night—might as well start now.

"Where are the girls?" she asked, getting mugs out of the cupboard.

"Playing at a friend's house." He was walking around while he waited, looking at all the pictures and knick-knacks. He stopped and peered into a glass-fronted cabinet.

It was full of books, but a framed photo sat in one corner, only just visible. He laughed, and took it out. "I forgot about this."

She came over to see. It was a bunch of teenagers, all in swimwear and sunglasses, captured in various crazy poses in front of the cabin. She squinted at the image, trying to see if one of them might be Jakob. No one looked like him—but if it was after his mother died, or while she was sick, he might not have been partying. She wanted to ask Fredrik, but judged it safer not to mention him.

"Looks like a fun day," she said.

He nodded. "We used to have great parties here." He put a finger on a grinning, gangly kid with one arm around a pretty girl, and the other holding a bottle in the air. "That's me."

Zoe was getting the impression that the various cabins scattered around the Swedish countryside were nothing but mini party venues. Her own teenage self would have loved it.

"You knew Oscar then? Greta and Bengt's son?"

"Everyone knows everyone here," he said.

"Which one is he?"

He pointed to a stocky guy with one arm around someone's neck and a bottle of beer in the other hand. Even at a low-resolution distance, she could see the resemblance to Bengt.

"What was he like, before he went to Australia?"

"I don't know." He shrugged and put the photo back in the cabinet. "Good at school, even though he never worked hard. Clever. Liked computers."

"Oh, like you."

He glowed at the implied compliment. "Thank you."

Oops. She'd meant the 'liked computers' part, but he didn't need any encouragement. She kept talking. "He wasn't outdoorsy, like Bengt?"

"Not really." He leaned an arm against the cabinet, over her shoulder. "Clever, did you say?"

There was a cursory knock, and Malin looked in from the doorway, still in her boots. Perfect timing for a rescue, thank God. While Fredrik was looking away, she stepped out of range.

"Let's go," Malin said.

"Already?" he grumbled. "What about my coffee?" But he went over to the door.

Malin poked him in the belly. "You need more exercise. Staring at the computer all day is bad for you."

He sighed in ostentatious resignation. "She's right. I won't get any exercise inside. Not the *skiing* kind of exercise, anyway," he added, with a wink at Zoe.

Ugh. She managed a weak smile. "Okay, well, have fun."

Outside, he finished putting on his ski boots, and stepped into his bindings. "We'll have coffee next time."

Zoe couldn't help being relieved. "Yes, of course." Or not. "Bye!"

They each put their sunglasses back on, a double dose of Nordic alpine style, then turned and glided away.

After that strange and brief visit, Zoe was even more ready for that coffee. Especially as she really would have to call The Shark back. Once again, she'd have to massage the truth—say she was working on it, still finding her way into the issues, getting a feel for the research. She'd got a feel for something all right, but there was no way she could tell Alcina *that*.

Yes, she was well and truly back to earth now. And unfortunately, the landscape was looking increasingly rocky. She dumped an extra spoonful of sugar into her coffee, and stirred it violently, sending a wave spilling onto the countertop. Sooner rather than later, she was going to have to face the reality of why she was really here.

★

Jakob wasn't at the office when she went up to start the volunteer jobs, so she set off on the snowmobile to check the eagle nest, the weight of her situation hanging over her. The fact that it had been such an amazing, sexy, abandoned night made her feel even worse. He hadn't even had the decency to be useless in bed. She picked up speed, letting the cold air burn her cheeks. Laugh or cry.

At the nest area she stopped and turned off the engine, then walked a short distance into the woods, surrounding herself with trees and quiet. Her footprints crunched as they broke the thin top layer of snow, and her breath was puffy in the cold air. She made herself breathe more slowly—in...out...in...out. It sort of helped...but not much.

She sighed and went back to the clearing. The nest still seemed to be uninhabited, and there was no sign of nest-building activity in any of the other trees. Maybe it was still too early, or maybe Greta was right, and home would be somewhere else for the eagles this year.

She started up the snowmobile, and started to drive away. But just off to her right, she spotted something—tracks running across the clearing, criss-crossing each other in loops and intersections. Pulling out the camera, she went to investigate. How many wolves had been here? Maybe Jakob would be able to tell. She took photos from every angle, then looked at where the tracks disappeared into the woods. It was tempting to follow them, but she was pretty sure that a healthy wolf wouldn't be as approachable as the one she'd found the other day. Plus, getting lost and freezing to death right now would be extremely inconvenient. She had things to sort out. Like proving something to The Shark without ruining things for Jakob, somehow...and deciding whether she should sleep with him again.

Images from the night before flickered in her mind. Candlelight, warm skin, her hands running over his body, his mouth awakening pleasure in every part of her...

Really, she shouldn't.

She shook her head and went back to the snowmobile, and set off towards the lodge.

She shouldn't.

But she knew she would.

Chapter Twenty

G reta and Bengt went off to their luxury bed-and-
breakfast getaway like newly-weds that afternoon, as
soon as the university club left. Zoe and Stina formed the
farewell committee, waving until Bengt's old Volvo was out
of sight around the corner of the long driveway. Then Stina
turned to her.

"Let's do everything fast, then we can relax."

"Sounds good to me."

They raced through the jobs at the lodge, working in
tandem to strip and remake beds, tidy the rooms, and get
the used linen into the two commercial-scale washing
machines in the basement. From there, it all went into the
equally supersized driers.

Jakob turned up at one stage, and found them working
in one of the rooms with a king-size bed. At the first sight of
him, Zoe felt a hum start up in her body. Memories of all
the sweet and sinful fun from the night before washed over
her, and her heart beat a little faster, a little lighter. But with
Stina there, she didn't give anything away.

"About time you came to help us," she told him, from
behind an armload of sheets.

His reply came with a wicked smile that told her he was
remembering exactly the same things. "Just making sure

you're working hard enough."

He dodged the pillowslip Stina threw at him, and had the last word from around the door frame, before he disappeared. "Bad shot."

Stina went to retrieve it from the hallway floor, and paused to watch him go. "When he's not grumpy, he's quite cute."

Zoe shrugged. "I suppose he is." She hoisted the pile of sheets higher to hide her smile.

When they finally stopped for dinner in the guesthouse kitchen—leftovers from the huge final meal Greta had prepared for the outdoor club the night before—Stina pulled a bottle of vodka from her bag.

"I thought we could toast their holiday." She took two glasses from the cupboard and splashed a generous amount into each one. "My dad will drive me home," she added, as she handed Zoe a glass.

"Well then—skål!" Zoe said.

"Skål!"

Stina grinned and threw back her drink with gusto, and Zoe followed suit. She shuddered as the sharply warming liquid went down, then held out her glass for a refill. Apparently her taste in drinks was getting harder.

They talked and laughed as they ate, and as the conversation went on, Zoe again found herself impressed by someone's language skills. Here—in a place that felt far from anywhere—she'd found nothing but immaculate English.

"Everyone speaks such amazing English," she said. "I wasn't expecting that."

"We all learn it at school," Stina said. "Not everyone *likes* to speak English—my sister is too shy. But most of us are happy to practise. A lot of companies want people who speak English too. And if you want to travel, you need it. That's why I'm doing a course taught in English. Most of the universities offer courses in English anyway."

"Really? I didn't know that. And I didn't know you were studying."

She nodded. "Psychology and counselling. Most of the

lessons are online, but I go to Stockholm sometimes. It's just a diploma, not a degree, but it will be enough to start."

"That must be interesting. Sometimes I think there's no way in hell we can ever say why people do the things they do." She put down her knife and fork, feeling suddenly flat.

Stina crinkled her nose in sympathy. "Are you thinking about the wolf?"

"Yes." She didn't add, *and myself.*

"People are terrible sometimes. And wonderful. And confused. I think it's the same everywhere. When I finish my course, I want to go to Australia and work."

"That would be fun. Maybe you can visit Oscar."

She pursed her lips. "I don't think so. I heard he's not very nice."

"Really? But Greta and Bengt are so lovely." It was impossible to imagine such a warm and generous couple producing unpleasant offspring.

"Oh, I'm sure he's fine really," Stina said, visibly backpedalling. "My dad heard he's living with an English girl over there. Anyway, he's much older than me. I don't think we'd have much to talk about."

"I'm older than you too," Zoe pointed out, but Stina shook her head.

"We're in the same decade, at least. Now, tell me more about *you*."

With that, the Oscar subject was closed, but Zoe added it to her list of unanswered Lillavik questions.

After dinner, she waved Stina off with her dad, then went back into the kitchen. Table wiped, dishwasher on, lights out. With no guests, there were no breakfasts to be made in the morning. She didn't know how Greta managed to feed so many people, week in and week out. Cooking was *very* low down on her own list of talents—although she might try the Janssons frestelse when she got back to London, just to honour Greta's enthusiasm for the dish. And the woman herself.

As she pulled on her boots by the back door, it struck her that she never thought of going 'back home'—only 'back to London'. For a person who spent all that time desperate to have one place to call home, she really was making a crappy job of living that reality. Was a decade not long enough to build something real? Become a proper grown-up?

She paused in the doorway, looking out towards the snowy woods. There'd been no sign of Jakob since he stopped in that afternoon to criticise their housekeeping. He'd probably gone to bed. Which was fine, really. It had been a long night last night, and he'd been busy all day doing...something. She didn't expect anything from him— didn't assume that just because they'd had two incredible nights, there would be more. No expectations.

But sure, she was *hoping*. Who wouldn't?

As she locked up the back door, ready to head to the cabin, she heard footsteps crunching on the snow, and looked up to see a dark figure approaching. Tall, dark, and Jakob. Her heart gave a little flip as he came out of the shadow of the house, and she saw his face.

"I thought you were in bed."

"Not yet," he said.

"Not *yet?*"

Her emphasis made him smile, and the rush of anticipation almost made her giddy. One more night.

"Thanks for the photos," he said.

She had uploaded the images of the wolf prints, and left a note to let him know.

"You're welcome. Can you tell how many wolves there were?"

"Not really. I'm just hoping there's no more poison out there. I checked as much as I could today, but I can't look at every metre of the forest."

"No."

"Anyway...I have something to show you," he said.

"Really? What is it?"

But he shook his head. "Let me in and I'll show you."

"Hmm. Okay."

He took the key from her and unlocked the door, and they went back into the guesthouse, their footsteps echoing on the wooden floor in the entranceway. He took her hand

and led her down the corridor towards the great room, but halfway along, she stopped. "It's so quiet. It feels weird knowing no one else is here."

"Just us and the wolves."

He pulled her to him, his intentions clear, and she let herself relax against his body.

She shouldn't.

Then he kissed her...and all her shouldn'ts fell to pieces. She kissed him back, heat flaring in her body, caution instantly thrown to the wind. When he broke away a moment later, she blinked, hazy with desire, and he laughed.

"Come on."

They went along to the great room, where guests spent evenings in front of the double-width fireplace, drinking, playing games, and swapping outdoorsy stories—there was no TV anywhere on the Nilssons' property. It was nice to be removed from celebrity drama, political machinations, and competitive baking for a while. Despite its high ceiling and alarming taxidermy, it was a comfortable, welcoming room, with heavy curtains, expansive sofas, and a well-stocked drinks cabinet.

He opened a door at the far end, and she looked through. A spa pool sat on a small enclosed deck, with views over the garden to the pond. White fairy lights were strung around the outer walls, and criss-crossed overhead, and steam billowed from the uncovered pool into the night air.

"I didn't know this was here," she said. "It looks *amazing*."

He smiled. "I asked Greta to leave it turned on."

She liked his initiative—but all she had in her suitcase was cold-weather gear. She hadn't expected to be swimming up here in the frozen north.

"That's such a nice idea, but I don't have my...oh."

He was taking off his jacket, a challenge in his eyes.

Okay. She wouldn't be needing any swimwear.

Welcome to Scandinavia—leave your inhibitions at the door.

Chapter Twenty-One

S lowly, piece by piece, they pulled off each other's clothes, leaving them draped over the armchairs. She knew no one would walk in, but still it felt oh-so wicked to be naked in here, standing in front of an equally naked man. She held her arms in front of her chest, suddenly self-conscious with Jakob watching her in the lamplight, even though he'd seen her from every conceivable angle the night before. High on the walls, the trophy heads from Bengt's hunting trips gazed over their heads, casting surreal shadows.

He came closer, and in turn, she let her eyes wander up and down his body. It wasn't a pumped-up gym body, but it obviously belonged to someone who did physical work every day—lean and strong and muscular, capable of handling anything nature could throw at him. And then there was that spot she had to tear her eyes away from—the bold proof of his unselfconscious wanting.

He took hold of her arms and gently unfolded them from her chest, standing close. Their fingers tangled, and her breasts, now hard-tipped, brushed against his chest. The answering hardness of his own desire teased against her belly, and every millimetre of her skin tingled with anticipation, but she stood firm, prolonging the delicious agony. She looked up. Did her own eyes hold the same drowning hunger she saw in his? They must do.

When his lips finally met hers, the tidal wave of need propelled her against him, and he pressed her close, closer, with a moan of relief. She heard herself echo the sound, a day of waiting too long without him. One leg around him, one hand on his broad back. His mouth on hers, his fingers in her hair. Both of them foregoing oxygen to breathe the urgency of their kiss. How had she thought she had any choice about whether to do this again? Only the tiniest, waggy-fingered part of her brain was opposed to it. Every other nerve and particle of her body and mind was a resounding, flag-waving, one hundred per cent in favour.

Then he broke away, leaving her heated and giddy, wanting more.

"Spa?" he said.

Was he freaking *kidding*? Oh God, apparently not. He was pointing to the door.

"I...suppose so," she managed, her breath uneven.

He took her hand and opened the door, and they stepped outside. The cold air hit her like a slap, cutting through the lingering heat of the kiss, making her gasp as she broke out in instant goose-bumps. As fast as she could, she clambered into the pool, too cold to care about what kind of view Jakob might be getting from behind her. With a groan of appreciation, she sank into the water.

"Oh, this is so, so good."

He stepped in, grinning, and sat opposite her. "*That* was good."

She splashed water at him, and he reached out and grabbed her, floating her across to sit on his lap. Everything above the top of her arms was exposed to the freezing air, but below, she was warm...and tempted.

"You're dangerous," she told him, wriggling closer, craving the feeling of him against her. *In* her.

"Maybe." He encircled her with his arms and slid off the seat, so that she was submerged up to her chin. She wrapped her legs around him, and met his lips with a heat that matched the steaming water.

"There is one Swedish tradition you have to do while you're here," he said, when they paused for breath. "We can do it tonight."

"What is it?" Please don't let it be something hideous to eat, she thought. Let it be, oh, some wild sexy move that only the infamously uninhibited Scandinavians knew.

"Roll in the snow," he said.

Uh, what? She frowned. "You must be joking."

"Usually we go from the sauna to the snow, but a spa pool is okay. Hot and cold, and hot again."

Personally, she preferred just the hot. But he was determined.

"It's good for you," he insisted.

"I don't see how it can be," she said. "It sounds like it would be very *bad* for you."

He smiled. "Sometimes bad things *are* good for you."

He had a point. In fact, he *was* the point. She gave in.

"Fine. But if I catch pneumonia, you're driving me to hospital."

"Deal." He took her hand under the water. "Ready?"

"No."

But when he stood up, she did too, the freezing air a shock against her bare skin.

"You have to roll," he warned her as they went down the steps, out of the fairy-light and into the moonlight.

All she could do was nod. She was already nothing but one giant goose-bump. This might be wild, but it was *not* sexy.

The snow under her feet burned like dry ice, and she danced across it like a possessed firewalker. Then Jakob gave the call—*now!*—and she flung herself blindly to the ground, all breath knocked out of her body by the chill. She rolled faster than she imagined was possible, gasping and cursing and inelegant. This kind of cold *hurt*.

As she stood up, ready to make the return dash to the pool, she suddenly registered the sound of a car turning into the driveway. Across the pond and down the hill, almost back at the road, headlights sliced through the darkness.

"Someone's coming," she hissed.

For a millisecond, they stood frozen—almost literally—then Jakob said, "It's Fredrik's car."

They raced back to the deck, and she leapt into the pool with surprising agility, considering that her body was now composed of stalactites. Or stalagmites. Either way, she *had* to warm up. Jakob only stopped to turn off the fairy lights before vaulting in to join her. They sank down to their chins, waiting.

"It would have to be *him*," she whispered.

He said nothing in reply, but the look on his face was the same as when he'd seen Fredrik at the party, and when they'd butted heads on her doorstep—absolute daggers. Again, she wondered what exactly had happened between them. They held their breaths, but there was silence. They waited, and waited. And waited. Was the car coming up, or not?

"Maybe he changed his mind," she whispered. "He might have turned around while we were making a run for it."

He nodded. "Maybe."

"Hopefully," she added. "How did you know it was him? I couldn't see that far."

"The engine." He kept his voice low. "He's the only person in Lillavik with an American car. A GMC pickup."

"Oh."

The flashiness of it seemed perfect for what she knew of Fredrik so far. But still, there was no sign of the truck coming up the driveway. After a while, she realised that they could be sitting here endlessly waiting for Fredrik to arrive or not arrive, and there were other more entertaining things they could be doing.

"Let's get out," she said.

He nodded, and held up one finger for her to wait. Then he got out and grabbed two towels that were sitting on a nearby bench. He handed her one as she stood up, and helped her step out. They both wrapped themselves up and crept inside, Jakob stopping to turn off the spa pool on the way.

"Why do you guys not get on?" she said, as she gathered

up her clothes.

He locked the door and pulled the heavy curtain across. "We get on."

There was only one small lamp left on in the great room, and shadows fell around them. She could hardly see his face, but the edge to his voice told her this was dangerous ground. The night was already half ruined by Fredrik's almost-interruption—she didn't want to barge on and wreck it completely by pursuing that question. Especially when Jakob had set up such a romantic tryst. Well, apart from the naked in the snow thing, but she would forgive him for that.

"Okay." She looked at her clothes, then back at Jakob. "What now, then?"

"We could go upstairs," he suggested.

"Oh...we could."

She thought of the two rooms with luxurious king-size beds. As Jakob well knew, she and Stina had put clean sheets on them only that afternoon, crisp and white and inviting. She wouldn't mind changing the sheets again, if she had enough of a reason...

He came closer, his armful of clothes meeting hers between them, and she could see him more clearly in the dim light. "Is that a yes?"

His face was a charming combination of doubtful and hopeful. She laughed—did he really have any doubts about her answer?

"Yes. Definitely a yes."

★

They made their way upstairs. By herself, this would have been spooky—tip-toeing up the creaky stairs in the half-dark, cold draughts on her bare skin, yet more heads of moose (or elk) and deer staring vacantly from the walls. But there was nothing scary about her hand in his, and the promise of another night of pleasure.

She pushed aside the nagging guilt about her secret.

Later, she promised herself. She'd figure it out later.

In one of the big bedrooms, they threw their clothes on a chair, and he lit a candle. She went over to the window, intending to pull the curtains. But the night-time view caught her attention. Beyond her reflection, the snow-covered landscape stretched away into the distance, the untamed country of soaring eagles, snoozing bears, and wandering wolves.

"I wonder where they are," she said.

He knew what she meant. "Out there somewhere." He put his arms around her, and rested his chin on the top of her head.

In the middle distance, headlights passed by, and all at once she was struck by the intrusion of humans into these wild places, and how everything was weighted against the wolves.

"It's horrible to think that people want to get rid of them," she said.

"Not everyone," he said. "That's why we keep working and fighting."

For a second there, she'd forgotten that she was on the other side of that fight. If he knew that, she was pretty sure he wouldn't be here in the candlelight, gently caressing her bare skin. His fingers traced a path along her collarbone, between her cleavage, and down her belly. With his other hand, he cupped one breast, grazing his thumb against her nipple. Through half-closed eyes, she realised he was watching their reflection—watching her body respond under his own hands. Seeing that image in front of her, she was hit with a charge of lust that made her twist around and press against him, overtaken, overwhelmed. With a deep groan, he lowered his head and kissed her, crushing her closer. No more talking. No more waiting.

Somehow they made it over to the bed, still entangled, and she tipped onto it, taking him with her. In the heady, muddled haze of desire, she could hardly think which country she was in—but she'd definitely left her inhibitions elsewhere.

Afterwards, they lay in the candlelight, the shadows

deep and soft, the covers tangled at the end of the big bed. He had one arm flung over his head, the other around her, and a distinctly satisfied aura, even with his eyes closed. Now *that* would be a picture to send Denise, she thought. Her own expression was probably much the same, given how extremely satisfied he'd made her. More than once. She stretched, luxuriating in the afterglow. She was a regular-sized sort of girl, but next to him, she felt positively petite. She pointed her feet, but he was too tall for her to reach his toes, so she twined her leg around his, and ran her hand down his muscular thigh.

"How did you get the scar?" she asked.

He didn't open his eyes. After a while, he said, "An accident."

"A car accident, or...?" Of course she did know that, but she was curious. Why had he never been the same afterwards, as Vera had said?

"Truck and car," he said. "I was a teenager. One of the drivers was sick, but we needed the truck. All the other drivers were busy, so my father asked me to bring it back to the workshop, but a snow storm suddenly came in..."

All at once she understood why he didn't like driving in bad weather. But she knew he wouldn't appreciate her mentioning that.

"He let you drive the trucks?" she asked instead.

"Just here and there."

"I'm impressed. Those are pretty big to handle."

She draped a leg over him, and he reached out and pulled her closer, tucking her against him. She felt him stir and rise against her again.

"Pretty big to handle," she murmured, laughing.

He grabbed her around the waist and tickled her, making her squeal. "Handle this."

She fought back, clambering on top of him and wrestling until his arms were pinned above his head. He'd let her win, but she'd take the victory anyway—after all, her prize was tall, buff, and hot.

"Now you vill tell me everyzing," she said in her best cartoon villain voice.

He pretended to struggle, then give in. "I surrender."

"Well, you have no choice," she told him. "Now where were we? Ah yes, your manly scar."

"Mark of the road warrior."

"But you're not driving trucks now," she said. "Alvar used the company to fund Defrost Digital, is that right?"

"He thought that could make a lot more money. He was right."

"Your dad's quite the entrepreneur. Didn't you want to work with him? He and Fredrik seem—"

"You saw what he was like," he said. "Would you want to work with him?"

"Maybe not work with him. But you're family. Wouldn't it be good to have that?"

For the briefest second, she saw something in his expression—a flicker of longing. Then it was gone. "No. He and Fredrik deserve each other."

He was tense underneath her, and his face had darkened, and suddenly she regretted bringing any of it up. Why the hell would she ruin the beautiful time they were having?

"Sorry, yes. I mean no, I suppose not. I just thought..."

He lowered his arms suddenly, taking hold of her and flipping her over, and she whooped and laughed as she arrived flat on her back, looking up at him.

"That's enough thinking," he told her, taking her hands and holding them against the pillow, a wild promise in his eyes. "Now it's your turn to surrender."

And, willingly, she did.

Chapter Twenty-Two

E merging into the morning air, Zoe took a deep breath and raised her face to the bright sky. Bright, because they'd slept in way beyond the usual time. Well, slept in...and stayed in to do other things. Things that made her swoony all over again to think about.

She'd left Jakob in the shower just now, whistling like the satisfied man he was. She'd decided to throw on her clothes and shower in her cabin, where she had clean underwear, and all her toiletries. Then she'd go back and change the bed. There would be no evidence—only a slight tenderness between her legs to remind her of the deliciously heated night (and morning) they'd spent. As she walked the curving path through the property, everything seemed even more of a winter wonderland than usual. She smiled. That's what he did to her. And damn, it was *good*.

Then—of course—her phone rang. She pulled it out of her coat pocket, the familiar ring-tone jarring in the snow-hushed setting. Gah. Trust The Shark to ruin her glow. She hesitated, not wanting to face the Monday-morning real world just yet...but she couldn't put off talking to her forever. She looked over her shoulder, then hit 'accept'.

"Hi, Alcina."

"Zoe, hello. You didn't ring me back."

Guilty as charged. "No. Sorry about that." She didn't offer any explanation.

Alcina was silent. Even without being able to see her, Zoe knew the silence carried a clear message. Her performance so far had been unsatisfactory. Her credibility, and probably her job, was on the line. She climbed the cabin steps with the phone pressed to her ear, and turned to take in the clearing, the sky, the frost-blessed trees, Jakob's little cabin. The world she usually occupied seemed very, very far away.

Then The Shark's voice snapped down the line, as cold as the tip of Zoe's nose.

"We have clients who expect a return on their investment. And right now, you are responsible for that. If you don't come through, *I* will have to answer to those clients."

Yes. The clients who were opposing everything Jakob was working for. Here she was, in his world, but living a lie—even though she was coming to realise that his was the side she belonged on. And maybe *by*.

She shook the crazily premature thought out of her head. Okay, she knew him a lot better now than before, in one obvious way...but they didn't really *know* each other. In particular, he didn't know her. The guilt rose up again.

"I know, Alcina."

"I didn't send you there for a holiday."

"I know," she said again. A bird flew past, its red front brilliant against the pale landscape, and in an instant she was back at the lake, by Jakob's boathouse. "Bullfinch," she said.

"I *BEG* your pardon," said Alcina, obviously mishearing in the worst way possible.

"Sorry, no, I said bull-*finch*," Zoe said hurriedly. "A bird just flew past."

"Stop thinking about birds, and whatever else you're wasting your time with, and get the information we need," she replied, icier than the frost on the porch roof. "If you want your salary paid, do the work. It's as simple as that."

Zoe bit the inside of her cheek to stop herself saying

something she'd regret. She couldn't go on like this. Still, if her parents could spend their days defending and tidying up after dodgy corporates, she must have it in her to put her conscience aside for the sake of work—whether she liked it or not. She just had to get it over and done with, with minimal damage.

"I understand." She went inside, closing the door on the fairy-tale landscape. "I'll email you as soon as I have something to report."

★

She stood in the office doorway, back from doing the usual morning tasks, and stared at Jakob, hearing his words but hardly able to make sense of them.

"What?"

He said it again. "Brynjar died."

Out in the forest, she'd been daydreaming about the teasing, flirty conversation they'd have when they saw each other again, after their lusty night (and morning). She felt like going out of the office and coming back in, to restart everything—but his face told her it would do no good.

She sank into her chair. "But he was going to be okay."

"He wasn't okay." His voice was edged with anger and frustration. "He had kidney failure."

"Oh, no. What would cause that?"

"Emil just rang. He says he was poisoned with antifreeze. The damage was already done. After a few days, his body couldn't cope any more."

"Antifreeze? But why would he drink that? Wouldn't it taste terrible?"

He shook his head. "It tastes sweet. Sometimes dogs lick it from the garage floor, if the car leaks."

"But he wouldn't have been in anyone's garage."

"No. Someone must have left it out. There have been so many tracks near here lately—they probably chose a place where the wolves have been passing."

It was deeply unpleasant to think that someone had

been out there doing something so nasty. "We have to find out who it is."

"I'm going to keep looking around. Maybe there will be a clue."

"And I'll keep my eyes open for anything suspicious when I'm out there," she promised. "Can I help you with anything else? Take the pressure off a bit?"

He sighed and rumpled his hair, thinking.

"There is one thing. We have the map tracking where the wolves travel. But for the last few years I've also been working on a more in-depth database of information about wolf sightings and interactions. We use the government data on the radio-collared wolves, but we also have people around the country who can log in to our system and add information for their area."

His accent—that strangely mesmerising blend of musical Swedish and Scottish burr—even made databases sound sexy. She longed to go over and mess up his hair even more, but after the grim news about Brynjar, it hardly seemed appropriate. Also, The Shark's words were still fresh in her mind. She forced herself back to the topic at hand.

"Are they all researchers like you?"

"Some of them. But anyone can contribute through the website, they only need to create an account. We've combined the government data and the information from our own people. It's in Swedish, but two of them have been translating it into English, so we can put together a report for the Scottish hearing."

She nodded. "Good idea."

"But before then, we need someone to check it and make sure the English is all correct."

"Me?"

"Yes. If you don't mind."

Here was the opportunity she'd needed—and he was handing it to her on a plate. *Var så god.* All the available information for the whole country, and in English, even. She really ought to be happier about it...

"I could do that. But your English is so good, I'm sure

you'd do a great job."

"Thank you. But it should be professional, and writing in English is harder than speaking."

"Well, I'm happy to help." Sort of.

He scooted his chair over to her desk and showed her how to log in to the database as an admin, his shoulder against hers. With a heavy heart, she listened, made notes, and watched as the information scrolled down the screen in front of her. This was the reality of why she was here.

When he turned to her and asked if it was all okay, she answered automatically, half her mind in some other place, with a Swedish *ja* instead of an English *yes*.

He smiled. "Very clever."

She had to laugh. Maybe Greta was right, and they'd make her a Swede yet. She loved the coffee, she was getting used to the climate…and it hadn't taken any time at all to embrace their infamous permissiveness. But then, she'd had extreme provocation—tempted by this complicated, compelling man.

Unfortunately, there were only twelve nights left before she'd be removed from that temptation. The thought made her want to break into a tantrum like a baby losing its blankie. But in this reality there was no time for tantrums, temptation, or even truth. She could only hope to get out with enough information to please The Shark without compromising the wolves, and without Jakob uncovering her lie.

And without leaving an iceberg-sized chunk of her heart behind.

Chapter Twenty-Three

At the sound of a snowmobile passing the cabin, Zoe looked up from her spot on the sofa. She'd made a good start on proofreading the database reports, and found nothing of note so far. After a few hours, she'd gone to get herself a late lunch, empty the dishwasher in the guesthouse kitchen, and change the bedding that they'd so thoroughly messed up the night before. With no appetite after the morning's bad news, Jakob had gone out on the snowmobile to check for anything suspicious in the surrounding area.

After finishing at the guesthouse, she'd come back to the cabin, planning to have a nap—the energetic nights were catching up with her. (Not that she was complaining.) But in the end, her mind was too busy to sleep, so she got back up and checked her email. There was a message from Paul, saying that Sarah was holding steady, and had even started to say a few words. With that small glimmer of light the best part of her day so far, she'd decided to do a bit more searching for Claire. Well, after she forced herself to send The Shark an update, saying that she had access to the database, and would let her know if anything showed up.

She'd hit 'send' with a decidedly queasy feeling.

Now, with a stab of shock, she saw through the French

doors that Jakob was towing the sled, heading for the forest on his side of the clearing. That could only mean one thing—another wolf down.

She slapped the laptop closed and ran out the front door in her socks, but he was already heading into the trees. Damn it. Well, he'd have to come back this way—and she'd be ready for him.

She pulled on her boots and grabbed her coat from the hook by the door. As she lifted the hood over her head, the faux fur trim in her hands gave her a flashback to Brynjar's rescue. She'd never been so close to a wild animal, and ever since then the experience had been replaying in her mind. The wolf's vulnerability and trust in them, Jakob's calm strength, and the surreal, unreal sense of connection with an animal from the furthest reaches of human myth and imagination.

The word 'feral' had always seemed to have a negative connotation. Not any more.

She waited on the porch, bouncing on her toes in the cold until she heard the snowmobile's engine again, then ran out to meet it. Jakob stopped just long enough for her to get on behind him, then set off again.

She looked over her shoulder, and her heart clenched. On the sled, a dark grey wolf lay under a woollen blanket, its eyes closed. This one was wearing a collar too—it must be another one of the animals being tracked by the government programme. It looked much worse than Brynjar had when they found him. She turned to face the front again, and pressed her forehead against Jakob's back. Please let it be okay…

Back at the garages, they swung into action, getting the unresponsive wolf into the four-wheel drive and setting off for the vet clinic one more time. It felt like a very long drive, the road flanked with endless trees, the sky steadily darkening. She turned back frequently to check on the wolf, but it showed no signs of life.

"Is it bad?" she asked at one point.

Jakob only nodded, his mouth set in a hard line. She bit her lip, and hoped.

When they arrived at the clinic, Jakob immediately got the wolf out of the vehicle, while Zoe went to the door. Like the first time, he had phoned ahead, so Emil and Vera were expecting them, and the door opened before she had a chance to knock.

"Again?" Vera looked at her as though the whole thing was her fault.

Jakob came up the steps, bearing the wolf, and glared at Vera. She stepped aside for him to go through, and Zoe followed. Inside, Emil held the treatment room door open for Jakob to bring the wolf through, asking quick-fire questions as they went. Vera went in too, and then the door closed behind them.

Once again, Zoe was left in the waiting room. This time, she knew what was at stake. Hopefully, now that they knew what it was, Emil would be able to start exactly the right treatment straight away. But how long had the wolf been sick in the forest?

She waited impatiently, alternately pacing the floor between a shelf of specialist cat food and a rack of squeaky dog toys, and perching anxiously on the window seat. When they finally came back into the waiting room, she leapt to her feet.

"Is he okay? Or she?"

"He." Emil pulled off his latex gloves. "We have to wait. It's not very good, but I will do everything I can."

Vera shook her head, and looked at Zoe. "It's strange how this all started when *you* arrived."

Zoe felt her cheeks instantly flare with heat at the unspoken but obvious implication. Jakob said something sharply to Vera, in Swedish, and she visibly backed off. But Zoe wanted to say something in her own defence.

"It's horrible," she said. "I know I'm new here, but I want to stop this just as much as you do."

Emil nodded. "Good. If you see anything unusual, please tell us."

Then he turned to Jakob, reverting to Swedish as he continued speaking. Vera swept her eyes over Zoe, and went back into the treatment room, letting the door swing closed behind her.

Stunned by the insinuation, Zoe sat back on the window seat while the men remained deep in conversation. If Vera was saying that here, right to Zoe's face, who else was she saying it to? Suddenly her lack of Swedish felt like a huge disadvantage—how could she defend herself when she had no idea what people were saying? On the other hand, maybe it was just Vera having a bitchy moment. She hoped so.

This time, Jakob didn't suggest they stay over. There was no snow falling, and although it was dark, the drive back was easy. Before they left, Emil had promised to keep them updated, and the whole way back she was half expecting Jakob's phone to beep with bad news. She was also quietly fuming over Vera's pointed comment. Finally, she had to say something.

"Vera seemed to think this has something to do with me."

He let out a disparaging *pfft*. "Ignore it. She doesn't know anything about you."

She looked out the car window. Neither did he. But it was good to hear him dismiss it. Hopefully anyone else would too.

They pulled into the garage, and Jakob turned the engine off. The headlights reflected back against the rear wall, throwing a glow over them. She hesitated. The day's events—one wolf lost, another in grave danger—had turned everything on its head, and the sweet, hot fun they'd had only the night before seemed a long time ago.

Suddenly she was overtaken by a yawn, holding her hand over her mouth.

"We should get some sleep tonight," he said, watching her.

She tried not to look disappointed. "Yes, I suppose so."

He opened his door, and the lights went out.

★

When she went up to the volunteer office the next morning, Jakob was already there, and the aroma of strong coffee filled the air.

"I checked the nest already," he told her, before she even said good morning. "Nothing to see."

"Oh...thank you." She poured a generous serving of coffee into her mug, and stirred in far too much sugar. Privately, she'd decided the eagles weren't coming this year, but Greta was so ecstatic about them, she didn't like to say so. "You must have been up early."

"Yes."

He turned back to the email he was writing, clearly not in a conversational state of mind. Well, fair enough. But there was one thing she had to ask.

"Have you heard anything about the wolf?"

He stopped typing, but didn't turn to look at her.

"He died."

She clapped her hand over her mouth. "Oh, no." She reached out, laying a tentative hand on his shoulder. Under her fingers, she felt him tense for a moment, but then he went back to typing, the keystrokes hard and bitter.

She took her hand back. "I'm sorry."

"Yes. I am too."

"What will happen now?"

"An autopsy," he said, and the very word made her flinch. "For him and Brynjar. And we have to tell the conservation department."

She thought back to the radio collar around the wolf's neck.

"Did he have a name? Can we look up where he'd been? I'd love to know where he came from, where he travelled."

He shrugged. "If you want to. The details are in Emil's email."

Clearly, she was back to having surly Jakob for company. She couldn't blame him—it was enough to make anyone despair, let alone a wildlife ecologist whose life's work so far was with the wolves. She decided to look it up after he'd gone.

In the meantime, while he worked, she continued with the database. As she read, she could see by the report count that more entries had been made in the last few days. Hopefully she could get through it all before she went back to London. Maybe there was something in there that could be given to Alcina...something that looked significant, but was vague enough to be of no practical use.

Eventually, Jakob packed up and left, saying he was going out on the snowmobile. She knew enough about him now to understand that out in the natural world was the best place to make him feel better.

The other place—in bed with her—didn't seem to be an option right now.

Once he was gone, she logged into the project email account, and noted down the wolf's number. Then she went to the map that tracked the wolves' movements. Where had the sooty wolf been, before he met his sad end? Increasingly, she felt a sort of affinity with all the wolves—travellers, on the move with their family, or without. It was the life she'd had, and rejected, but for them, it was everything.

She entered the wolf's number, and found that his name was Sten. A quick Google search showed that it meant 'stone'—maybe he was named for the colour of his fur. She looked at the convoluted trail he'd left around northern Sweden. Wow. He'd been captured and collared way up north, by the Finnish border. Over the next few years, he'd made his way south and west, roaming in a squiggly line through forests and counties, until he arrived in this area. She clicked in closer, wondering if she could see exactly where he'd been near them. Combined with Google Earth, the system gave an amazingly detailed record of where he'd been. She clicked in...and in...closer...and closer.

Oh.

There was the lodge, and their clearing, with the two little cabins. And there was the red line of the wolf's route, passing right through. Just a day or two ago, he had been right outside her window, probably while she slept. He'd had no idea that inside lay a person who was working to eliminate his cousins from the Scottish Highlands.

She frowned. Her white lie was becoming blacker with every day that passed.

Chapter Twenty-Four

S ometimes you just need to get away for a few hours to clear your head.

Zoe found a parking space in the square, and made a beeline for Lillavik's best café, where they'd had prinsesstårta after ice skating that day. Well, there were only two cafes. But Lena said the cakes were better in this one, and when it came to cake, Zoe was wise enough to rely on the word of a six-year-old girl. With Greta and Bengt not back until tomorrow night, and the lodge spick and span, she had time to think. God knows she needed it.

The café door set off an old-fashioned bell as she entered, and every person in the place turned to look at her. It felt like she was making an entrance into an old-time saloon, except that the cowboys were blonde and gorgeous instead of grubby and lawless, and they weren't cowboys, but models from an H&M catalogue. She smiled weakly, and went over to the counter, feeling self-conscious with her mousy-reddish hair and her not-flawless complexion. A childhood under various latitudes of sun had left her with enough freckles to trace out a constellation on each cheek. Oh well.

She said hej to the girl at the counter, who immediately replied with a *hello*. Was her pronunciation so incredibly crap that no one trusted her with a word of Swedish in reply? Admittedly, any more than a word would leave her lost, but still. She sighed, and decided to be grateful for the good manners that compelled every Swede to instantly switch to English at the sight of her.

With a lunch of hot soup and crusty bread rolls in front of her (and a cupcake for afterwards), she settled in to eat. Her phone whistled, and she read the text from Denise, and laughed. She missed that crazy girl. They texted backwards and forwards as she ate, a silly round of jokes and innuendo, with Denise still on her 'get a Swede drunk and see what happens' track. Zoe gave as good as she got, but stopped short of revealing her fling with Jakob. If that was what it was. Which of course it was. Of *course*. What else was he thinking—she was only here for three weeks, and what guy wouldn't be up for a no-strings, limited-time, good time? And how many other volunteers had done the same thing? She wouldn't blame them either.

Well, now she'd depressed herself all over again.

Denise sent a final text full of hearts and cheeky faces, finished off with a whale and a poo—her secret code for Alcina, in the absence of a shark emoji. Good luck, Zoe texted back, with an assortment of encouraging symbols. Somehow, they never got old.

She ordered a coffee from the girl who came to clear the table, then opened the book she'd been reading on her phone. While Jakob escaped into the wilderness, her own best escape was into a story. It worked every time. She picked at the edge of the cupcake while she read and waited for the coffee to cool.

After some time, she became aware of someone standing by her table, and looked up. "Oh! I didn't see you there."

Fredrik grinned. "I saw you."

So that wasn't stalkerish or anything. She pasted on a smile. "How are you?"

"Good, thank you," he replied. Then he glanced over his shoulder.

She looked in the same direction, and saw Alvar

Lundberg coming towards them. Oh great, the more the merrier. Thank God Jakob wasn't here now—all the negative energy would surely trigger some kind of spontaneous combustion.

"Zoe, you remember Alvar," Fredrik said, by way of introduction.

"I remember," she said. "Nice to see you again."

Funny how complete and utter lies could pass as good manners.

He nodded. "Sober this time," he commented.

She stared at him. Really? "Yes. Now I've been sober fifty per cent of the times we've met."

He regarded her with a level stare, and she met it. What a prick, as Jakob would say.

"Well," Fredrik said. "We'll join you, if that's okay."

What could she say? He was already sitting down.

Alvar sat down too. With one of them on each side, she felt like the filling in an extremely hard to digest sandwich.

"How are things with the Nilssons?" Fredrik asked.

"Good," she said cautiously. "Bengt and Greta have been away for a couple of days." She wanted to mention him coming the night before last, but if she did, it would be obvious that she'd seen his car, but not come out to see *him*. She waited to see if he'd bring it up, but he didn't.

"Yes, I heard they were having a break."

Alvar took a few sugar cubes from the bowl on the table, and dropped them into his coffee. "Very bad news about the wolves."

"Yes, it's terrible," she agreed.

He and Alvar looked at each other, then Fredrik came right out with it.

"Do you know anything about the poison?"

She felt her cheeks go red, despite herself. "No, I don't."

Her voice may have been slightly too loud—the couple at the next table looked over at her, then away, and whispered to each other in Swedish. Well, shit. Let them talk. She had nothing to hide.

Fredrik said something in Swedish to Alvar, then turned back to Zoe. "We heard a rumour, but I knew it wouldn't be true."

"What kind of rumour?" She was going to make him say it.

"That you are poisoning the wolves."

Thanks a lot, Vera. Not just a bitchy moment after all. She worked to keep a lid on her temper, and her voice even. "What possible reason would I have for poisoning the wolves?"

"I don't know." Fredrik shrugged. "That's what everyone is trying to figure out."

"Everyone?" Bloody hell.

"Oh, well, not *everyone*, I'm sure." He gave her his best ABBA smile, white and wholesome. "Of course I don't believe it."

"Thanks for the vote of confidence." She looked at Alvar. "What about you—do you believe it?"

"It's nothing to do with me." He took a sip of his coffee, nonchalant.

Something occurred to her. "But it does have something to do with you, doesn't it? Jakob is your son, and the wolves are his life's work. Don't you care at all?"

Under her questioning stare, he adjusted one sleeve of his fine wool jumper. "I do care."

She rolled her eyes. "Doesn't look like it to me."

"Why do *you* care so much?" he threw back at her.

"Well, because..." She glanced at Fredrik, who was obviously waiting for her reply. She scratched around for the right answer. "Because I think the environment is worth fighting for."

Alvar laughed. "Really? I was at that party. I think you're more interested in Jakob than in the environment."

"And I think my interests are none of your business." She put her phone in her bag, then stood up and pulled her coat on. "Very nice to see you again, *Fredrik*."

He glanced at Alvar, then stood up too, maintaining his so-called manners. "Yes, very nice. See you again soon."

With a nod, she turned to go, but stopped after one step. Reaching back, she grabbed her cupcake from the plate, then made her exit.

Chapter Twenty-Five

Jakob was sitting on the front step of her cabin. From his expression—even darker than yesterday, if that was possible—she knew he wasn't feeling any better. Which was fair enough.

She wasn't exactly feeling crash-hot herself, after yet another Jakob-free night. This morning, she'd had to drag herself out of her (empty) bed, and she'd felt every negative degree on her snowmobile trip to the (empty) eagle nest. And only half an hour into work at the volunteer office (also empty), she'd had to give up and come back here for paracetamol.

Now here he was. She stood at the bottom of the steps, so they were at eye level, and offered him a smile. "Hej."

But she got no smile in return. He stood up, towering over her. "What is this?"

His tone instantly got her back up, but she made herself take a breath. He was going through a tough time, after all. She came up the steps and squinted at the label on the bottle he was holding. "I don't know. It's in Swedish."

"I'll translate it for you." He ran his finger along one of the words. "An-ti-freeze."

"Oh. The stuff that poisoned the wolves."

"Yes."

The way he was watching her, waiting…a sick feeling started to creep in, and her headache intensified. "So…" She didn't know what he wanted her to say.

"I found it under your cabin."

The silence that followed, and the expression on his face, said everything.

"It's not *mine*. And why were you even looking there? Are you listening to Vera after all?"

"No," he said. "I don't need to."

He was still holding up the bottle. How had it got under her cabin? Her mind was racing, but she tried to keep her voice calm.

"There's no way I'd do that. You know me well enough to know that." Well, he didn't really—but they'd been getting there, until things started going wrong with the wolves. "Why would I do something so awful?"

"That's what I'm trying to understand."

This was going nowhere. She turned away and opened the door. "There's nothing to understand. It wasn't me."

As she went inside, she heard him following, but he stopped in the doorway. She hung her coat on the hook and took her boots off, all under his doomsday stare.

"Jakob, why would I have told you about the first wolf, if I'd done it myself? That doesn't even make sense."

He raised an eyebrow, and she could see what he was thinking—so that no one would suspect her.

"I came here to *help*." As she spoke, she tried not to remember that, actually, she hadn't come to help at all. Not that he knew that. He was still standing in the doorway, looking grim. "Are you just going to stand there, or what?"

"No," he said. "I'm going to go. And I think you should too."

With that, he went down the steps and back to his cabin, leaving her in shock.

Where the hell had that stuff come from? She wouldn't even know where to buy it, or how to ask for it in Swedish. Her brain raced in her pounding head. Who…and how? Then she remembered. That night…Fredrik's car in the driveway…or maybe the day he'd come by on skis with

Malin. He could easily have been around before that. Skied silently onto the property and left the poison without anyone ever knowing, and planted the bottle under her cabin. One way or another, it must have been him.

But if it was, why had he chosen *her* to implicate? Maybe she was just a convenient scapegoat to hang the whole thing on—just her bad luck to be the volunteer of the moment. Whatever the reason, she was *not* going to let him pin it on her.

★

With Greta and Bengt still away, and no guests, it was very quiet, and the crunch of her footsteps was loud in the still air as she went back up the winding path through the trees to the volunteer office. She sat at the computer and opened up the database. If she was here, she'd do the damn work— until Greta and Bengt came back, anyway. She couldn't leave until then, and at this point, she didn't know what else to do. She'd do the work, and hopefully she wouldn't find anything, and then she could go back to London with no evidence to derail Jakob's Scottish project. And if that meant she proved nothing to The Shark, so be it. She could say she'd done what was asked of her, up here in the almost-Arctic—a job that none of the others were willing to front up for.

As she was getting started, she heard the door open, and her entire body tensed. But it wasn't Jakob. It was Stina.

"Hej, Zoe," she said. "Are you busy?"

Zoe rolled the chair back from the computer, and shook her head. "No. And some company would be good."

Stina looked doubtful as she perched on the edge of Jakob's chair. "Well, okay, but...I have to tell you something." She hesitated, chewing her bottom lip. "I've been hearing things...about you."

Oh, hell. "What things?" But she already knew.

"People are saying maybe you..." She paused, her sweet face conflicted. "I mean, not *everyone*, but...some people. It's about the wolves."

Zoe threw up her hands. "It's okay. I think I know."

"You do?"

"I saw Fredrik and Alvar yesterday, at the café. And Jakob came to see me this morning."

"But he doesn't believe it."

"Maybe he didn't believe the rumours. But he found some antifreeze under my cabin. That's what killed the wolves. So that's evidence, I guess." She shrugged.

"But why would there be...why would you hurt the wolves? He can't think *you* did it!"

Zoe shook her head, trying not to let Stina's astonishment feed into her own disappointment. Because so far, she'd concentrated on being offended and indignant. If she lost her grip on that, it could get messy. She'd let herself get way too deep with him, way too fast, and now she had to drag her heart back out.

"That's exactly what he thinks. But who else would have done it?"

Stina tapped a finger against her lips, thinking. "Vera said Fredrik told her he heard someone talking about it at the systembolaget, so—"

"Wait. Fredrik told Vera?"

"Yes. She texted me to ask, because she knows I work here."

"Okay..." Her assumption was being turned upside down. "I thought Vera told Fredrik."

Stina frowned. "Well, everyone seems to be telling everyone now, so..." Seeing Zoe's face, she cut the sentence short. "Sorry. But *I'm* telling them it definitely wasn't you. I said that to Malin when I saw her in town yesterday."

"Not Malin too?"

Stina's expression said it all, and Zoe sank back in her chair.

"Well, that's just great." Then she remembered what Jakob had said. "Do you think I should leave now?"

"Why should you leave if you haven't done anything wrong?"

"Because everyone thinks I did."

"But they're wrong, aren't they? The truth will come out. It always does. Especially in a small town like this."

The truth will come out. Zoe looked out the big window at the clear white landscape. If only her conscience was as pure as the driven snow outside. Maybe she wasn't completely above board, but on this one question, she was innocent. Innocent until proven guilty, right? Well, maybe not in the opinion of the Lillavik locals. She'd have to go soon enough, but not like this. All she had to do, somehow, was prove that Fredrik was the culprit.

Stina left her with a hug, and went to get things ready for the next guests. They were arriving the next day, only a couple of hours after Greta and Bengt were due back. Zoe dreaded them hearing the gossip about her, but it was inevitable. She'd have to talk to them before anyone else did.

She did her best to put the thought aside, and went back to the translated report. There was the occasional spelling and grammar error, but it was pretty clean overall, and after a while her attention started to wander. She skipped forward to the most recent entries, which had come in from all around the north of the country. Someone had found wolf tracks in the forest behind their house. The previous entry mentioned an actual sighting—three wolves, spotted from a distance. All good. But the entry before that made her heart stop. A hiker had been attacked by a lone wolf, out in the countryside. He'd survived, but with bite injuries. His friends didn't have guns, but managed to scare the wolf away. They saw it run off in the direction of the nearest village.

She leaned back in her chair. Jakob wouldn't have seen this yet—and it was the last thing he needed to find out right now. On the other hand, this information was exactly what she'd been sent here to discover, and exactly what The Shark was waiting for.

She stared at the screen for a while. Then she turned off the computer and went up to help Stina in the guesthouse.

She couldn't un-see what she'd just read.

Now she had to decide what to do with it. Or not.

Chapter Twenty-Six

B engt got out of the car and went round to open Greta's
door. He reached for her hand and helped her out, the
whole procedure as elegant as movie stars arriving at the
red carpet, except in khaki pants and puffer jackets. They
were glowing like returning honeymooners.

"Welcome home!" Stina waved her flag wildly. She'd
insisted on giving them a proper reception, and Zoe had
already learned that almost any occasion demanded a
Swedish flag.

"Welcome home," she echoed, fluttering her own flag.
Had they already heard the rumours about her?

But Bengt was cheery as usual. "Hej, hej," he boomed.
"Everything okay here?"

"Yes, fine," Stina said, glancing at Zoe. "All good!"

"Excellent!" He took their bags from the car, and they
all set off towards the house.

"Did you enjoy yourselves?" Zoe asked, as they went
up the steps.

"We did," Greta said, giving Bengt's arm a squeeze.
"But what a nice welcome back! And I'm looking forward
to seeing my little girls, too."

"Are Lena and Ebba coming?" Stina asked.

Greta smiled at the prospect. "Yes, Malin has an

appointment, so she's bringing the girls here for the afternoon." Then she switched into business mode. "Is everything ready for the guests?"

"Yes, there's nothing for you to do," Zoe said. "Don't worry."

Greta looked from her to Stina. "You girls are wonderful. Thank you."

"You're welcome," Stina said.

Zoe felt anxiety rising at the thought of how not-wonderful Greta would very soon think she was. Stina must have noticed, because she took her arm and tugged her back down the steps.

"We'll let you unpack," she called to Greta and Bengt. "We'll double-check the guest rooms now."

Greta gave them a wave as she went inside.

As they walked across to the guesthouse, Zoe felt butterflies in her stomach. Actually, it felt more like eagles. Maybe that's where the missing birds were. Either way, she'd have to talk to Greta and Bengt sooner rather than later.

"You'll be fine," Stina told her.

"Yes."

It must have sounded very unconvincing, because Stina gave her arm a shake.

"You will! Do you want me to go with you?"

"Thank you, but you're right. I'll be fine. I'll go back over soon."

Stina's phone beeped. She checked the message, frowning. "I need to go. I forgot I have a Skype tutorial for my course—getting ready for my exam tomorrow. Will you be okay?"

"Yes, of course. Go."

"Thanks." Stina gave her a hug, and raced back to her car.

In the guesthouse, Zoe did the rounds in the upstairs bedrooms, checking that everything was ready. In the big room where she and Jakob had spent the night, she avoided looking at the bed. Stay mad at him, she instructed herself.

She heard Malin's car arrive and leave again, and then

there was a bustle downstairs as Greta brought the girls in. Giggles and chatter came from the great room, and the old printer in the office sprang into life. Greta must be working already, while the girls played.

There was only so much fussing around she could do upstairs to put the moment off. Eventually, with everything straightened and adjusted twice over, she squared her shoulders and went down to talk to Greta.

★

"Mama!"

As she came to the bottom of the stairs, Zoe stopped and listened. Was that one of the girls? She could hear Greta talking on the phone, but there was no noise coming from the great room.

The little voice rang out in the air again, but this time it was a desperate scream. "Mama!"

Her heart suddenly pounding, she ran out the front door, down the steps, and towards the voice.

Towards the pond.

She flung herself down the slope to the water's edge. Lena was standing on the shore, crying hysterically.

"Ebba," she sobbed. "*Ebba*."

Zoe looked to where she was pointing. Near the middle of the pond was a dark hole in the ice, and in that hole was Ebba, her little face paler than her hair as she clung onto the jagged edge. Oh, no. Even a few minutes would be too long for such a tiny waif in that freezing water. She looked wildly around, but there was no one else.

"It's okay," she said, as she kicked off her boots. "It's okay!"

The words were as much for herself, as for Lena.

As she took the first step onto the ice, she heard a crack. If it had given way under Ebba's insignificant weight, there was no way in hell it would support her. But it was a pond—how deep could it be? She took a breath and ran towards the hole in her woolly socks, taking the longest, lightest strides she could.

Within two steps, the ice broke through, and she was in the water. Every bit of air was instantly sucked from her body by the wicked cold, and she gasped, desperately heaving oxygen into her lungs. She flailed for the bottom, but there was nothing, only weed grasping at her legs. With a mammoth effort, she started to swim, breaking through the ice as she went.

Ebba.

The short distance became an epic battle as her leaden limbs struggled through the water. *Why* was this goddamn pond so deep in the middle? There was no sound from Ebba now, just the serious white face watching as help came closer.

Just before Zoe reached her, her eyes fluttered closed, and she slipped under the water.

"Ebba!"

The sound of Lena's scream in her ears was replaced by the roar of water as she dived under. The water was surprisingly clear, and she could see Ebba's little figure just within reach. She grabbed her, and hoisted her up until her head broke the surface. The weight seemed twice what such a tiny girl should be.

As she turned for shore, she saw Greta holding a wailing Lena. And she saw Jakob, ploughing through the water towards her. She passed Ebba to him, and he took her with ease, then reached out a hand. But she waved him away.

"No. Go. Take her first." She watched him swim away, her own frozen limbs rapidly becoming useless in the water.

He soon had Ebba to shore, and as Greta hurried into the lodge with the precious burden, he swam back and scooped Zoe into his arms. She was ready to protest—why would he help a supposed wolf killer?—but the cold had sapped every ounce of strength from her body. He got them to solid ground, and carried her all the way up to the lodge. As they went in the door, water streaming off them, she was shaking so violently that her teeth were literally chattering. But she could hear the bath running in the downstairs bathroom, and the sound of Greta's voice.

"Ebba?" she managed, her voice as shaky as her body.

He called out something to Greta, and she replied. The only word Zoe could pick out was 'okay'. It was the only one that mattered.

"Ebba is in the bath," Jakob said, heading for the stairs. "She's okay, but Greta is calling the ambulance."

All she could do was nod, and let her head sink to his chest. It was freezing, but there was immeasurable comfort in it.

Even though he hated her.

Upstairs, he took her into one of the guest bathrooms, shut the door, and set her on a chair while he turned on the shower. It was over a tub, so it slowly started to fill. He pulled her to her feet again, and set to work taking off her clothes. She would have shoved him away, but the cold had permeated to her bones, leaving her weak and useless. So she stood like a child as he undressed her, occasionally holding her steady when she wobbled. Then he helped her over the side of the tub, so that she was standing under the stream of hot water. She closed her eyes, arms wrapped around her body. She could feel the heat on her skin, and steaming water was rising around her ankles, but the shivering didn't abate. Inside, she was permafrost. It seemed appropriate.

She opened her eyes as Jakob got in next to her. His skin was cold too, but he held her under the shower, turning her slowly so the water ran over every part of her. After a few minutes, the tub was full up to their knees.

"Sit down," he said, and she obeyed.

He sat down too, and pulled her against him between his legs, her back against him. With the hot water rising around them, her shaking finally started to ease. He had unhooked the shower head, and used it now to run a constant flow of water over her body, down one shoulder, then the other. As her body started to defrost, so did her heart, and then the shock set in. Without warning, a huge sob suddenly wracked her body, and then she was overtaken by the relief and fear and anger and confusion of the last few minutes, and days, and then of life, the universe and everything. Even as one part of her knew how ridiculous it was, the rest of her was lost to the strange grief that gripped her, forcing its way out as her body escaped the icy chill.

He silently held her close as she cried, his arms around her, their bodies drawing heat from the water and each other, slowly returning to a normal temperature.

In his embrace, feeling his chest rise and fall against her back, she had a sudden clear knowledge. She wasn't going back to Vertex. How had she ever thought she could stay somewhere so wrong for her, let alone want a promotion? She might not even go back to London, except to quit and pack. She couldn't stay in Lillavik, that much was obvious. Even if she had enough Swedish, and a job, everyone was looking sideways at her. She might have had stupid fantasies about staying here with Jakob, but suspicion had been enough for him to cut her off, and it had taken a near-death experience to get them naked together again. She wasn't planning on any more of those, even for the sake of feeling his lean, strong body against her one more time. She'd spent all those years fighting the gypsy life, in order to have somewhere to call home. And for what? She should have just kept moving. It was in her blood.

With that, a huge pressure seemed to lift. Her tears stopped, and her breathing calmed. She could feel his breath against her neck, his muscular forearms against her breasts, his fingers where they lay on her skin. It was quiet, the only sound the drip, drip, drip of the shower head where he had wedged it behind the taps.

Then his lips were on the side of her neck, one slow, gentle touch. Despite all the time she'd spent swearing off him, something stirred in her exhausted body. At the small of her back, something of his stirred too. How could their bodies even consider this, after the trauma they'd had?

And how could *she* consider it, after everything that had happened?

She turned around in the water, and hugged her knees to her chest. She couldn't.

Before either of them had time to say anything, they heard a siren in the distance, then the sound of what must be the ambulance coming up the driveway. Jakob stood up and got out, and she focused on the water, trying not to look at what she might have had. When she looked back up, he had a towel around his waist, and was laying another on the edge of the bath for her.

"I'll go and see Greta and the girls," he said. "Will you be okay?"

She held her position, a perfectly self-contained unit under the water.

"Yes," she replied. "I'll be okay."

He looked at her for a long moment, as though he understood the finality of her tone. Then he smiled, although there was a sadness in it that pricked at her heart.

"I thought you would be."

Then he was gone.

Chapter Twenty-Seven

"Zoe, please let me in."

From her makeshift bed on the sofa, Zoe heard the voice at the door. But she had no energy for a visit from Malin—especially as she'd apparently joined the ranks of the Zoe condemnation society. Also, the fire was warm, and she was tired. She lay her head back on the cushion, and watched the flames leap and dance behind the glass.

Malin knocked again. "Please let me in. I want to thank you."

She pulled the blanket higher over her shoulders.

"Zoe, please. Imagine if it was your daughter."

She groaned, and dragged herself up off the sofa. "Coming."

Tonight, all she wanted was to go home. Wherever the hell that was. The cupboard-sized bedroom in Bayswater, the crush of London crowds, the grubby streets, the competitive machinations of her colleagues...none of that spoke of home. Which was why she wasn't staying there either. Maybe she'd go and visit with her parents for a while, before she decided what to do next. She didn't need to cling onto the idea of home anyway. Yes, for the briefest moment, she'd had some ridiculous romantic notion that this place was somewhere special. Somewhere that could be *the place*. But now she knew it was the combination of the utterly foreign, fairy-tale setting, the escape from her everyday life, and the burning attraction to a guy who was surely not right for her—and who had turned his back on her along with everyone else.

She wondered about Claire. Had her own escape turned out to be everything she'd hoped for, or did real life catch up with her too?

She opened the door for Malin and stood back to let her in. Then she went and sat back on the sofa, pulling the blanket over her knees.

"How's Ebba?" It was the only thing she wanted to hear about.

Malin perched on the armchair, looking drawn. "Shocked, but okay. They're both in bed. Greta wanted them to stay at the house, and keep warm."

"Good idea."

She wasn't going to say anything more. Ebba was safe, that was the main thing.

Malin looked her up and down, assessing. "Are *you* okay?"

"I'm fine."

Compared with the little ones, who were nothing but tiny wisps, she had a decent amount of padding, and she had Jakob to thank for getting her warmed up. Now, dressed in thick flannel pyjamas, two pairs of socks, and a huge fluffy dressing gown of Greta's, she felt like a gigantic marshmallow—but at least she was back to a normal temperature. In all the drama, she hadn't mentioned anything to Greta about the wolves, and the suspicion that was falling on her. And after the ambulance arrived, and it was clear that Ebba was okay, Jakob had left without speaking to anyone. There had been no time to tell him about the wolf attack report either.

Malin leaned forward. "Thank you," she said. "*Thank you*. My girls are everything. Without you..." The words caught in her throat, and she teared up.

"You don't have to thank me. Anyone would have done that."

It *was* nice to hear it though, especially after all the accusations that had been flying around. And she knew that Malin had the same suspicions.

Now Malin pressed her palms together, twisting them this way and that. "There's something else."

"What?"

She fiddled with the tissue in her hand. "You know Fredrik is obsessed with you?"

"Oh, no." She crinkled her nose. "I mean, he's obviously a terrible flirt. Like, *terrible*. But I don't think he's obsessed."

Malin slumped back in her seat. "He is. He has a sort of...what do you call it? Personality problem?"

"Personality disorder?"

"Maybe. His brain is like one of his computers. One plus one equals two. But he doesn't see how he makes people *feel*. And there's always one thing he's focused on. Right now, it's you."

"No." That was creepy to hear.

"I shouldn't say it," Malin continued. "I'm his sister. But he's not right."

Zoe thought back to the times he'd said inappropriate things, and faced off against Jakob. She'd thought him a bit obnoxious from the start, but then again, she'd come across plenty of guys in PR who were just like that. It didn't necessarily make them some kind of sociopath—just an overachieving jerk. But if she was right, and he was trying to pin the wolf poisoning on her, that was more than just being socially inept.

"Well, he has been...weird."

"Not just weird." Malin shook her head. "I know what he did."

Her whispered words triggered a warning in Zoe's mind.

"What? What did he do?"

"I'm so sorry," she said. "I should have known it wasn't you."

"It wasn't me who what?" Malin shifted under her scrutiny, but Zoe knew what she was implying. "You mean the wolves?"

Malin nodded, her eyes teary. "I'm sorry."

She wanted to be absolutely clear. "Fredrik poisoned the wolves."

"I think so."

So she *was* right. But even with her suspicion confirmed, one piece of the puzzle still didn't fit. "Why?"

"Because of you and Jakob. I told you he was obsessed."

"Wait. He wanted to make me look guilty, so Jakob would hate me?"

"I'm sorry," Malin said again.

"But before the first wolf got sick, Jakob and I hadn't even...you know."

"Maybe." Malin smiled a little. "But it was obvious to everyone at the party that Jakob liked you."

"Really?" For a second, she hugged that information to herself. Then she remembered that it was over, and that would be obvious to everyone too.

Malin nodded. "And if Fredrik wants something, he won't let Jakob have it. Those two are a nightmare."

This was unbelievable. "Okay, now I agree with you. He's not right."

"But Zoe, please don't tell anyone."

"Don't *tell* anyone? He succeeded—everyone thinks I did it! Even Jakob."

Malin pressed her hands to her face. "I really am sorry."

Zoe watched her distress, but her own betrayal was too raw to feel any sympathy.

"Why did you wait until now to tell me?"

"He's my brother. I don't want it to be true. But now...I owe you something so big. Ebba..."

Zoe sighed. "No, you don't. All you owe me is the truth, so I can clear my name. You have to tell Jakob about Fredrik. You have to tell *everyone*." When Malin hesitated, she added, "If you don't, I will."

She tried not to think about whether anyone would believe her—Malin *had* to be the one.

Finally, Malin nodded. "Okay. I will."

Zoe glanced out the French doors towards Jakob's

cabin. She knew he must be there. "You can go and do it now."

"Okay." Malin got to her feet, and stood uncertainly in the centre of the room. "Can you forgive me?"

She hesitated, then gave her answer. "Yes."

The relief on Malin's face was like a light turning on. Well, she had no right to withhold forgiveness when she'd been living a lie herself, hoping all along that Jakob might forgive *her* if the truth came out about her job. She was still walking a tightrope on that one.

On the other hand, she wasn't *that* noble—her forgiveness didn't extend to Fredrik. When she saw him again, she'd have a few things to say.

She saw Malin out, and watched from the doorway as she trudged through the snow to Jakob's cabin. He opened the door, and listened as she spoke. At one point, he glanced in Zoe's direction, but she couldn't make out his expression. Finally, Malin finished and turned to leave, and he closed the door.

Zoe closed her own door too, and stood by the fire, warming up. Now what? Now that he knew it wasn't her, did that change things?

She'd been so angry that he'd walked away, the same as everyone else, based only on circumstantial evidence. Only hours ago, she was so clear on what she needed to do, or *not* do. Nothing had changed, apart from Fredrik being confirmed as a complete bastard.

So why was she hungering for one more time with Jakob? Was it just for the sake of I-told-you-so, or maybe for that elusive state, closure? Maybe it was nothing more than the left-overs of their attraction, still smouldering. After that moment in the bath, she knew part of him must have still wanted her, even when he thought she was guilty. But even if they had another chance, she was still living a lie about her work. She might have been proven right *this* time, but that undiscovered secret could end everything all over again.

However she wanted to analyse it, it came down to one thing: she still wanted that last chance.

Chapter Twenty-Eight

Pacing around the cabin, trying to keep herself awake, she waited for him to come over. Surely he would come. Wouldn't he? It was only a few hours before that he'd swung into emergency mode, stripped her down, and put her naked in the bath. And joined her there. For her own good, of course. Medicinal body heat, to ward off hypothermia. Apart from that kiss... Standing in the cabin, she could almost feel his warmth behind her again, the lightest touch of his lips on her neck.

He thought she'd killed his wolves, but he still took care of her. He still kissed her. And his body still wanted her.

From the kitchen window, she could see over to his cabin. The light was on. Maybe she should just go over. She started to pull on her boots, then changed her mind. After all, he was the one who'd judged her guilty without trial. Now he knew the truth, he should come to her.

As the evening wore on, though, she had to admit to herself that it was looking very unlikely. She jabbed at the fire with the poker and added another log, watching as the flames twisted, licking at the wood.

Gah. If she wanted to say something (or hear *him* say something, in this case), she should stop the agonising and go. One boot on and one off, she argued the case backwards and forwards in her head. Finally, she tugged off the one boot and tossed it to the door. What was that saying? Doubt means don't. And right now, doubt was dragging her down as ruthlessly as the dark, icy water of the pond.

Seeking a distraction, she stopped by the cabinet where Fredrik had found the photo of Oscar and the summery teenagers. She opened the door and brought the photo out. The guys all looked so coltish and ungainly, with their long legs and arms. The girls, though, were like mini Victoria's Secret models—blonde and tanned and perfectly formed. It was sort of unfair how girls seemed to overtake boys in the growing-up process. She looked again at each boy, but none of them were Jakob. What had he looked like as a teenager? Did he always have that same air of self-containment and distance, as though he'd rather be away from everything? Maybe that had come when his mum died.

In contrast, Oscar looked goofy and cheerful as he raised his beer bottle, one arm flung around a sweetly pert-nosed girl. As she looked at them, something stirred in her memory. Stina had said that he was living with an English girl in Australia.

An English girl.

Was there any chance...?

She put the photo back in the cabinet and went to get her laptop. It was late now, and she was bone tired after the day's events, so she climbed into bed and set the laptop on her knees. This time, she wasn't searching for Claire—not directly, anyway.

First stop, Facebook. She typed 'Oscar Nilsson' and 'Australia' into the search bar, and hit enter. The first Oscar looked about sixty. The second looked about sixteen. The third Oscar's profile picture was Brad Pitt in Fight Club, and the cover photo was a picture of the outback. But amongst the squares of friends on the side, something caught her eye. Claire Nilsson. And the profile picture was an illustration of Nova No-Show, Claire's kick-ass girl gamer character.

She leaned back against the pillows. As easy as that.

She clicked through to the profile but it was set to private, and the only photo was Nova. She hesitated, then sent a friend request, and a message.

Need to tell you about family news. Please get in touch with me or your dad.

She hesitated, then added, *Miss you.*

Now to wait.

★

She checked Facebook on her phone as she walked to the volunteer office the next morning, but there was nothing from Claire. Well, Australia was in the opposite time zone. And she had no idea whether Claire even used that Facebook profile, or whether the message would get lost in the usual torrent of spammy messages from strange men...or whether she might ignore it. Surely not. Even though Claire had cut herself off so thoroughly, she'd want to know if there was something important happening with her parents. Maybe she should have been more specific.

There was a note from Greta, thanking her again for the rescue, and saying that Malin had collected the girls, and she and Bengt had taken the new guests on an overnight snowmobile safari. It was a reprieve—one more day of them not knowing the shadow she was under. Maybe she could ask them for Oscar's contact details...before she had to go.

Back from the usual run to the nests, she parked the snowmobile by the volunteer office and went up the steps. She untangled the little Swedish flag hanging there, and the low rays of the morning sun illuminated the gold and blue. Then she reached for the door handle.

The door was locked.

She tried again, jiggling the handle and giving the door a push, but it wouldn't give. Then she understood. After the antifreeze, he was locking her out—literally as well as emotionally.

This was ridiculous. She went back down the steps and

charged off towards his cabin. Doubt, in this case, meant damn it to hell, I'm doing it anyway.

She knocked on the door straight away, before she had the chance to rethink. When it opened, the sight of him— tall, jeans-clad, serious—tipped her heart sideways. She searched around, and found a word.

"Hej."

"Hej," he replied.

Ack, where had her fortifying rage gone? Suddenly, she was on the back foot. "Um...the office is locked."

"Yes, it is."

"Right. But...Malin came to see you?"

He gave a short nod. "Yes."

Oh, for God's sake. Did he still have to be surly Jakob? She almost turned around and waded back through the snow to her cabin. But then, seeing him standing alone in the doorway, she suddenly remembered what Greta had said about his mum. How he'd been so lost, and his father was no comfort whatsoever. (She could believe *that*.) Maybe surly Jakob wasn't so far from that teenage Jakob. Plus, surly Jakob was—inconveniently—still damn sexy. She ploughed on.

"And she told you about Fredrik?"

"Yes."

Was that it? She stifled a sigh. "It's really cold out here. Can I come in?"

He stood back so that she could pass, then closed the door.

She hesitated on the woven rug in the entrance, unsure whether to go and sit down. It hadn't exactly been a fulsome welcome. She wasn't waiting for gushing apologies, but it seemed reasonable to expect *some* recognition that she wasn't guilty after all. Especially when they'd gone from wild lusty nights to cold hard zilch, in one brutal step.

"So...it wasn't me who poisoned the wolves."

"No." He hadn't moved from his spot by the door.

Jesus, he was killing her. Didn't that count for *anything*? She dug her fingernails into her palms, fighting the swirl of feelings that threatened to well up—most of all, frustration.

"So there's no need to lock me out. I didn't do it. I *told* you I didn't."

Instead of the smile or even the embrace she'd hoped for, his face darkened further.

"There was something else you *didn't* tell me."

Oh, no.

No.

Instantly, she knew what he meant. She was busted, exposed for the fake she really was.

Except one thing was not fake—her feelings for him. They were new and raw, not yet ready for the harsh reality of this situation, but they were real. At the hardness in his eyes, her hopes tumbled like a demolition site under a wrecking ball.

"Who told you?"

"You'll think this is funny," he said, in a tone completely devoid of humour. "Fredrik told me."

Oh, perfect. Of course it would be him. She didn't bother asking how Fredrik knew—the damage was already done.

"I went to see him after Malin talked to me," Jakob continued. "He says he didn't do it either."

"He would say that. You didn't believe *me* when I denied it."

"I don't believe anything Fredrik says—unless it's on Google too. Vertex PR has some interesting clients."

Shit. Despite Alcina removing her from the website, apparently there was something left linking her to Vertex. When Claire wanted to disappear, she could wipe herself from the internet, but Zoe was still trackable. Great. How the hell would she talk her way out of this? If ever she needed spin, it was now.

"This looks bad, I know. But I can explain, honestly. And the wolves—Malin wouldn't blame her own brother for nothing. I would never, ever harm them. Can't you give me credit for that, at least?"

He shook his head, apparently already at zero tolerance. "Why are you here expecting me to apologise, when everything you did was a lie?"

"Not *everything*," she said. But he had a point. "I mean, I'm sorry. I really am. I didn't come here expecting to..." She stopped. There was nothing to gain now by confessing her feelings—but nothing left to lose either.

"Expecting to what?" he asked. "Use my own research against me?"

"No." She might as well say it. It was too late now anyway. "To fall for you."

He laughed, a hard sound that petrified the edges of her heart.

"You can stop playing the game now. And you didn't have to sleep with me for that information. All the volunteers can see it."

"It's not a game," she said. "Couldn't you tell, all those nights? It was the real me."

But he opened the door, put one hand behind her back, and gently, firmly, stepped her out to the porch.

Why wouldn't he just listen? Stubborn-arsed Swede. Why had she jumped into bed with him practically the moment she arrived? Now she was sorry they'd done all those things. All those irresistible, addictive, insanely hot things...

She twisted away from his hand. "I didn't force you to sleep with me! I'm sure the other volunteers made it just as easy as I did."

He shook his head. "There weren't any others."

It sounded so much like the truth that she wished they could go back to that first porch kiss, when she'd still had a chance to tell the truth and set them on a different course.

"It was just a job," she said, giving it one last desperate try as he closed the door. "I was just doing my job."

"Maybe it's just a job for *you*," he said. And the door clicked shut.

Chapter Twenty-Nine

S he stomped back to her cabin, trying to maintain her anger, because if she didn't have that to hold on to, an avalanche of shame and disappointment would overwhelm her. Unfortunately the snow was too deep for proper stomping, and her black-tempered forward momentum made her top half go faster than her feet could keep up with. Twice she face-planted into the snow, cursed, and got back up again. She didn't look back.

Inside, she dragged off her boots and threw herself on the sofa. How could he have thought she was sleeping with him to get information? Didn't he see that she'd let him in, trusted him with her heart as well as her body? The swirl in her head was matched by the churning in her guts. And now he knew the truth about her lie. He had every right to be angry about that, but maybe he'd let her explain once he'd calmed down...although he seemed perfectly, horribly calm already. And even if she got the chance, how would she explain? It was what it was, damn it. She was what she was.

What she *wasn't* was a wolf killer. Like Fredrik.

She had a few things to say to *him*.

And hey, no time like the present, when she was aflame with indignant rage. Anyway, it had better be now, because once Greta and Bengt knew the truth about her job too—her heart clenched at the thought—she would definitely have to leave. She hated that she'd been deceiving them all along. Kind, quirky Greta, and funny, practical Bengt—they'd become like family so quickly. She shoved the thought out of her mind, and pulled her boots back on.

In Greta's guesthouse office, she grabbed the car key. She'd face her truth with the Nilssons soon enough. But first...Fredrik.

★

Once again, the Defrost Digital reception area was empty. Zoe hesitated, looking at the bell. With all the real action happening online, she supposed there was no need for an actual person sitting at a desk, way up in the wilds of northern Sweden. Which was pretty convenient—no one to talk her way past. She went behind the desk, and reached for the door. It was unlocked.

Inside, she paused. Every desk in the big open-plan area was empty. She looked at her watch—lunch time. Had they really all gone out and left the place wide open? Between the frosted windows, the walls were covered from floor to ceiling with illustrations, posters, and photos, evidence of years of creativity and fandom. She walked slowly between the desks, looking for Fredrik's. Most of them held two big screens, as well as various other devices and gadgets, alongside headphones, empty energy drink cans, and figurines (apart from Star Wars and Minecraft characters, she didn't recognise any of them). Under one desk, a tiny dog raised its head as she passed, making her jump. She held her breath, but it just yawned and went back to sleep.

Finally, at the back of the room, she came to two walled offices. Was one of these Fredrik's? Choosing the one on the right, she tentatively pushed the door open—and just about had a heart attack. Alvar was sitting at the desk, headphones on, working at his computer. He stood up when he saw her, his chair shooting backwards, but the headphone cord jolted him back to the desk. He pulled the headphones off and came towards her, obviously ready to escort her out.

"Zoe." His voice was faux-welcoming, with a guarded edge. "What are you doing here?"

"I'm looking for Fredrik."

"He's not here. I'm so sorry." He didn't sound sorry. "Let me show you out."

But she'd seen something pinned to the wall, amongst all the drawings and designs and certificates and awards. One tiny, familiar illustration.

Nova No-Show.

As he reached for her, she planted one hand on each side of the door frame. "Wait."

It came out with such authority and determination, surprising even her, that he stopped.

"You did know Claire."

He made a sound somewhere between a bluster and a *pfft*. "We've already had this conversation."

"We have. But you didn't tell the truth." Pot calling, but hey.

"I don't have to—" he started.

But she elbowed past him and pulled Nova from her spot on the wall. Holding it up, she thought she saw him waver for the briefest moment. Then he smiled.

"I told you a lot of people want to work here," he said, as though explaining to a child. "They send me all kinds of things. Some of them end up on the wall." He waved around the office, the walls barely visible under everything stuck on them.

She narrowed her eyes. Nothing got her as riled as being talked down to.

"Listen, there's a reason why I need to find Claire. Her mother is sick."

At this, some of the condescension seemed to drain out of him. "Her mother?"

He looked at Nova, then back at Zoe. Something had changed in his face. For the first time, she felt like she was seeing something closer to the real Alvar. Suddenly she made the connection. Claire's mother. Jakob's mother. Did he have a heart in that peacock-puffed chest after all?

"She's really sick. And I want them to have the chance to see each other before…before it's too late."

He rubbed his chin. "Well…"

"How terrible," interrupted a voice from the doorway. "I really hope you find her. What a shame we can't help you."

Fredrik.

"I don't want *your* help," she told him. "Right now, I want your lying head on a silver platter."

He laughed heartily.

"What spirit. And what a fucking nerve, from a liar like you."

"From one liar to another," she snapped at him. "I know it was you who poisoned the wolves."

His lip curled. "I don't know why you've chosen *me* to blame, out of everyone in Lillavik."

"I didn't choose you. Malin—" She stopped.

"Malin told you?" He laughed. "She's always been crazy. What do you think all her appointments are for? And why do you think her husband never comes home?"

She flinched on Malin's behalf. And here she'd been thinking how sweet their sibling teasing was.

"Come on, think about it," he said. "Why would I be bothered about the wolves? They're nothing to do with me."

"They're nothing to do with you, but they're everything to do with Jakob. And I was something to Jakob." The past tense *was* gave her a stab of regret and loss.

"So what?" His arctic blue eyes were icicle-cold. "Plenty of women have been something to Jakob, just like his dirty old man here."

With that one sentence, he struck at all three of them: Zoe, Jakob, and Alvar. Fighting the urge to lunge at him and punch his stupid, perfect, high-cheekboned face, she looked to see what Alvar would do. No matter how much she resented The Shark, she would never speak to her boss like that.

But Alvar did nothing.

"You can leave us now," Fredrik told him, and to Zoe's surprise, he did.

Fredrik kicked the door shut behind him.

"Sit down," he said.

She sat.

"We have some choices to make," he said, leaning on the desk in front of her like an FBI interrogator. "I'll keep it simple. Here are the facts. I have no motive for killing wolves. You do. And everything started when you arrived."

"Jakob doesn't believe your denial." Never mind that he didn't seem to believe hers either.

He shrugged. "Who would the authorities believe?"

She shifted in the seat. He was right—not that she'd let him see that. "Knowing some big English words doesn't make you right."

He smiled. She smiled back.

"You're very confident," she said. "But you obviously know your way around the Nilssons' place on skis. And we heard your truck in the driveway, the night before the second wolf got sick. Jakob knew it was you."

The confidence slipped slightly, but he regrouped. "That wasn't me."

"Sure," she said. "It was that other guy in Lillavik with a GMC."

"It must be. I was away in Stockholm with Alvar."

She snorted. "Oh, come on. I saw you that morning—you and Malin were going skiing."

"We left that afternoon." His smile was back. "You can ask Alvar."

"Fine. I will."

She stood up and made for the door, and was surprised (and relieved) when he let her go past into the open-plan area. There was no sign of Alvar there, or in the other separate office. She went down a hallway and looked in a lunch room and a meeting room, but found nothing.

Fredrik was leaning against a desk, toying with a Darth Vader figurine as he watched her search. "Don't bother. Alvar can't tell you anything you want to know anyway."

If only a lightsaber was within reach. She made do with a burning stare. "Screw you."

He laughed. "Maybe one day. The offer still stands."

Behind her, she heard the door open, and turned around. The staff were coming back from lunch. She bit down on the reply she wanted to fire back at him, and left.

★

Outside, she stood for a minute by the car, letting the freezing air cleanse her lungs and her mind. God, he was beyond creepy. He deserved everything he was going to get—if she could figure out how, before she left.

Her phone rang, and she pulled it out and looked at the screen. Paul.

"Hi," she said. "Is everything all right?"

His voice came from a long distance, not just in miles. "She's had another one."

"Oh, no. Oh, God." She stood in the car park, the grey sky pressing down above, and felt the weight of the news settle on her heart. "How is she?"

"Not great. Lost all the progress she'd made, and gone backwards even more."

"Oh hell. I'm so sorry."

"That's okay," he said, even though it wasn't.

"Did you hear anything from Claire?"

There was a silence on the line, then he sighed. "Yes."

"So you've talked to her?"

"Yes. She got your message. She said that..." He cleared his throat. "That they didn't speak before, so there's not much point in coming now she can't speak at all."

At that moment, she understood that the Claire she'd known was no more. Or maybe that Claire had never been a real person at all, just the idealised version of Zoe's lonely teenage longing for a sister, and a friend. But then...things went both ways. There'd been years' worth of chances for Sarah to reach out to her daughter. The longer they'd each left it, the harder their hearts must have become. And there was Paul stuck in the middle, a nice man, but hapless, somehow not equipped to stand up to his wife, even for her own good. For the good of them all.

There were so many things she wanted to say, none of them helpful at this point.

"I don't know what to say," she managed. "That's just…"

His laugh was hollow. "I know. Now I'll let you get on with things there."

"Okay. I'll come and see you as soon as I get back."

She didn't tell him that her work had met a sudden end, and she'd be home sooner than planned. Need-to-know basis, for now.

"Lots of love," she said as usual, but this time the phrase couldn't say enough.

"Right back," he said, and her heart broke at the simple words. She was the only one he had to say them to.

There in the snowy car park, an idea crystallised in her mind. Claire's mother. Jakob's mother. Back in the office, she had definitely seen something in Alvar's eyes. Everything else might be a mess, but before she made her ignominious exit, maybe there was one last thing she could do.

Chapter Thirty

S he went up the driveway between towering trees, bare and frozen now, but still impressive. Alvar's house, Hofsvik, was like a scaled-down stately home sitting on the rise ahead—dusky pale gold, with beautifully symmetrical rows of windows, a high peaked roof, and a small tower at each end. It was elegant, historic, and just grand enough—evidence of the small fortune Alvar had made with Defrost Digital.

She followed the circular driveway around, past neatly clipped, snow-dusted shrubbery and double-sided stone front steps, and parked facing back down the driveway. Her arrival had set dogs to barking inside, and when she reached the top of the steps she could hear them scrabbling and leaping on the other side of the enormous front door. She took hold of the knocker—the same double D as the company logo—and rapped firmly.

Alvar opened the door, and two leggy hounds shot out and milled around her, yelping and snuffling. In contrast to their enthusiasm, Alvar looked less than pleased to see her.

"What do you want?"

She didn't bother with any niceties either. "Can I come in?"

"Why?"

"Because it's freezing, and your dogs are going to eat me."

He sighed and called them off, and they went back in, all drool and waggy tails.

"Come," he said, jerking his head towards the inside, and it took her a second to realise that he was talking to her now. Nice.

She followed him through the airy entranceway, where a tall antique clock stood next to an armoire of palest dove grey. The dogs jostled her as they went down a wide, white hallway, and she peeked into the rooms they passed. Everything was exquisitely decorated in that traditional clean, whitewashed Swedish style—but it felt impersonal. There were no family photos, no cheerful muddle of daily living, nothing that said anything about the person who lived here.

Then they turned left into a living room, and Alvar went to sit in an armchair with wide rolled arms by the fireplace. It looked like his regular spot—there was a footstool in front, and dog beds close by. The coffee table alongside was scattered with newspapers and magazines, and a laptop sat open next to an iPad. It was an oasis of real life in the cold perfection of the big house. He picked up a half-empty glass of something golden, and emptied it in one go.

"Sit," he said, and she and the dogs obeyed. At that, a smile twisted briefly on his face, but quickly disappeared. "How did you know where to find me?"

"I knew the name of your house." She didn't want to say that Greta had told it to her. "I googled the address."

"Hmf." He refilled the glass, threw back the contents, then poured himself another serving. "And why are you here?"

She could have done with a wee something herself, but she wasn't about to ask. She reminded herself of that moment in the office today, when she'd had a tiny glimpse of a more genuine Alvar. Maybe he hadn't been a good father so far, but there must be something good, somewhere in his DNA, if he'd managed to make a man like Jakob.

She plunged in.

"I'm here because of Jakob."

"That is not your business."

Maybe, but she was doing it anyway. "Yes, I'm butting in, and I know nothing about you, but I know something about Jakob. Don't you think he deserves a father, even now?"

"It's not possible." He shook his head as he emptied the last of the bottle into his glass, then lifted it unsteadily to his lips. How much had he put away since he got home?

"It *is* possible," she said. "Don't just give up on your family. Life's too short."

He slugged the drink and set the glass back on the table, hard. "I *know* that."

"Of course...I'm sorry. Your...Brigitta. She was so young."

"She wasn't *my* Brigitta." He went to a cabinet in the corner and pulled out another bottle, then sat back down and refilled his glass. "She never was."

"Well...I'm sorry," she said again. She didn't really know what their relationship had been like, or why it hadn't worked out. But why hadn't he tried to be a father to Jakob, when each one of them was all the other had? "But Jakob is yours. And you're his. And you're both here still."

He tipped back his head and laughed.

"You have been here for five minutes, and you want to fix us? Who are you, anyway?"

I'm a fake. Maybe he didn't know it yet, but he would. And it seemed like she was nothing to Jakob now—worse than nothing—so she went with the other, less incriminating facts.

"I'm a volunteer at the Nilssons' lodge. And I'm Claire's friend." She didn't need his help to find Claire any more, but his previous denial was niggling at her. "I know she was here—she went to Australia with Oscar Nilsson. You knew her, didn't you?"

"Yes," he said. "I did."

He stood up and took a packet of cigarettes from the mantelpiece, and pulled one out. She watched as he lit the cigarette and inhaled deeply, his eyes narrowing.

"So why did you tell me you didn't know her?"

He flicked ash into the fire, and shrugged. "That was in the past. She wasn't here long."

"That's not a reason to deny it. I needed to find her, for her mother." She saw the chink in his armour again, and pressed her point. "And why would Fredrik deny it too?"

He took one last long drag on the cigarette, and threw it into the flames, unfinished. "It's nothing to do with Fredrik."

"You were going to tell me something, before Fredrik came into your office. Why do you let him be so..."

She couldn't think how to say it exactly, and looking at his face now, she knew she probably shouldn't go there. But the way Fredrik had treated them both made her blood boil. "Why does he act like he owns you?"

"He does not."

He turned abruptly and reached for the bottle, then saw that it was empty. Sensing his mood, the hounds jumped up, whining as they trailed after him to a liquor cabinet on the other side of the room. He plucked out another bottle and made his way back, his unsteady gait betraying the amount he must have had to drink. Then one of the dogs darted in front of him, and he fell over it, landing heavily on the pale woven rug. The bottle hit the dog's back, and it skittered away with a yelp, then turned and slunk back for reassurance.

She got up and went to help, shooing both the dogs out of the way. But he shooed her away too, so she stepped back and knelt just out of arm's reach.

"That's exactly how he acts," she said quietly. "It's not right. And why won't Jakob talk to either of you?"

He sat himself up, the unbroken bottle back in his hand. "This is not your business."

"Okay. Fine." She let it go, for now. "But Fredrik told me to ask you one thing. Were you in Stockholm with him last weekend?"

"I was."

Oh. "Really? You were?"

He fixed her with a withering look—as withering as anyone could manage from the floor, surrounded by dogs.

"What do you want—train tickets? Hotel receipts? A note from my mother?"

"Fine." She stood up. So much for that. On the other hand, maybe he was just being a yes-man for Fredrik—that seemed to be their dynamic. There must be some reason behind it. And she was pretty sure it must have something to do with Jakob not speaking to either of them.

"I didn't poison the wolves, you know," she said. "Fredrik did it—his own sister told me."

He pulled himself to his feet, swaying slightly. "He has no reason to do that."

"He works for you. Don't you want to know the truth?" she asked. "For Jakob's sake, at least? The wolves are special to him."

He kneed a dog out of the way, and went back to the mantelpiece for another cigarette. Avoiding her eye, he lit up again, taking his time to inhale, then exhale, as she waited. Inhale, exhale. Inhale, exhale. She stifled a cough.

"I think you do care," she said.

He went over to the door. "Thank you for coming."

She stood for a moment, then took the gigantic hint. As she went through the door, she looked directly at him.

"Go and see him," she said. "Please. At least try."

He just held out a hand, inviting her to go ahead of him.

She went. She'd tried her best.

It had started snowing while they were talking, and now the dogs rushed outside, snapping at the snow and racing around like lunatics. She had to smile, enjoying their lollopy joy at being out in the glorious white stuff.

She'd miss this.

She turned to say goodbye to Alvar, but he just nodded. Then he called the dogs in, and shut the door.

In the sudden quiet, she sighed. Maybe Fredrik would win this one after all—but maybe, today, she'd done one good thing for Jakob. It would have to be enough. Because tomorrow, when Greta and Bengt were back from safari, she'd finally have to confess all...and pack her bags.

Chapter Thirty-One

S he drove back into Lillavik and out the other side, then settled in for a slow, careful journey to the lodge. The snow was thickening now, and she put the windscreen wipers on. Hopefully it wouldn't get too heavy—before now, she'd never driven in anything more than a few flakes. But the road was empty, the headlights were on (standard procedure year-round, day and night, apparently), and Bengt had said that the car had its winter tyres on. All she had to do was keep it steady, and she'd be fine.

Well, as fine as a person on her way to face the music could be.

And then, around a bend in the road, she was suddenly facing something else—a huge elk, making its leisurely way from one side to the other.

With no time to think, she swerved, and the car shot across the opposite lane and off the road. It hit a snow bank with an impact that knocked all the air out of her body, and whipped her head back. Dazed, she worked to catch her breath, her whole body shaking.

Greta's warnings—so funny at the time—had been all too prescient.

The engine was still running. She turned it off, then got out of the car just in time to see the animal trotting away unharmed. At least it was okay. No one could accuse her of being an elk killer too. She rubbed her chest where the seatbelt had tightened across her body. And she was okay, it seemed. But the car...the front of it had ploughed into a snow bank, and she wasn't sure how much damage might have been done. She scraped away what snow she could, then got in the car, restarted the engine, and tried to reverse out. But the wheels spun uselessly.

Outside, the snow was still falling heavily, and she realised that she needed help before it got dark. She reached for her phone. Thank God there was a signal. But who could she call? Bengt and Greta were away with the guests who-knew-where, Stina was sitting her exam today, and she didn't have anyone else's number.

Apart from one other person.

She peered through the windscreen. Even though he couldn't drive in bad weather, he might know someone who would. Despite everything that had happened, she was pretty sure he wouldn't let her freeze out here.

Mostly pretty sure.

She took a breath, and dialled the number. After what seemed like a hundred rings, he answered.

"Zoe."

His tone held not a speck of encouragement, but she had no choice.

"Jakob...I need help."

★

It was one of the better ways to die, she'd read. Unpleasantly cold at first, sure. But after a while, your body slows down, and you just drift off into oblivion. She looked at her phone. Twenty minutes since she'd phoned Jakob. Right now, with the car running and the heating on, she was comfortable. Toasty, even. But if it ran out of petrol, how soon would the chill set in, and frostbite start to nip?

Then she heard a truck pass by. She jumped out of the car and struggled up to the roadside, but it had already gone. She looked one way and the other along the empty road. Maybe she should wait there, in case someone else came past. But it was only her, and the road, and the endless, inscrutable pines. That damn elk was probably watching her from behind a tree trunk. After a few minutes she was so freezing, she *had* to get back into the car. No point in hurrying into hypothermia.

After that, she didn't hear any more traffic go by.

Surely it wouldn't be long before someone arrived. In their brief conversation, Jakob had said someone would come and get her, but she didn't know who. She checked her phone again. Forty minutes. Maybe he'd decided to leave her there after all, a satisfying payback for her deception.

Then she heard an engine. She got out, feeling the air sharp in her lungs, and scrambled up to the road, snow falling thickly around her. A four-wheel-drive was making its way towards her, agonisingly, excruciatingly slowly. She narrowed her eyes, trying to see. It looked like Jakob's truck—but who had he lent it to?

An eternity seemed to pass as it drew gradually closer. It came to a stop on the side of the road, and the hazard lights started flashing. Now, Zoe could see the driver. He got out and came around to her, his face tense.

"What are *you* doing here?" she asked, more surprised than grateful.

"Rescuing you, remember?"

"Yes, thank you, but—"

He turned away and went down to where the car was stuck, running a businesslike eye over the scene.

"We need a winch," he called up to her. Then he reached into the car and pulled out her bag, and the keys, and locked the car. With long steps, he climbed back up to the road, and gave them to her. "Bengt has one on the truck."

She nodded. "I'm really sorry. I just automatically swerved to avoid the moose. I didn't want to hurt it."

"Elk," he said. Then he opened his door. "Let's go."

She got in the passenger side, and he started the engine. She glanced across at him. Even in his heavy coat, she could see the set of his shoulders, and his jaw was rigid. Apparently, he was still as mad at her as he'd been that morning. She supposed he would be for a long while yet. She kept quiet as he checked the mirrors, put on the indicator, and then did a careful U-turn and started back in the direction of the lodge.

With her bottom on the heated seat and death by hypothermia averted, she started to breathe a little easier. Even with things so wrong between them, it was a huge relief to be safely here with Jakob.

She looked out the window. They really were going very slowly.

Very, very slowly.

She looked at him. His hands were gripping the steering wheel like a drowning man clinging to a life preserver. He seemed to be gritting his teeth. And was that a bead of sweat on his brow? She reached out and touched his arm, ever so gently.

"Are you okay?"

His eyes stayed glued to the road ahead. "Mnh."

"Are you sure? Because you don't look okay."

No answer. A small pulse throbbed in his temple. They were travelling at the pace of a moderately speedy snail—no wonder it had taken him so long to get here.

She tried again. "Jakob."

He kept driving, a look of grim determination on his face.

"*Jakob*. Why don't we stop for a minute?"

The way he was ignoring her was making her nervous. But then they came to the turnoff for a small side road, and he pulled into it, tugged up the hand brake, and turned on the hazard lights.

She leaned towards him. "Are you all right?"

He let out a hard breath of air, and frustration. "Since the accident, I..." He passed a hand across his eyes and turned away from her. "Shit."

Hearing him swear in English usually made her want to laugh, but there was nothing funny about the vulnerability in his face now.

"It's all right. That's perfectly natural." She put a hand

on his arm again. "Why don't I drive for a bit?" She wasn't exactly super confident in this weather herself, but it would be better than seeing him have a gradual nervous breakdown at the wheel.

At her suggestion, he looked like she'd offered to carve his manhood on a platter. But then he undid his seatbelt.

"Okay."

"Okay," she echoed, keeping her tone light. "Let's do it."

Neither of them spoke for the rest of the trip. She focused on not running into any more wildlife, and he looked out the side window. It felt like a long drive.

Back at the lodge, she carefully parked in the garage, then turned off the engine and looked his way. His expression took her back to the dark-and-angsty Jakob of their first days. Now, she'd started to understand where all that came from. And how difficult it must have been for him to make that drive.

"Thank you for rescuing me," she said, passing him the keys. *I know it was hard,* she wanted to add. But she didn't.

He nodded curtly, his hand already on the door handle. "Thanks for driving."

In the face of his detachment, she wanted to remain equally unmoved, not letting him see any of her own angst. But as he started to get out, something inside her cracked.

"Jakob," she whispered, her voice betraying the ache in her heart. "Please."

The briefest hint of regret crossed his face, and for one heart-stopping moment, she thought there was a chance. Her fingers itched to reach out and touch him, retrace the places they'd been on his skin, remind him of what they'd had together.

But then the moment was gone. And so was he.

By the time she climbed down from the driver's seat and came around, he was already walking away. She stood and watched him go, and he didn't look back.

One save for another—one drive each. On that count, they were even.

But they were still at zero.

Chapter Thirty-Two

Home wasn't somewhere else this year. It was here after all. For the eagles, anyway.

Zoe stood in the clearing, breathing the icy morning air, and stared up. High, high above, a golden eagle had finally made itself at home in the nest. Another bird—its mate, she supposed—was sitting on a branch nearby.

She'd decided to sneak in one last trip to the nest before going to see Greta. And here they were.

"You took your time," she told them.

But way up there, they couldn't hear her quietly spoken words. They poked about, getting settled in. There seemed something telling in the fact that they'd arrived just as she'd be leaving. Out with the interloper, in with the true inhabitants.

Captivated, she watched them. They were glorious. Not conventionally beautiful—they had mottled colouring, yellow legs sticking out from feathery pantaloons, huge talon-tipped feet, and small heads with a hooked beak. Not to mention a truly daunting expression, and the sound they made was somewhere between a squawk and a squeak. But they were perfectly, powerfully themselves, exactly where they were meant to be.

Then she remembered that she was supposed to take photos.

"Don't move," she told them, reaching into the deep pocket of her coat to find the camera. Zooming in, she took a bunch of close-ups, then backed up and took some wider-angle shots. Just as she'd got exactly what she needed, the second bird took to the air, and she realised how big they really were. It circled around effortlessly, hardly needing to flap its wings despite its impressive size. Watching it, she felt a pang of jealousy. Oh, to be so free.

She took some shots of it on the wing, then walked back to the other side of the clearing, where she'd left the snowmobile. Greta would be beyond thrilled at this news. Maybe—hopefully—it would soften the other news that Zoe was about to confess.

For her, home *had* to be somewhere else.

★

As she approached the lodge buildings, she could see all the snowmobiles parked in a row in the usual spot. Bengt was bustling around with some of the guests, unloading the sled. They waved as she pulled up and turned the engine off.

"Hej," she said, in reply to their greetings. "How was the safari?"

"Great," said one of the guests, her nose pink and her smile bright.

"Cold," said someone else, and everyone laughed, in good spirits all round.

Zoe smiled, remembering how shattering she'd found the cold when she arrived. "Definitely goes with the territory." Then she turned to Bengt. "Is Greta inside?"

"In the office, I think," he replied, passing a bag to its owner.

"Okay, thanks." She hesitated. "Has Jakob talked to you about the car?"

He nodded. "We'll get it later."

"I'm really sorry. I hope it isn't damaged."

"Don't worry," he said, seemingly untroubled. "It's not your fault. And we have insurance."

"Okay. Thank you."

"No problem," he said, uncoupling the sled. "Just a shame we won't have elk for dinner." He winked, and she had to laugh.

Relieved—about the car at least—she went inside. Jakob mustn't have told him anything about her secret. Leaving her coat hanging in the entranceway, she took the camera down to the office. Greta was sitting at her tidy desk, talking on the phone, so she waited by the door. Even though she didn't know what the conversation was about, the rollercoaster sound of the language was becoming familiar now, and every now and then, she thought she recognised a word. She wouldn't hear much of that back in London...or wherever she ended up.

Greta ended her call, and turned around.

"Zoe," she said. "You are okay."

"I'm fine. I feel bad about the car though."

She waved a hand. "It's not the first time for Bengt to pull a car from the snow. I told you the elk are dangerous."

"You did. He was handsome though."

"Oh, yes. They all are." She noticed the camera in Zoe's hand. "Have you been out?"

Zoe passed it to her. "Look."

She turned it on. At the first image, her face lit up, and she looked at Zoe. "Today?"

"Yes. Two of them."

She scrolled through the photos, oohing and aahing and exclaiming. Then she looked at Zoe. "How wonderful!"

"Yes. I'm glad I got to see them."

She hesitated. Showing Greta the photos should have been such a fun moment—if she was a real volunteer. She couldn't put it off any longer.

"Greta. There's something else I need to talk to you about. It's about me...about my job."

She sighed. "Jakob told me already."

Already? She felt the heat in her cheeks. "I'm sorry for misleading you all."

Greta shook her head. "We have to talk. Come on."

They went into the kitchen and Greta made coffee,

while Zoe fidgeted at the long table. "Does Bengt know?" she asked, picking wax drips from the side of a candle.

"Yes," Greta said. "He knows."

"Really? I just talked to him outside, and he didn't say anything."

Greta set two mugs down on the table. "He knows that you and I will talk."

"Oh." She looked down into her coffee. The liquid slowly settled and stilled, but her stomach kept churning.

"So let's talk," she said. "You start."

"Um...okay."

She tried to explain how it had happened—her frustration at work, and how she ended up being the one sent on this assignment. The more she talked, the less convinced she felt about it herself.

"Work is...I don't know. It was a chance to prove something to them. I never expected to get here and find all of you."

"And Jakob?"

"No. I never expected to find him." Out the kitchen window, she could see treetops and winter sky. He was out there somewhere, mad at her. "He's so angry. You said once that if anything happened to his wolves, that would be the thing to set him on fire. You were right."

Greta nodded. "I thought so."

"But I'm not giving any information to the company. I'm going to resign. They'll have nothing from his research." She squished the wax between her fingers. "I know it won't make any difference to what he thinks of me though."

"Maybe," Greta said slowly. "But Jakob is not just on fire about the wolves. We have never seen him like this before. The way he looked at you."

Zoe wanted to cry. "He doesn't look at me like that any more. You should have seen his face." Then she paused. "I thought you'd be angry too."

Greta gave a wry smile. "When you get to this age, you know that life is always more complicated than it seems."

That much was definitely true. "And Malin says it was

Fredrik who poisoned the wolves. What do you think?"

"Well, we knew that it couldn't be you hurting them. When you saved Ebba, we could see who you really were."

"Why couldn't Jakob see it then?"

She raised an eyebrow. "Maybe he could."

Zoe thought back to the way he'd put her in the bath, his arms around her, his heart beating against her back. Maybe he'd still wanted to believe in her then—but after that, discovering her volunteer deceit was too much for him.

"I don't know about that." She looked at Greta. "I suppose…I should still go though."

She nodded. "I think that would be the best thing."

Even though she'd been preparing herself, hearing Greta's words sent a pang of finality through her heart. "Okay."

"There's only one train a day," Greta continued, putting her mug in the dishwasher. "Malin is coming with the girls again this afternoon, but Bengt can take you to the station."

"What time?"

"You'll have to leave here at about two o'clock."

Zoe nodded. Only a few hours away. She wouldn't try to see Jakob again. But she did want to say goodbye to Stina, when she came this afternoon, and the little ones of course. She still had mixed feelings about Malin.

As she tipped her undrunk coffee in the sink, she remembered something else. "Greta…there was one other reason I agreed to come."

"What is it?"

"Remember how I said my parents moved around a lot for work, so I went to live with family friends?"

She nodded. "Yes."

"Their daughter Claire left home as a teenager, and basically disappeared. And now her mum is sick, and she needs to know."

"How awful."

"Yes. And her dad thought she came here years ago, so he asked me to try to find her."

"She came here?" Her voice was cautious.

"She did. It was Claire Evans."

At that, her face seemed to zip up. "Well. You do have a lot of secrets."

"Apparently. But that's not a bad one, is it?"

She just pursed her lips, so Zoe continued.

"I found out that she and Oscar went to Australia…but you're not really in contact?"

"No." She put the milk back in the fridge, shutting the door with a resounding thump. "We're not."

"Do you—"

"I need to go back to work," she said firmly. "And you need to pack." Then her voice softened. "You'll be able to say goodbye to the girls before you go."

"All right."

But she was speaking to Greta's departing back. Whatever had happened with Oscar and Claire, she wasn't telling.

Well, Zoe herself knew that Claire didn't do family especially well. Mind you, neither did she. She still hadn't had that Skype with her parents in Singapore…but maybe sometimes a bit of distance was the best thing anyway.

As she went off to pack, she tried not to think about the thousand or so miles of distance that would shortly be between her and Jakob.

Chapter Thirty-Three

This bloody suitcase would never close.

Cursing, she rearranged things, shoving rolled-up t-shirts and scrunched knickers into whatever spaces she could find. It was all the same damn stuff that she'd squashed in for the trip over—why wouldn't it fit now? She finally managed to close the zip, and sat back with her hair on end and her mood black.

She looked at her watch. Still a couple of hours until two o'clock. What to do? She was getting hungry, but it didn't seem appropriate to go up the guesthouse. Plus, she didn't think she could bear to see Jakob. So she made herself a coffee and ate the last of the breakfast things—probably the last filmjölk she'd ever have in her life.

Then she sat on the sofa with her phone and checked her messages. There was an email from Alcina, still waiting for news of something juicy that would advance their client's cause. Well, that wasn't going to happen. She deleted a bunch of newsletters she'd subscribed to but never read. Then she found a Facebook message from Claire.

I talked to Dad. Sounds like Mum is hanging in there. She always was a stubborn cow. Even if she could talk, I have nothing to say to her. She never had anything to say to me. Btw, how did you track me down?

Wow. That was truly heartless. She thought for a moment, then typed a reply.

I'm volunteering at the Nilssons' lodge in Lillavik. Think you were here? Put two and two together and guessed about you and Oscar.

She sent the message, then checked the time in Australia. Ten hours ahead. It was late there, so she might not see it straight away. But the 'seen' notification came up, and soon after that a reply arrived.

Well that is a small fucking world. Don't stay there too long. If the cold doesn't kill you, the locals will drive you insane. I got the only good one.

Hmm. She paused, her fingers hovering over the keys. Should she ask? Yeah, she would. Claire wouldn't hold back, so why should she?

What happened here? Seems like no one wants to talk about you.

She hit return, and waited.

And waited.

Maybe that not holding back thing didn't go both ways after all.

But then Claire was typing, and the message arrived.

I worked for Defrost Digital for a while, but I got in an accident. That was when the owner's trucking company was still funding DD—startups soak up money, even when they look successful from the outside. And his son ran into me with one of the trucks, fucking idiot. We found out that it didn't even have winter tyres on. My car was wrecked. I could have been killed, but luckily I got away with bangs and scrapes—sprained wrist, whiplash, bruises.

Zoe's heart was pounding as she read on. Maybe Claire had survived almost unscathed, but she didn't mention—and obviously didn't care—that Jakob had been injured.

Oscar wanted to bring in the police, but in the end we came to an arrangement with Alvar (the owner). And then it was better to just go. Small town politics. You know.

The implications of Claire's story jostled in Zoe's head. That was Jakob's accident. No wonder Fredrik had been so determined to mention Claire's name over and over again

217

that day, when Jakob had brought her the skates. Jakob had never asked her anything about it, though. She needed to know more, but she couldn't let her shock show now.

How awful, she typed. Nothing there to imply that she thought it was awful for Jakob too, even though she did. *What kind of arrangement was it?*

How much would Claire reveal? She crossed her fingers. Then she remembered, and held her thumbs instead. But Claire, unaware of Zoe's entanglements in Lillavik, seemed to be on a confessional roll.

Don't know if you've met Fredrik? Later that night he saw Alvar putting winter tyres on the truck, trying to cover himself. If the police had found out, it would've been curtains for the trucking company, probably. And the funding for DD. Oscar and I wanted some seed money for a project we'd been working on, and Alvar was able to help us with that. Oh and Fredrik wanted a piece of DD, so that worked out well.

Zoe realised that her mouth was literally hanging open. With breathtaking casualness, Claire had pretty much admitted to blackmailing Alvar. Claire and Oscar, *and* Fredrik. Now things were starting to make sense.

And it seemed like Jakob didn't have any idea.

Careful to remain neutral, she typed a reply.

And how did your project go?

A thumbs-up emoticon appeared.

Really well. We had worked on it at DD, so we got it up and running pretty fast. You might have heard of it—Kaleidoscoop. We've released a few more since then, but that's still our biggest.

She hadn't heard of it, but that wasn't saying anything. She wasn't a gamer. But she did know that taking a project developed as employees at DD and selling it themselves was probably not ethical, and maybe illegal. Before she had a chance to reply, another message came through.

Have to go, going out with Oscar. Oh and for God's sake don't tell his parents you know me. Not the favourite daughter-in-law, haha. TTYL.

And that was that.

Zoe leaned back against the pillows. No wonder Alvar was putting up with the unbearable Fredrik. How much of this did Greta and Bengt know? Enough, obviously. And what about Jakob?

She had to tell him what she knew.

★

Up at the house, a flashy black beast of a four-wheel-drive sat in the driveway next to Malin's VW Golf, with an American flag on the rear window. She looked at the badge—GMC. That could only be Fredrik's. What the hell was he doing here? Well, okay. Maybe he could answer some of her questions.

There was no one at the house, so she went over to the guesthouse. At the back door, she hesitated. She didn't feel like one of the team any more. She *wasn't* one of the team any more. In truth, she never had been. She stopped herself from knocking, and went in.

The first person she saw was Malin, coming out of the bathroom. Seeing Zoe, she stopped, and her face changed. Obviously, she knew.

"Hej," Zoe said.

"Uh...hej," she replied. She looked over her shoulder, as though she didn't want to be caught. "So...you're going?"

"Yeah." She didn't have time to tiptoe around. "Is Jakob here? He wasn't in his cabin."

"I haven't seen him."

"What about Greta?"

"She's in the office."

"Thanks." She started to walk away, then turned back. "I'd like to say goodbye to the girls, if that's okay."

Malin's face softened. "Yes, that's okay. Fredrik was watching them while I came to the bathroom. We don't leave them alone in here any more."

A red flag went up in Zoe's mind. "Really? Do you trust him with the girls, if you think he poisoned the wolves? The other day, you said he's not right."

Her cheeks went pink. "He wouldn't hurt his own nieces."

They went down the corridor and through the big entrance hall.

"Why is he even here?" Zoe asked.

"I suppose he wanted to see you before you left."

That seemed doubtful. Or maybe he wanted to gloat over his victory. Well, she had some information on *him* that she was ready to share before she left. He may have won their skirmish at Defrost Digital, but he wouldn't win the war. Neither of them would—but it would be a kind of triumph for her anyway.

In the great room, it was quiet.

"They must have gone to see Greta," Malin said. "They can't leave her alone. They asked her to take them skating on the lake again—even after Ebba fell in the pond, can you believe it?" She sighed. "I'm the mean mother, always saying no."

They went back through the entrance and along the corridor on the other side, past the kitchen to Greta's office. She looked up when she saw them.

"It's too early," she told Zoe. "Bengt has taken the guests out on the snowmobiles, but he'll be back in time to take you to the train."

Malin was frowning. "Where are the girls?"

"With Fredrik," Greta said.

"Okay. Where is Fredrik?"

For a moment they looked at each other, then Malin turned and sped down the corridor, with Greta and Zoe right behind. "Lena!" she called, the underlying fear in her voice obvious. "Ebba!"

"Go and look outside," Greta told Zoe. "I'll send Malin to look upstairs."

Zoe followed her instructions, but there was no sign of them anywhere outside. To be sure, she ran a circuit around the guesthouse, stumbling where the snow sat more deeply off the path. As she went around the side, she noticed that every single snowmobile was gone—including the one she usually used. Dread clenched in her stomach as a horrible thought occurred to her. Surely he wouldn't.

Back inside, a tearful Malin was on the phone. "She's

trying to call Fredrik," Greta said.

But Malin shook her head. "Voicemail."

This wasn't good. "Um…should *all* the snowmobiles be gone from outside?" she asked.

Instantly, Malin burst into a stream of Swedish. Even with her limited vocab, Zoe knew the words weren't pretty. Greta nodded as she replied, obviously trying to reassure her. Then she switched back to English.

"We have spare machines in the barn," she said. "Let's go."

"Are we going to the lake?" Zoe asked as they raced out to the barn, Greta and Malin doing up their coats as they went.

"Yes." Greta maintained a positive expression. "I'm sure it's fine."

Inside, amongst the hay bales and assorted vehicles and tools, Zoe followed her lead.

"Of course. Men are just thoughtless idiots sometimes." She pulled the tarpaulin off the snowmobile Greta pointed her to. "I bet they're just having fun."

She started it without too much difficulty as Greta's machine roared into life too.

"It will not be fun for Fredrik when I kill him," Malin said, over the sound of the engines.

And I'd be happy to help, Zoe thought as they headed off, with Malin sitting behind Greta. Now *that* would be something to report back to Claire.

Chapter Thirty-Four

They stopped by the boathouse where Jakob had showed her Brigitta's sleigh. Zoe's snowmobile was parked there, next to another older one. Out on the ice, there were four figures—Fredrik and the girls, and a frail-looking old man Zoe didn't know. But he was holding a fishing rod, and nearby was a little tent with a sled base. It must be Hakon Halvarsson. He and Fredrik were talking, but looked over when they heard the snowmobiles approach.

"There they are," Greta said. "Everything is fine."

Malin tugged her coat down and headed for the lake. "Not fine for him."

Relieved, Zoe got off her machine and watched as Malin mama bear went to retrieve her girls. Between the wrath of his sister, and the grief he was going to get from Zoe, Fredrik was facing a serious tongue-lashing—and hopefully, the repercussions of his blackmail.

But as Malin approached, Fredrik suddenly pushed Hakon out of the way. The old man fell awkwardly to the ice, his fishing rod sliding away, and the girls screamed. Fredrik grabbed one of their arms in each hand, holding them hard.

Malin stopped on the shore, Zoe and Greta right beside

her. Ebba had started to wriggle and cry, but Lena stood stock still.

In Swedish, Malin yelled something to Fredrik. He looked at Zoe, then answered in English.

"There's no problem," he said. Then he glanced at Hakon, who was trying to get up. He gave the old man a shove with his foot, and Zoe gasped as Hakon fell back to the ice. Then Fredrik met Malin's stare. "I just want you to do one thing for me."

Malin stepped onto the lake and started towards him, carefully shifting her weight from one side to the other like a penguin so she wouldn't fall.

"You should stop," he said, and something in his voice made her do exactly that.

Heart pounding, Zoe turned to the side and carefully took her phone out of her pocket. Trying not to let Fredrik see, she texted Jakob as fast as she could, forgoing punctuation or sense, but hoping he'd understand.

Help girls danger lake Fredrik hurry

Then she slipped the phone back into her pocket.

"Fredrik, please," Malin said. "Why are you doing this?"

"Alvar called me," he said. "After *she* talked to him."

He looked at Zoe again, and Malin and Greta did too.

"What did you say to him?" Malin's question was more of an accusation.

She felt her face flush with heat. "I just…I wanted him to try again with Jakob. Because life's too short to give up on your family." Had Alvar decided that he couldn't live under Fredrik's thumb any longer, no matter the cost? "And…I told him that you said Fredrik had poisoned the wolves. But you already told Jakob that—you were going to tell everyone."

Her expression was daggers. "There must be something else."

"No. That was it. Except…" She glanced at Greta. "We talked about Claire."

Malin kept her eyes on her daughters. "You know about that?"

"Yes, I—"

She stopped as Ebba squealed again. Fredrik was lifting each of the girls higher, twisting their arms. Ebba twisted in his grip, kicking his leg, and he finally let her go. She struggled over the ice to Malin, who held her tight.

"Tell them the truth," he said to Malin, his face contorted as he clutched Lena's arm.

Malin's face was white. "The truth about what?"

"Tell them who poisoned the wolves. I'm not losing Defrost because of you."

Zoe's hand went to her mouth. Had her words got through to Alvar after all? After the years of blackmail and manipulation, maybe the wolves—Jakob's wolves—were his breaking point.

"Fredrik, please. This is crazy." Malin spoke slowly, steadily, but there was a quaver in her words.

"*You* are crazy," he shot back. "Your husband knows it. Everyone knows it. You're crazy enough to kill the wolves to protect your children."

Greta gasped, but Malin shook her head.

"You *want* everyone to think that."

Then they heard another snowmobile, and Jakob emerged from the trees. He skidded to a stop by the boathouse. He must have been out checking for wolves—Zoe could see the tranquiliser gun slung across his body. As he came towards the lake, he took it off and aimed it at Fredrik.

Seeing it, Fredrik laughed. Then he picked Lena up and turned to dangle her over the hole.

"Tell them you did it," he said to Malin, his voice as hard as the ice under their feet, as cold as the fathoms of water beneath.

Zoe looked from Fredrik, to Malin, to Jakob. Apparently, they were *all* crazy.

"Okay, I did it!" Malin screamed. "I did it! Now let her go!"

He put her down.

Then Jakob fired.

Fredrik screamed as the dart hit him in the back of the

neck, and twisted this way and that, trying to reach it.

With Malin still holding Ebba, Zoe took her chance, and raced forwards, skidding and slipping, thankful for her rubber-soled boots. She scooted out of reach as Fredrik clutched at her, and grabbed Lena. They both fell over, but struggled to their feet, scrambling and sliding away, until Lena was back with her mother and sister.

"I let her go!" Fredrik shrieked at Jakob, as Malin bundled the girls away. "You're going to kill me!"

"No loss," Jakob said.

Zoe remembered what he'd said about the tranquiliser—even a small dose can be enough to stop a human's heart. Oh, shit. She knew now exactly what Fredrik had stolen from Jakob—his inheritance, his father—but surely Jakob wouldn't actually kill him. She looked at his face, dark and unforgiving. Or maybe he would.

All at once, Fredrik had composed himself, and was coming towards Jakob. "Give me the antidote," he called.

Zoe came closer, but Jakob held up a hand, warning her away.

"First, I want a confession too," he told Fredrik. "Tell me why my father gave you everything."

"Give me the antidote, and I'll tell you," Fredrik countered. "If you don't, it'll be too late. I won't be here to tell you anything, or care about your family drama."

That vein throbbed in Jakob's neck again, but his voice was deathly calm. "Then both our problems will be over."

At this, a shadow of doubt came over Fredrik's face, but he wouldn't be the one to cave. "No," he said. "You will have a whole new problem."

"Jakob," Zoe said calmly, as though settling a wild animal. "Do you have the antidote?"

He shrugged. "No."

At that, Fredrik snapped. Despite expecting to drop dead at any moment, he summoned up all his energy, and attacked. Jakob was ready. The men came together, violence exploding in a flurry of slams and punches that had obviously been brewing for years.

"Stop," she shouted. "Jakob, stop. He's not worth it. I know what happened."

With one huge shove, Jakob pushed Fredrik to the ice. As he fell, she could see that there were grips attached to the bottom of his shoes. No wonder he'd been standing firm while everyone else was skating. She noticed now that Jakob had the same on his shoes too.

He turned to her. His lip was split, and there was fire in his eyes.

"What do you know?"

But before she could reply, Greta interrupted.

"Jakob," she said. "This is serious. We have to help Fredrik. I do not want you in jail for murder."

They looked down at Fredrik. There were bright red splashes on the ice around him, from his bleeding nose, but he was still very much alive.

"Fuck you," he hissed at Jakob, then spat out a mouthful of blood.

Jakob smiled, very slightly. "The dart was empty."

Then he turned and walked away.

Chapter Thirty-Five

"Sit *still*, Fredrik."

Greta dabbed at the blood on his face, possibly more roughly than was medically advised.

"Ungh," Fredrik said. His nose had ballooned up, but Greta said it didn't seem to be broken. Privately, Zoe hoped it was.

Malin was getting the girls settled on a blanket in front of the TV to watch cartoons and have a snack. They seemed remarkably unfazed by their ordeal, and by the presence of their insane uncle in the kitchen. No one had suggested calling the police, and Zoe could see why. With all the complications in this situation, it would open a can of aged and extremely stinky worms. No one was coming out of this looking good.

After much fussing from Greta, Hakon had packed up his fishing gear and headed unsteadily for home. He was indignant, but luckily unhurt.

"Poor Hakon. That was probably the most exciting thing that's happened to him for years," Greta commented as they watched him go. "He'll have something to tell his wife today."

"Thank God he's okay," Zoe said, and Greta agreed.

Then they went back to the house, Greta with the two

girls squeezed on the back of her snowmobile, Zoe with Malin behind her. She wasn't exactly a welcome passenger—Zoe was fuming at being taken in by her double-cross confession about Fredrik being the wolf killer. But it had to be done.

They left Fredrik to start walking back, now that he was no longer on death's door. Once the girls were safely inside, Greta went back to meet him on the path, saying she'd better get him safely out of the forest at least, and make sure he was okay to drive.

When they got back to the house, Zoe came and found them sitting at the kitchen table, where Greta was trying to clean him up. His nose had started bleeding again, and he winced and pushed her hand away as she stuck a cotton ball in it to stem the flow.

Zoe sat down opposite, and looked right at him. "I know you blackmailed Alvar after Jakob's accident."

"What?" Greta said.

Fredrik shook his head. "That old fool. He's lying." The injury made his voice thick, but the disdain was clear as day.

"He didn't tell me. Claire did."

At the mention of Claire's name, Greta tensed over the first aid kit, but Fredrik didn't miss a beat.

"She's an idiot," he said, adjusting the cotton ball. "She's as guilty as any of us. Alvar, and Claire, and Oscar." His eyes flicked to Greta, but she remained silent now, her lips pressed together.

"You took Jakob's place in the business." Zoe said. "And you took his father too. You know things were shaky between them anyway—forcing Alvar to shut him out of the company must have been the last straw."

"So dramatic." He rolled his eyes. "Jakob doesn't want to sit behind a computer all day."

She knew that was true, but it wasn't the point. "He deserves a father."

"He always hated Alvar," he scoffed. "Even after his mother died."

"You really are an asshole," she told him. "There's still time for them. You might be a narcissistic, egotistical loner who's incapable of having a real relationship, even with your own family, but other people aren't like you."

He looked at Malin, who had just come in. "Some people are," he said.

But Zoe was on a roll now.

"Why did you lie to me, even after I rescued Ebba?" she asked Malin. "You said Fredrik fancied me, so he was trying to drive Jakob away. What bullshit. You said you owed me, but you still lied to me."

Fredrik snorted, then cursed as a fresh gush of blood rushed from his nose, taking the cotton ball with it. He pressed a handful of tissues against it as he spoke.

"*You* lied to everyone, from the day you arrived."

"Yeah, we covered that already," she snapped at him.

He grinned. "You know, you're single again now. My offer is still there. You don't know what you're missing."

"Oh, piss off Fredrik." She turned to Malin. "You know the truth about me now, so come on—let's even the score."

Malin looked nervously at Fredrik, but he just shrugged, so she perched on a chair. Zoe sat opposite her.

"It was you who left the antifreeze under my cabin."

She nodded.

"And did you come here in Fredrik's car last weekend, to leave poison for the wolves?"

She hesitated, and Zoe leaned forward. "We know it was you already."

At that, she nodded again. "It was me."

Zoe had a sudden thought. "Who was looking after your children? Did you leave them alone and drive all the way here?"

Finally the words flowed. "No! I would never do that. I had a babysitter. I want to keep them safe—and they're not safe with the wolves around here."

"But they're not a danger to people." At least she'd thought they weren't, before she saw that report.

"Well, there was that attack north of here..." Fredrik pointed out.

Malin went white. "I didn't see anything online about that."

"Huh. You must have missed it," he said casually, tipping his head back and dabbing at his nose.

But Zoe stared at him. "How did you know about that?"

In the second it took for him to compose his reply, she knew he was lying. "I saw it on a...news website," he said.

My God, why didn't she think of it before? "*You* posted that report on Jakob's database."

With everything blown open now, he didn't bother denying it. "It was too easy."

"Malin, see?" Zoe said. "The only report of a wolf attacking a human was made up by your screwed-up brother."

But Malin wouldn't be convinced.

"If you had children here, it would be different," she said. "I'll do anything to keep them safe. You don't even know how many miscarriages I had before they arrived. I can't lose them." The tears started, and she grabbed for the tissue box.

Oh, no. Zoe reached over and patted her arm. She couldn't even imagine how awful that must have been. She looked at Greta, who nodded, and a look of empathy passed between them.

But Fredrik groaned, showing zero sympathy. "You shouldn't even have children. They'll grow up and be as crazy as you."

Malin got up and slapped his face, catching his nose, and he roared in pain. Then she went to leave, pushing past someone in the doorway.

Jakob.

Seeing Fredrik there in the kitchen, he turned on his heel and left.

Despite the pain, Fredrik laughed, and Zoe wanted to follow up Malin's slap with a smack in the head. But then she laughed too.

"It *is* funny, isn't it? I have my job, but now I don't want it. You want your job, but now you won't have it. Maybe you should come to London and work in PR. I think you're made for it."

As she stood up, Stina walked in. She took in the scene—Fredrik bleeding, Greta shocked, Zoe riled up—and confusion and concern came over her face.

"Malin says you're leaving. What's going on?"

"It's a long story," Zoe said, grabbing up her coat from the back of the chair. "Really, really long. Fredrik will tell you."

Then she went after Jakob.

Chapter Thirty-Six

B y the time she got out the front door, he was already going back down the path to the cabins.

"Jakob, wait," she called.

He didn't stop, but his pace slowed a little, and she caught up and walked alongside him. His lip was swollen, but overall it looked like he'd come off better than Fredrik.

"Are you okay?" she asked.

He stopped and turned to her.

"Why was he there?"

"Greta didn't want him to drive until she knew he was okay."

He looked off to the trees, his jaw clenched.

"Come on," she said. "What if he wasn't okay, and he had an accident and hurt someone?"

As soon as the words were out, and she saw his face, she realised what she'd said. "I didn't mean it like that."

"It's fine," he said. "I know what you meant. You were all worried about Fredrik."

"We were worried about you too, but you left. And I know you didn't want to see *me*."

His eyes flicked to her face, then away.

"I'm going, okay? That's what you wanted. I'm not doing my last week. I'm going today, at two o'clock."

She waited, but he made no protest. There would be no last-minute declarations, no sudden request for her to stay after all. But she knew that already. She looked at her watch. One thirty. Half an hour left to breathe the same air as this complicated, compelling man. To look at his beautiful, angry face. To fix things.

"Don't you want to know what Claire told me?"

The set of his shoulders eased just a little. "Yes. I do."

She nodded. "Come on then."

They went down the snow-dusted path, under the bare, tangled branches, and across the clearing to her cabin. Ever the gentleman, he opened the door for her. As they went in, she saw him notice her luggage sitting in the entrance, but tried not to look at it herself.

"Sit down," she told him as they took off their coats.

Twenty-eight minutes. She'd better talk fast. Even if it made no difference to the two of them, she might leave him with some kind of family again.

She sat opposite him, took a breath, and launched in.

"Okay, here's what Claire told me. After your accident, Fredrik found your dad replacing the truck tyres with winter ones, to avoid prosecution."

His head jolted back, as though her words had flown across the room and hit him. But she kept talking.

"I suppose Fredrik saw a chance there. Basically, he blackmailed Alvar into giving him a share of Defrost Digital, and also giving Claire and Oscar money for their own startup project, because she was injured. He's been holding it over Alvar ever since."

She watched as the implications of her words sank in. He was silent, but the anger and pain were evident on his face. She longed to go over and touch him, hold him, kiss the darkness away—but he wasn't hers to comfort any more.

"What a freaking mess," she said. "I was thinking...were you even old enough to be driving the truck?"

He nodded. "I was old enough. But I didn't have a commercial license."

"So…maybe he was protecting you too?"

"If he wanted to protect me, he would have made sure the truck had winter tyres."

He looked so agonised that she tried to think of another angle. "Or the driver should have?"

"It doesn't make any difference now." He closed his eyes and squeezed the bridge of his nose, obviously trying to process everything she'd just told him.

"Is all this why you left to go travelling? Before you went to university?"

He nodded. "I just had to get away."

She remembered Vera's comment that he hadn't been the same after the accident. Now she understood that it wasn't just the accident itself, but what happened afterwards.

Then he sat forward, looking at her. "Why did you go to see Alvar?"

"I knew there was something wrong about the whole situation. Turns out I was right. And…I thought there might be hope for you two yet."

He sat back. "Hmnf. I doubt it."

But she could see the idea sinking in.

"I'm not all bad, you know."

Was there a new softness in his eyes, as he looked over at her?

"I know," he said.

"By the way, you kept a secret from me too," she pointed out. "Why didn't you tell me Claire was the other person in the accident?"

He ran a hand through his hair, leaving it rumpled. "Because if I did, you might not—"

"What?" He didn't reply. "I might not what?"

He got up and walked over to the fireplace, the woodburner empty now. "Might not want…" The sentence hung, unfinished, as he looked at the cold ashes.

Possibility leapt in her heart, and she stood up. Better to put herself on the line now, than go back to England wondering and regretting.

"I know about wanting," she said.

She reached out and laid her fingertips on his back. At that, he turned and grabbed her up, lifting her against him, kissing her as though her touch had released all his simmering, unbearable tension. She put her arms around him and held on, not believing that it would last, but taking everything while she could. He turned them around, pressing her against the smooth stone of the fire surround, and she wrapped her legs around him as he kissed her harder, deeper, making up for all the lost days. There was no fire lit, but between them, the wanting had sparked a blaze of its own.

Finally, they paused for breath, but their bodies were still burning.

"Between a rock and a hard place," she murmured, pressing his hips to hers.

"Should we stop?" he asked, his face buried in her neck.

"N...ohhh." He flicked his tongue against her skin, and with his warm breath on her neck, his roaming lips, his wandering hands...no. She did *not* want to stop.

But she'd remembered something else—something she had to check with him.

"Wait, though," she said breathlessly. "Did you see the report of the wolf attack, in the translation? It was new."

He let her slide down to her feet. "You saw that?"

She knew what he must have been thinking—that she'd take that information back to London with her. In her darkest moment, she'd almost been tempted to email Alcina. But she didn't. She couldn't, and wouldn't.

"Yes, I saw it," she said. "But I didn't tell them anything."

He raised an eyebrow. "Why?"

"Because now I understand. I came here to prove a point to my colleagues and my boss. And then I met you...and the wolves..." She met his gaze, freed by the knowledge that there were no secrets left. "And you were more important."

He ran his fingers along the curve of her jaw, his thumb brushing her lips, and the echo of his touch ran through her body. She wanted to grab hold of him and drag him to the bedroom, show him how important she could make him feel. Amongst other things.

But she had to tell him one other thing.

"And anyway...I found out just now that the report was false," she added. "Fredrik posted it."

In an instant, his expression changed, and he blew out a hard breath of anger, his fists clenching and unclenching. "I should have killed him after all."

She couldn't help it—she laughed.

"I can't believe you let Fredrik think he was going to die. You're almost as bad as he is."

His grin was wry, and a little dangerous. "It's all the time we spend in the dark. Makes us a bit twisted."

"Yeah, I see where that whole Scandinavian noir thing came from now," she said.

He took a step closer. "Speaking of time in the dark..."

She looked at her watch. Eleven minutes to two. Whether she had eleven minutes left, or a week, she knew how she wanted to spend it.

Then, in one swift movement, he lifted her up and headed for the bedroom. Apparently, he knew it too.

Epilogue

E xactly on time, the train pulled smoothly into Lillavik station. Zoe peered out the window. Under a full, pale sky, snowflakes were falling in gentle drifts, occasionally chasing each other here and there in slow whirls and flurries. The park trees, the familiar stone buildings of the village, and the dinky model-railway station were dressed in frosty Christmas white.

Usually, this snow-globe beauty would have filled her with joy. But in this case, it only meant she'd have to wait longer to see Jakob. She sighed. Still, it would be nice to spend the car trip catching up with Bengt or Greta, whichever one of them made the drive to collect her.

But as she stepped down from her carriage, she saw a tall, broad-shouldered man coming along the platform. No hat or scarf. Dark hair dusted by the falling snow. A smile.

"You!" she said.

Without a word, he scooped her up. Foreheads touching, they looked into each other's eyes, the chilled puffs of their breath mingling as they laughed. God, she'd missed him. Well, she'd only seen him a few weeks ago in Scotland, but still. When their lips met, she felt like she'd been starving all that time, and his kiss was the only sustenance that would save her.

"You could have grown a moustache for me," she said, when he set her back down.

His eyebrows knit in puzzlement. "What?"

"Never mind," she laughed. "Kissing is better without it, anyway."

"Are you sure?" he said, leaning closer again. "You might need more data to confirm that."

"You're right." She tipped her head. "Are you available to cooperate on a full research project? There might be a number of variables to test."

He maintained a serious expression. "I'll do anything for good science."

"I like the sound of that," she said, giving in to laughter.

"Me too," he said, and there was a hunger in his voice that made her stop laughing and kiss him again.

When they finally broke apart, he straightened her woolly hat. "Come on," he said, picking up her suitcase. "You must be cold."

On the outside, she was cold...on the inside, not so much. But she *was* keen to get back to the lodge and start this urgent project. In fact, it was feeling more urgent by the minute.

At the top of the station steps, he took her hand and tucked it through his arm.

"No falling over this time," he said. "We need you in good shape for our experiment."

"Sensible boots," she said, lifting one foot to show him, and he grinned.

At the car, he opened the door for her as usual, then put her suitcase in the back. She made no comment about his driving, but he looked at her when he started the engine, and they both knew. She was, just quietly, proud of him.

They drove to the lodge in the settling dusk, Zoe's hand on his thigh, his hand on top. For the last year, they'd done the long-distance thing, meeting whenever and wherever they could, and with Jakob based between Scotland and Sweden, and Zoe still in London, they were racking up the miles. She'd left Vertex (cheered on by Denise) and set up as a freelance copywriter, and was building a list of clients she could work with from anywhere in the country, or even the world. She could up and go at a moment's notice, if she wanted to...or if she had a reason to. Jakob's invitation to spend a week in Lillavik over Christmas definitely qualified.

They made it to the lodge without elk or incident, and Jakob parked the car in the garage. "Everyone's in the guesthouse," he said.

"Everyone?" she asked.

He pulled her suitcase from the car. "Just the most important people."

She knew that Fredrik wouldn't be there. He'd signed his share of Defrost Digital back over to Alvar, and left for a job in Sydney. Hopefully he was driving Claire and Oscar mad down there. And although Alvar had asked Jakob to work with him, they both knew—as everyone did—that he was happiest following his heart, and his wolves.

They walked across to the guesthouse, breaking the crisp surface of the snow with each footfall. On the steps, they stopped for a moment before going into the light and warmth, and the hum of voices. She breathed deeply in and out, savouring the clean northern air, drinking in the view—dark forest under a snow-heavy sky, and the big Norway spruce by the pond glowing with enough golden-white lights to rival the Eiffel Tower. He took her hand, and she leaned into him. There was nowhere in the world she'd rather be.

In the great room, they found Bengt and Greta, Alvar, Stina, and Malin and the girls. While Fredrik had been exiled, Malin had kept up with her counselling and treatment, and was coping much better, even though Anton was still spending long stints away. Lena and Ebba seemed about six inches taller and three times sweeter, and Lena even spoke a little English. Stina was home from California for Christmas, having changed her mind about Australia and found a job soothing the successful-but-stressed residents of Silicon Valley. Alvar and Jakob shook hands and slapped each other on the back, a greeting that would have been impossible a year ago.

There were no guests over Christmas, so Greta had decided that everyone should stay together in the guesthouse. Zoe received hugs from them all, and when they wished her Merry Christmas, she replied with *God Jul*, demonstrating just a little of the Swedish she'd been learning. There were murmurs of approval all round, and Greta handed her a mug of potently warming mulled wine, called *glögg*.

"Welcome back," she said. "I said you would be a real Swede."

Zoe smiled as they toasted each other. "I'm getting there."

That night, they celebrated a real Swedish Christmas Eve, with a *smörgåsbord* of ham and herring, little sausages and meatballs, gravad lax, and of course more glögg. They Skyped with Paul and Sarah, who had amazed everyone with her recovery, and was getting a little stronger every month. Then they exchanged gifts.

Zoe had struggled to think of something for Jakob, but in the end she'd found a 1906 first edition of Jack London's *White Fang*. In a world of wolf-themed TV programmes and movies, he was one of the original fictional wolves. The look on Jakob's face when he opened it told her that she'd made a good choice.

"Thank you," he said, kissing her. "I love it. You have to wait until tomorrow for your present," he added, leaving her wondering what it could be.

Later, Alvar mysteriously went missing, just before Santa Claus—otherwise known as *Jultomten*—knocked on the door bearing presents for the girls. *Are there any good children?* he asked, in a booming Father Christmas voice, and as Lena and Ebba jumped up and down, Zoe saw him catch Jakob's eye.

It was the nicest Christmas Eve she'd ever had.

And it was even nicer later on, back in his cabin in the clearing, when they gave each other a very grown-up Christmas present indeed.

★

Neither of them was in any rush to get out of bed the next morning. It was a rare luxury to wake up together...and then wake each other up even more.

"Merry Christmas," he said softly, running his fingers down her spine, making her arch towards him.

"Happy Birthday," she replied, reaching to find the most awake part of him.

He had no answer to that, only an appreciative rumble as her hand closed around him. Choosing a Christmas gift might have given her trouble, but she knew exactly what his birthday present should be.

Afterwards, they ate breakfast in bed, lazy in the shared afterglow.

"I have someone for you to meet today," he said, passing her a pastry.

"Really? Who?"

He shook his head. "You'll see. He's helping me with your present."

And that was all he'd say.

They showered, then walked up to the guesthouse. Everyone was there, drinking coffee and chatting, and there was a heavenly smell of baking coming from the kitchen. After some giggling and joking in Swedish—which had Jakob looking bashful—they switched to English for Zoe.

"Don't listen to a word they say," he told her, as he and Bengt left to shovel snow from the paths.

The women just laughed, and Malin shuffled over on the sofa, making space. Lena and Ebba were sitting on the floor in front of her, playing with dolls.

"Come and sit with us, Zoe," she said, her voice hopeful.

So she did. What went around came around, and she'd long been forgiven for her own deception. Lena came to lean against her knee, showing her one of the dolls wearing ice skates, and they were back in action.

A little while later, Bengt came back in. "Would you like to come outside?" he asked Zoe.

"Oh...okay."

She stood up, and everyone else did too, a frisson of

excitement suddenly in the air. Something was up. She helped Malin fasten the girls' coats, then they all trooped outside. The snow was glittery underfoot, and the girls danced around, invigorated in the sparkly cold.

Bengt cupped his hands at his mouth, and called out across the yard. "Okay!"

First, they heard the sound of Christmassy bells, as though one of Santa's reindeer had gone rogue overnight. Then, from the direction of the barn, something wondrous appeared—a stocky little horse with a golden mane and tail, pulling Brigitta's sleigh, with Jakob in the driver's seat. The sleigh looked just as she'd imagined it, that day in the boathouse—the new paintwork rich and red, the black runners glossy in the winter sun, and the delicate gold trim retouched.

They came to a stop in front of her, and Jakob got down and came to stand by the horse's head.

"This is Atli," he said. "Atli, this is Zoe."

"No way." She looked at Jakob, amazed. "This is the most beautiful thing, ever."

The little horse shook his head, making the harness bells jingle. The sound rang clear in the pure air, magical and Christmassy and nostalgic all at once. Zoe ruffled his wild flaxen forelock, and he pressed his head against her front, letting out a steamy sigh in the cold air. She laughed and dropped her head to his, inhaling that oh-so-good pony smell.

"Atli's grandfather was one of my mother's Icelandic horses," Jakob told her.

Seeing the emotion in his eyes, she touched his arm. "That's perfect. It's like you closed the circle."

"I know." Then he smiled and held out a hand. "Shall we?"

He helped her up onto the newly recovered seat, and covered their knees with a thick blanket. A mini-paparazzi scrum ensued as Malin and Stina took pictures with their phones, and Greta pulled out the camera, while Bengt grinned. As they drove away, the little ones chased after the sleigh, giggling and squealing. Atli shook his head, but kept his stride, unbothered by the fuss.

"Everyone's snap-happy today," she commented, looking back over her shoulder. Greta gave her a wave, and took another photo, and she waved back. It must make a pretty picture, she knew, and Greta did love her Swedish traditions.

"Snap-happy?" Jakob asked.

There were so few English terms he didn't know, she was always secretly pleased to teach him a new one. "Like, going crazy with their cameras."

"Oh. Yes." He just smiled, and gave Atli a tickle-up with the reins.

He drove them to the lookout point over the lake, where she and Bengt had stopped that day and seen him checking one of the cameras. Since then, the wolf population seemed to have increased in the district, if the reports from volunteers were accurate. Which they probably were, now that Fredrik had left in disgrace. But this winter, Jakob had told her, there hadn't been any sightings or prints near the lodge, like last year. He thought the two local packs were spending more time around the western side of the lake. She was relieved—even if they weren't on the Nilssons' turf, it was more remote out there, and safer for them.

They sat together taking in the view, and she leaned against his shoulder. For Jakob, every inlet and peak was familiar, but she was still learning the lake's secrets.

Atli pawed hopefully in the snow, looking for grass to nibble.

"I'll just, um, check the harness," Jakob said, and got out, tucking the blanket around her knees as he went.

Just then, she heard a bird's call, and looked up. A bullfinch was soaring above them.

"Oh, look at that," she began—and then stopped.

He was kneeling on the snow by her side of the sleigh.

Taking a deep breath, he started to speak slowly, as though making sure not to forget a word.

"Zoe. You might be the one who's always falling over, but I was on my knees when I met you. Me and the wolves, that was it. Then you came to be a volunteer. Or not."

Her heart was pounding. "I thought you would never forgive me after that."

"I know." He paused for a minute, seeming to gather his thoughts. "But your lies uncovered every truth I needed to know. You made everything the way it should be. Almost everything." He pulled off his gloves and reached into his pocket. "There's one more thing."

Just before he said the words, she saw the flash of a diamond in his hand.

"Will you marry me?"

"Oh..." She didn't know whether to laugh or cry. Maybe both.

He breathed out. "I wanted to say it perfectly."

She'd never seen him so uncertain—and it was very charming. "You *did* say it perfectly."

He shifted slightly on the snow. "Does that mean yes? Because I think my knee is frozen."

"Sorry!" Laughing, she jumped out of the sleigh and reached down to pull him up. "It means yes," she said, watching relief wash over him. "That was perfect."

Still serious, he tugged at the tip of her left glove, and she pulled it off. Then he took her hand and slid the ring onto the appropriate finger, as she held her breath. It was stunning—tiny diamonds set in an art deco design on both sides of one big diamond, all sparkling to rival the northern frost. Her right hand went to her mouth.

"This is incredible. Is it an antique?"

He nodded. "My mum inherited it from *her* mother, but she never got to use it." He held her hand tightly. "I think she'd be happy for you to have it."

Okay, here was the crying part.

Now it was his turn to laugh, and he pulled her close, kissing her with such tender passion that there was no time for crying, only lips and breath and love.

When they parted, something occurred to her. "Where will we live? Not London, I suppose."

"I don't know," he said, laying teasing kisses on her mouth between each word. "Probably not, if you marry a wildlife ecologist. Do you mind?"

"No. I can work anywhere now. The only thing I mind is not being with you."

She'd never felt so set free, and so anchored at the same time.

It was a good feeling.

In front of them, the bullfinch tipped its wing over the frozen lake where they'd skated under the stars that night, neither of them knowing what was ahead. On her finger, the heirloom ring shone in the light. And behind them, Atli shook his head, setting the harness bells ringing sweet and clear again.

No matter where they ended up, everything had been made right, here in this north that started out as a lie, and became something so true.

Thanks for reading *A North So True!*
For more information about Serena and her other books,
visit www.serenaclarke.com. While you're there, sign up
for her VIP newsletter to receive new book news, special
offers, and exclusive extras.

Reviews help other readers find the kind of books they love. If you enjoyed A North So True, please do consider leaving a rating and comment at your favourite online retailer or review site. Your review is greatly appreciated!

Acknowledgements

It was just me at the keyboard writing, but all kinds of people helped to bring this book to life—even if we didn't know it at the time. Thank you...

Adam, Nate, and Zach—my own true north.

Mum, for watching me leave time and again, but always cheering me on.

Dee Kidd, for Tuesdays in the window seat, and always.

Johan Sjöberg (a.k.a. Johnny Seamountain), for all things Swedish.

Vanessa Gulik, for edits, encouragement, and enthusiasm.

Stephen Pollard, who said exactly what I needed to hear, exactly when I needed to hear it.

And most of all, Eva, Iwan, Erik, Göran and Maria, the Ehring family, Bo and Elisabet Griwell, Cathrin Damsholt Andersson, Sharon Johanson, Nicki and the Mörrum gang, and everyone in Sweden—then, and now. *Tack för allt.*

Also by Serena Clarke

The Same But Different
All Over the Place
One Distant Summer

 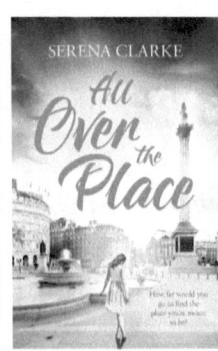 

About the Author

Serena Clarke writes escapist romantic fiction set all over the world. Readers have described her books as engaging page-turners, with sigh-worthy happy endings that will leave you smiling.

Her own story? She's lived in thirty-nine houses, in seven cities, in four countries. She's been a riding instructor, edited a medical journal, worked at a London law firm, and taught English as a second language to wayward teenagers. And now she's found her own happy ending—living near the beach in beautiful New Zealand with her family, writing the kind of feel-good books she loves to read. She hopes you'll love them too!

Find her online at www.serenaclarke.com.